THE SUNDAY KILLER

THE CASE FILES OF HEATHER MOODY

JEN LOWRY

Book Cover Design: Thirty Quills Press by Tish Bouvier at www.
tishbouvier.com

Editing: Kimberly Macasevich kmacasevich@gmail.com

✤ Created with Vellum

PRAISE FOR JEN LOWRY

PRAISE FOR JEN LOWRY

THE SUNDAY KILLER is a slow burn that grows into a roaring fire as the story develops! TSK is a masterclass in toeing the line between edgy and clean fiction This book comes highly recommended for a reader wishing to find the rare book at the intersection of crime fiction and Christian values. Can't wait to see what Heather Moody (and by extension, Jen Lowry) does next!

— PETER FENTON, AUTHOR OF ABANDON ALL HOPE

DEDICATION

To Eli, for loving me
   To Solomon and Samuel, my darlings forever
   To Aunt Dot, my greatest cheerleader
   To Mom and Dad, for believing in me

1

When my brother was seventeen, he chased me with a Colt .45. I was thirteen and should've been gossiping over boys, not locking my bedroom door at night and praying I'd live to see another day. The day he tried to kill me, I found my calling. Sandals pounded on hot concrete as I fled to the police station down the street in our tiny, dead-end town of Millbrook, North Carolina. Looking for safety. Distance. For any place but back where he was.

The chief's musty office smelled of cheap cigarettes piled in an ashtray that hadn't looked to be dumped in days. Adrenaline pumped as I watched sunlight filter in through blinds, one cracked and bent by the dispatcher's adopted cat. More than the sun lurked outside the window. He was waiting somewhere. Seething because I'd gotten away and plotting for my return. I'd have to—or would I? Was there another way? That was the only day I ever saw my mother cry. I don't remember the chief's name, but the memory crashed out of the blue as I slipped the heavy police vest over my head.

The chief let me try on a uniform shirt he had hanging on a peg in his office. He thought it would distract me from the fear still pounding through my veins, and he rolled up the long sleeves and tucked them under to make the appearance seem fitting, even though the extra-large shirt swallowed me whole. It was the day I realized I needed to be a protector and fight for those too weak to do it. I grew up that day. Up and strong. Running from a gun could do that to you. Running to the Virginia line to get away from my brother could do that, too. Starting over. Confused as to how a family could appear so perfect yet be so terribly wrong. Now, I run towards the fear.

I secured my Kevlar®armor in place and pulled my dark hair under my cap. It was that kind of day. When we geared up, there was an eerie silence that always followed the buckling of clasps. The lock-tight protection was only superficial, though. The silence was a part of our knowledge. It was that moment between us that spoke volumes. Being a cop was never easy. With one wrong step, death could knock against any of our doors. That realization kept us all tightly knitted together. We all understood without having to say a word.

I'd been on the force for seven years, and on the anniversary date of my swearing-in, I got the call to head upstairs to meet the captain. It was unannounced and very unexpected since my team was about to close in on a huge drug raid. The entire department knew it. We'd just discovered the gang had a hostage, some big political connections that were going to blow up soon, so I figured it was one of those speeches of how I couldn't mess this one up, and everything was riding on the bust.

Captain McBride was waiting for me by his door, his bulky bull frame blocking me from entering. Not to mention the large brown boxes with incoherent scribbles on the sides, old dates, and dust on the top. He was never one for small talk and put the files down at my feet. "Heather, check out the files. Take them. Do better this time."

Confused, I looked down at old dates staring at me as if eyes were still pleading from the grave. "And where do you want me to drop these off at? Isn't Joe Jackson working on cold cases?"

The captain's brow crossed as he made his way back to his chair. He motioned for me to take a seat, and I braced myself for a letdown. Here it was. All I'd worked for and all I could think about was it was my turn to be let go. What had I done?

"You are over the cold cases now. Did I not make myself clear when I said take these? I don't look at you as an errand-runner. I've got my own people for that."

The surprise hit me full force. "I thought this was about the Delgado gang. Sir, with all due respect, we're about to roll out. We've got a marker on . . ."

The captain cut me off. He was notorious for that and didn't care what others thought about his incessant interruptions. "You've got a new assignment and promotion coming. You've been here for how long now?"

"Seven years today."

"Then, it's time to get off the streets. I'm making you a detective and head of a unit. For once just smile and say thank you."

"Sir, I'd really like for us to wait to . . ." All thoughts collided like a police chase gone bad. The foot race I could play with my mind would often get the best of me. "But . . ."

"Sit down," he barked. "I can't deal with excuses. If you haven't noticed, I'm in the corner office for a reason. I push your paycheck and I have already approved your promotion. So, don't deny me the satisfaction of handing you a career advancement. Do you know how many others I could've given this lead position to? I don't have time to interview. I don't have time to second guess this decision, so don't give me a reason. Your reputation has gained traction. I was impressed by how you worked to resolve that Marcus Pew case and trust me when I say nothing impresses me anymore."

How could I put it into words without sounding ungrateful? "Thank you, sir, but I'm really fine where I am. Maybe in a few years I will be ready for a new position."

Anniversary gifts aside, promotions and the rank of detective meant more on-call time, more responsibility, and with all that came more paper pushing. I didn't want to end up like Joe Jackson. I shook off the thought. No matter how many reports I'd have to file in my life, a million and two, I'd never be like Detective Joe Jackson or fired Joe Jackson. He was a scumbag times a million and two.

"Let's just say we aren't fine with where you are. There's been talk about how these cases aren't moving and something isn't right about them. When we consulted with the FBI, they concluded they're too random to be a serial, but something is nagging at me about the series of murders we've had over the past few years. Jackson wasn't fit for the job, as you and everybody and their momma knows. I've worked this beat for thirty years, and we had our occasional scuffle, revenge, jealousy, a robbery gone wrong, but what's in these coffins right here," he pointed to the boxes, "isn't that. We need fresh eyes. You're not turning down the promotion. I'm offering you the lead detective of the unit. Take it. Goodbye."

He knew I wouldn't turn it down in the end. Every reason I should say no left me when I felt the weight of the boxes and what they meant. Someone's family couldn't move on because of what was in these boxes. Who would fight for them? I knew I'd paid my dues. Worked hard for the department and built solid ties, but I didn't want to leave my guys and my partner. They were my team, like the brothers I never had. I trusted them, and that took time to establish. Working a box of cold cases was void of the luxuries of time. Quiet killers didn't wait for anyone. If it wasn't a one-and-done kill job, the confidence of the killer could rise because whoever was out there doing the crimes, they'd got away with it the first time. Easy to think they'd try again, or the thirst would begin. Or they'd skipped town long ago, leaving no way to solve it. I feared open murder cases would gnaw at my heart like no other.

"Sir, I do appreciate the offer. Can I think about it? I'd like to talk it over with . . ."

My heart started to pound harder and my arm was getting that sensation again. I knew my blood pressure was rising just at the thought of having to confront the guys.

"Alex? Harris? They know already."

"You told them before me?"

"They had a few choice words between them about not wanting to lose you and how much of an asset you were on the team."

He knew as well as I did when departments shifted, so did relationships. I would be so involved with the cold cases, there wouldn't be much time for me to continue those relationships. And they were mine for the past three years. I couldn't just turn that off in a day. I'd seen firsthand what happened when people transferred units or went to work for another department. They'd say they'd call. Never would. They'd say they'd keep in touch. Never heard from them again. I didn't want to disrupt my life. It was easy to manage for the first time in a long time. I'd finally found some footing. Now, I felt it slipping away and clutched the boxes closer to my chest as if it were some reminder that this might be more of my own selfish needs and comfort making me deny this move.

He said, "These cases need not only your fresh eyes but your instincts. You took down Pew when the bigs at the state couldn't. You understand it isn't open for discussion here. It's yours. You'll report to your team tomorrow morning. Take off the gear. Leave it here, and then follow me."

"Can't I go down and at least . . ."

"I told you, they know. Better to just break ties hard. You'll still see them on the elevator."

He passed over a photo badge and flashed a smile at me. I saw my same picture human resources had on file since my first week in the Crystal Falls Police Department. Such a young face. Thinner. Wide innocent green eyes stared at me. Oh, what you would see in your years, dear girl.

I waved the badge back at him. Lead Detective, Heather Moody, was inkjet printed on hard plastic gloss. "Were you sure I wouldn't deny the position? This sure?"

"You could've denied me. Sure. We all make choices in life. Just know that if you don't follow my lead around here, that keeps us at a standstill, and I can't have that. I can't support insubordination. Ask Joe. I can't let Crystal Falls get out of hand, and with that smile of yours you can be the face for the press. Joe wasn't the one to take the pressure and was a ticking time bomb. If you need the complaint reports I received from families as proof of the foul mess he spread with the press, then that'll be enough to know why. I need someone with your way, your . . . talents . . ."

I questioned, "Tact?"

"I was going to say faith, but that, too. Both are hard to come by these days."

I wanted to reply that they all needed a little more Jesus around there, the whole world but left it. It could surely clean up their language in the break room.

"When you start in on the files, I'm sure you'll know the cases well enough from the news. Maybe you'll be able to see through the mistakes of Jackson and put an end to this for the families. When it's a kid, it's different, Heather. You don't have kids, do you?"

"No," I said.

I had no children, no relationships since college, and one sour date with a State Trooper who asked me to pay for my half of everything before we were walking in, announcing it loudly to the hostess that he wanted separate checks before we even sat down. He only talked about the job, and a rig he'd stopped with stolen goods, or how he'd saved a boy from drowning once. I needed to get away from the job, not spend nights out drowning in it.

"You've got six months to solve these cases. Prove to me I didn't make a mistake with you."

Scribbled on the side of the worn box was a date from over five years ago. I'd cracked the Marcus Pew case, but it wasn't a cold one. It was an active pursuit, and I had an inside connection to that one. Not to mention, he'd slipped up with his arrogance. There was no one I knew that came out the gate wanting to work on unresolved cases.

"But sir, as doom and gloom as this sounds, cold cases are hard to work. Leads and memories fade. Time and distance create a hardship that easily can't be overcome. Six months might not . . ."

"That's about right, and that's why it's time to put these to an end." He rose from his desk and grabbed the boxes again, pushing them my way. "The clock is ticking. Move."

He didn't want me to start until tomorrow, yet he set the

stopwatch to go. "Can you tell me more about Jackson's team?"

"You mean, your team? Pretty solid. A rhinestone cowboy, a diva, and a quick draw McGraw. Should be easy to pick them out as soon as you meet them. They're just like any other team in this place. You included."

"And what am I?"

"Fresh eyes. That's what you are."

I grabbed the boxes from his hand. "And I'm abandoning the team just when we're closing in on the hostage situation, so can I . . ."

"You're only a floor away," he said dramatically, as we waved his hand out to the new domain. "Welcome to the big show."

"Thank you, sir."

I wanted to add, 'I hope you know what you're doing,' but I let that one go. I should've felt blessed for being promoted and put in as the lead. With only seven years in, that was an accomplishment in a department that was so structured and solid. People rarely left once they got desk jobs. Dale, who started training with me, was still chasing pedestrian violators and trying to pedal down muggers on the old speeder bike.

"Now, go on. Spend some time with the files before you walk in gung-ho, all blazing and ready to bring justice to these families. Start with the Emma Sanders case. That's a haunting one right there if there ever was one. Poor little girl. I go to church with her family. Let that one be the first on your list."

He pointed to a side office with no windows and a tiny metal desk. The sunlight streaming in on the second floor didn't pair well with my headaches, and my eyes preferred a darker room. Save for the cracked glass on the door, the room felt like an escape portal I could crawl in. I smiled at my little Hobbit hole. It would do.

I smiled. "This is perfect."

He acted surprised. "You like this closet?"

"I prefer it to all of that out there," I said.

My eyes followed the trail of a small-time criminal I recognized from a road stop bust a couple of months back being escorted for booking, a couple distraught over some tragic news, a baby crying hysterically, and a worn-out mother trying to calm her with the phones ringing off the hook to top off the country song on the station.

"Then, call this your office. I'll get you a sign one day. Send me a list of supplies and remind me to put in the work order for your plate."

His tone let me know he didn't want to be bothered with trivial tasks. I wouldn't remind him. I didn't need a title or my name on the door. I just needed quiet, a dark room, and Jesus. All of that could be found right there where I stood. I sat at the desk and rolled back the ripped leather desk chair, worn from some heavy setter for sure. It was caved a little in the middle and was way more comfortable than it looked.

He sighed before walking out, acting as if he wanted to say more but refrained. "HR will be around later to have you sign some forms. Expect them."

"I'm not going anywhere," I said.

I was sure the case files would keep me occupied well after clocked hours. If I only had until tomorrow morning to familiarize myself with the case, I knew there would be takeout in my future and a sleepover. That would suit me, too. I opened the first cardboard box. Manilla files waited impatiently. Sad. All crammed and ordered by date. Voices of the dead screamed at me as my hands slid across each one. 'Help me,' they cried. 'Please.'

Families called out and their voices rang in my head, reminding me that no matter what I'd been through I did make it out alive. I was fighting for the ones that didn't. I was here for them. I didn't know how I would do such a thing that the investigative team already assigned to these cases couldn't do, considering they also had resources from the FBI, but I would give it all I had. There was no other way.

2

A knock brought me back from reliving the crime scene of Emma Sanders. My nerves were shaking. It didn't take long for Alex to find me. I tried to even my breathing and smile as he leaned against the small glass cutout, making stupid faces at me. I motioned for him to come in, but as soon as he opened the door, I realized he wasn't alone. A guy from Human Resources was right behind him carrying a folder and waving a pen. Next, a heavy brute of a weightlifter walked in looking like he could've boxed Tyson and given him a run for his money. He wheeled in a flatbed piled with more case file boxes.

Alex put my computer bag beside my desk. Before he could start on me, I got, "Where do you want these," and "Sign your new contract." I motioned for the corner and swished my name haphazardly over the line. My eyes only took the Lead Investigator title in for a second, and my face flooded with guilt. Alex deserved this more than me. He was two years my senior.

When Alex and I were alone, t, I started in the only way I knew how. "I'm sorry."

He smiled and appeared to be as relaxed as anyone about to be on the brink of the biggest bust of their life. There was no anger in his posture.

Alex's voice was smooth. "I'm not."

I feigned surprise. "So, you're glad to see me go."

"Actually," he said, leaning over the desk a little. "I've been praying for it."

I laughed. "So unlike you, Alex. Well, God does answer a sinner's prayer. Evidence points to that when . . ."

He raised his hand. "I didn't come here for Bible study, Heather. I came for something else."

"Let me guess," I said, leaning back in the chair. The little squeaking noises were already familiar, and I liked it. "You want to pick at me endlessly about this?"

"I might. But I also want to tell you I'm happy you've got this gig." His phone rang. Typical. We never really could get full conversations around this place. I watched his face drop the smile as he answered the call. "I'm on the way. Got it."

He slipped his phone back into his pocket and nodded. "You know the drill."

"Yep. Go get 'em, Alex."

"Without a doubt." He waved his arm across the files sprawled out on my desk and the newly delivered stack of boxes in the corner of my little hovel. "And I'm confident you'll do the same."

Again, I tried to smile at him but couldn't. Watching him walk out of the door and leaving me here gave me a feeling I didn't want to connect with. I should've been with Alex, Harris, Rodriguez, and the guys all piling up in the back of the van. Going over the plan one more time while we jostled together over the speed bumps taking us out of the parking lot of the department into the wild backstreets of Crystal Falls. Waiting for Alex's stomach to start rumbling and the conversation would stray on what celebratory takeout we were going to choose this time after we locked the gang securely away. It was my turn to pick, and I was going for sushi. Loved to see the faces the guys made when it was my turn, taking them away from their typical burgers or steak runs. Last time I got us all noodle bowls, which they all said were just appetizers, joking with me to ask where I was hiding the real food. If I wanted sushi today, I'd be calling in an order alone.

I looked back down at the coroner's report, rubbing my temples to fight the demons away in my head. This was just a stress headache, nothing major. I leaned over and took a couple of pills and washed it quickly down with the last of the water bottle sticking out of my bag.

Alex came back in, this time without knocking. "Here. Looks like you might need this." He placed the coffee on the corner of the desk, the steam swirling in a welcoming dance.

I couldn't help but smile this time. A real one. A sign he wasn't truly angry at me. This guy was a keeper. My team was, and that's why it was so hard.

"I thought you had to go."

"The Delgado's can wait another two minutes. The third-floor break room has a Keurig station with a fancy spinner with all the flavors of the universe at your disposal. And you should see the fridge. It's stocked."

"Oh, you were that nosy."

"I am a detective. Wait until Rodriguez hears about this. He'll be making impromptu visits just to check this place out—and to see you, of course."

I blurted out, "Who's taking my place on the team?"

Captain hadn't told me, and I was too numb to ask him.

"Gary Sweeny. He's got experience on the task force and

has been on a couple of runs with us. You know, the bald guy."

"As long as it's not . . ."

"A woman? I'm surprised by you. I wouldn't have thought it was like you to be jealous."

I eyed him narrowly over my coffee and took a slow sip. "I was about to say, Jackson, but I heard he got fired. Just hard to believe. I just figured they were taking him off the case and stuffing him behind another desk to avoid the backlash."

"No. He's out. I heard they got some pretty heavy stuff on him."

His phone went off. "Yeah, yeah. I know. I had to stop by to take a leak."

I tried to muster the strongest evil eye I could. "Go to the bathroom. Don't lie."

"I'll stop by on my way down to clear your conscience. I promise." He held up his scout's honor fingers.

"It's not my conscience I'm worried about. Be safe out there."

"Always."

I yelled as he left out, "And thanks for the coffee."

My eyes fell to the case files that would consume me for the next six months. What would happen to me if I didn't solve these cases? Should I look for another job now? My old chair was already being warmed by Sweeny, so my place was lost. I'd seen enough in my seven years to know that if Captain McBride gave me six months or else speech, he meant it. There were no empty threats here.

I had a crawling sense of doubt taking over that whatever was in these boxes wasn't enough. If Jackson was fired for pretty heavy stuff as Alex said, then that meant he would have cut corners on the notes and follow-ups. I knew this would be more Cliffs Notes reading and for any case, especially of this magnitude, that meant I'd have to start over.

I closed up the third victim's file and went back to Amelia Eastman, age sixteen. She would've been a freshman in college by now, about to close out her first year. The crime scene photos were so unnerving it was hard to stare at them for long moments, yet I needed to pick out as many details as I could. When I was a child, I would spend hours in spy picture books, picking out buttons and thimbles, finding red yarn and a needle. I focused on one object at a time, anything other than the body, which was hard to ignore, inversely suspended.

A cleanup crew found her in an abandoned warehouse near the docks that the owner hired to clear out the old grain bins before putting it up on the market. There was contractor equipment piled haphazardly on the scene. The murder weapon, if there could be only one tortuous object to claim ownership of the crime, was tagged as evidence marker three. Blood was visible on the tool and pooled around it like a pillow. Attached to the monkey wrench were chunks of skin and hair matted on the metal. It looked like he might have done a little digging with it, extracting pieces of brain matter with the adjustable jaws.

The medical examiner called the time of death between 3:00 and 6:00 a.m., noting fracture of the vault of the skull and asphyxia by vomitus as the immediate cause of death but a quick look at the cuts on the wrists let me know she would've bled out in a matter of ten minutes if left alone. Not to mention the crushing weight of her chest cavity on organs.

Poor girl.

To bring it all up to the family would be a painful reminder of all they lost, a sharp hurting that took my breath away at even the thought of digging it all up again. But, just like I knew how hard it was, I also realized it never got easier either.

Why wait for tomorrow? It was never promised. If Captain McBride wanted me to lead this case, then it would at least be on my terms. Let the team know I wasn't one wasting time in a corner office, brooding over a cold paper trail. It was time I faced whatever waited for me outside this door.

As surely as I knew faith found those who called His name in a second, evil also waited for no man. This psychopath would not wait for me to go through all the files to piecemeal clues together, and he would not stop. I couldn't wait either with the questionable dealings of what Jackson left behind. I couldn't distract myself with how much he might've botched this case and just covered enough to get by. If I only had six months to clean up his mess and catch a killer, then today was the day to start the manhunt. Captain McBride would just have to deal with me breaking his orders. Tomorrow could fend for itself.

3

———

The open design of the third floor was some new decorating scheme to bring a collaborative spirit to the homicide floor. I turned to look back at the closet, my new office, tucked away in a place where a passerby would probably mistake it as a janitor's closet, and knew I could easily retreat. 'Just take steps forward. Do this. Today.'

I surveyed the room. Captain McBride wasn't in his office, but from his open windows, I could tell he could be the micromanager of the teams he surveyed. We were pretty much on our own just one floor down.

A beautiful woman with long, silky black hair from one of those hair product commercials approached me. She smiled and immediately I knew she had to get those teeth whitened.

She extended her hand. Long manicured nails with tiny pearls glued in the center reached out to greet me. "You're Detective Moody, right? We were told they assigned you to us. Don't be upset, but we did a little snooping around. The fault of the job, I guess."

I smiled at her. Her voice was kind. I awkwardly shook her hand. She then reached down, since she stood a full head taller than me, and swooped me in a quick hug. "That's how I do things around here." She let out a huge sigh as if she was the one with the bottled-up nervous energy. "That's better. I'm Jade. Jade Cain."

"Nice to meet you, Detective Cain."

The tall beauty laughed. "Don't even dare think about that. That's my daddy, and I'm never living up to those size thirteen shoes. How about Jade? That'll do."

"Well, if I would've known I was going to be assigned a new team, I probably would've done the same thing. Stalked you all. Then, I would have known about your father, too."

She grinned. "Figured you didn't know about your promotion by the looks of you."

I shrugged. "Captain didn't give me many details."

"Other than I was a diva, right? I can't stand that stereotype. Just because I love my nails done and tend to pay closer attention to my fashion than he does. Lord, bless that man's heart. Have you seen him out and about with his wife, Dee. She's got her hands full with him. I've also heard people around here think I'm the one who is bossy and demanding or that I'm some kind of socialite. So far from the truth."

"That's good to hear." It was my turn to hide a giggle. Working with a diva wasn't on my to-do list ever in my life, but she sure was a talker. She seemed so down to earth, right smack gorgeous, but pleasant and charming all the same.

She took me by the arm. "Let me take you on the two-cent tour. It's not much."

"My old partner thinks it's too much. He was impressed with the break room. I think we might need to put a combination lock on the door. My guys will be coming up here to scope it out, and when I say that I mean raid the fridge."

"Now, that isn't a stereotype. The guys and food and the fridge deal. That's the truth."

She spoke as if we were friends. Her chit-chat wasn't contrived. I couldn't even count on my hand how many women I had as friends. Outside of the office, there were no friends. Who had time for a life outside the job? I was impressed with those who could keep relationships going. They must have had a well of faith or a truly patient partner in crime. The guys were all I had and now they were probably off celebrating with steak plates, and I was headed over to a corner table surrounded by a barricade wall on wheels. Pinups of some of the crime scene photos were haphazardly strewn together, with a to-do list as long as the wall itself. They had checked nothing off. No wonder the cases were cold.

Jade motioned to a stout man, a former college football star by the looks of his build, and smiled warmly. "That's our ol' Mike, "The Rhinestone Cowboy" Hampstead."

He stood up and nodded. "Well, I see our new Holy Roller has arrived. No offense to that, Moody. It's not a bad thing."

"None taken," I said, trying to hide the shaky feeling. 'Appear confident until you are,' I thought. Words I often prayed silently as if I were a third grader about to step out on the stage for my first school play. I could play lead detective until I owned it. Until it fits. Until I earned it.

He continued, "I have a little faith myself. Well, because of Maude mostly."

Jade said, "Maude is Mike's wife. You guys are what now . . . thirty-five years?"

He patted Jade on the shoulder. "That's right, Jade. You

better remember the date this year. Did you get it on your calendar in that fancy gadget of yours? Maude says this is the big one. Wants me to take her on some Caribbean cruise ship. I've had enough drowning cases in my lifetime to never step near the water but she doesn't get that one bit."

"It's not a fancy gadget," Jade said, waving the newest cell at him. "It's just way more efficient than the flip. I still can't believe you carry one of those around."

"So, you're the one he called Rhinestone Cowboy."

Mike laughed. "I like that. Cap got me covered. He's the one called you Holy Roller. I figured I kinda liked that nickname for you. Reminds me that all things are possible. We can have a sermon right here on the third-floor mount. You'd have my attention."

I liked Mike and Jade. Both of them were just good people. If there was one thing I prided myself on was the fact that I could get a pretty good read on people. Maybe it was one of my gifts of the spirit—discernment. Maybe it was just I listened beyond what they said to what was felt behind the words. Either way, I knew they were going to accept me in. Being the lead didn't mean I needed some kind of seal of approval, but at least I needed to establish some type of camaraderie with them to establish a rapport that could lead to trust. It was starting on the right footing. Even though Jade was working in a set of six-inch heels with a leopard skin inlay and Mike wore leather cowboy boots that reminded me of an old western hero who still held on to his chaps, mixed in with her my low plain flats, I felt at ease.

"Aren't we missing someone?" I asked, pointing at the third desk pushed together in their pod. One was clearly Jade's, potted plants and glitter stars were sticking out of the ceramic pots. She needed fairy lights and her desk would be complete. Mike was leaning up against his neat and tidy desk, without an inch of disarray. Then, there was a messy stack on the other— piles of papers, a paper bag leftover from Lacy's shop on the corner, and a large disposable coffee cup from Joe Machines.

Someone called from four desks over, which let me know there wasn't much chance for a private conversation on the third floor. He put his hand over the receiver and said, "I'm almost done with this call. I'll be right over." He went back to talking, and my eyes lingered a little too long.

When he stood up, my first impression of him was that he was tall. Heck, everyone was tall compared to my five-foot-two frame. He had sandy blonde hair, fraying at the ends like the way a ribbon curls at the end of a pull of a scissor against it. It was this way and that, long over the ears. The disheveled look was his way. From desk to hair, to untucked slim dress shirt that needed a good ironing, looking as if he'd slept in it. He wore a pair of dark jeans that fit him well. Maybe a little too well. I hadn't noticed a man in that much detail until it was time to describe a scene to a sketch artist for a class I had taken on criminology and profiling. Something about him made me notice every single thing. That scared me more than the promotion. That I could maybe handle. The man approaching me, maybe not so much.

He held out his hand to me. Worn hands. He was raised on a farm. Clearly. Weathered skin, a healthy glow to him. Muscles moved against the shirt as he moved.

His voice was warm. "I'm Ben Caraway. Nice to meet you. You must be Heather."

"Benjamin of the twelve tribes." I couldn't stop myself. Why did I just say that?

He laughed. "So, she is the Holy Roller. Let me see, I

never had a comeback like that. Mike, what did she give you? The history of angelic beings?"

Mike's grin spread wide, letting me know he was going to lay another one on me. "She's been talking to Maude if she would've because that wife of mine swears I fell right from the sky."

"A fallen angel, more like it," said Jade, throwing her hands up in the air. "Don't mind these two. You'll get used to them. It's taken me a couple of years, but it'll happen."

Even though Ben's brown eyes held a hint of playfulness behind them, his words took on a more serious tone. "So, boss lady. Are you ready to whip us into shape? Have us do exercises and all that?"

"No," I said, falling right into taking off the pinned photos. "I think we don't need to touch our toes but meet minds. Can we start from the beginning? Pour through this from day one?"

Jade's brow deepened with a quiet fury. "Finally, someone came in and picked up all the pieces Jackson scattered to the wind."

Mike said, "We tried, Heather. We did. I don't want you to judge us based on what you've heard about Jackson."

I didn't want to tell them I hadn't heard much, and I sure didn't want to keep stirring around the negative energy. "We're past that now. It's a new day. Let's not waste daylight hours. I want to visit the crime scenes."

Ben raised an eyebrow, surprised I might start in this direction. "Which case?"

Captain McBride thought we should start with one before the others. "Emma Rose."

Mike said, "That was two years ago. I'm sure there's nothing left."

"I'm sure of that, too. I want to get a feel for the place. Shall we take a ride or do I do this alone?"

Mike grabbed his keys. "I'm the driver in this here neck of the woods. Let's go little lady. Out to the Bronco."

I laughed, my eyes following him from his newly added cowboy hat, how he adjusted his belt buckle, down to the spurs on the back of his boots. We were in North Carolina country, but that was an old-timer country.

"He would have a Bronco, right?"

"Of course, he would," said Ben, the light in his eyes softening his features. "He has horses, too. Those kinds of broncos, too. Mike's the real deal."

"I've never ridden a horse before," I said absentmindedly. It was something I'd always wanted to do. Wait. This was small talk, not case talk. I needed to play the boss lady, not Ms. Chatterbox.

Mike said, "As soon as this nightmare is over, we'll go riding. I've got a good twenty acres you can explore. The trails are all cut back, thanks to this here hired hand."

"You don't pay me," chuckled Ben. "I do it all out of the goodness of my ever-loving heart."

"He hunts the land for free," said Mike, out of the corner of his mouth. "He ain't doing nothing without getting a due."

"I heard that. I do this for free," Ben said, sweeping open the door so we could walk through it.

"Ever the gentleman," said Jade.

There was easy banter between them, reminding me of what I'd lost earlier that morning. The step beside, the walking out of the building where our strides matched, looking fierce. This time, I heard the ching of the spurs hitting the gravel, Jade's heels pounding, Ben's smooth loafers, and my flats. I was two steps behind them, letting them lead the way to the shiny red and white Ford that had to belong to Mike.

"Hop in, little lady," he said. "She's riding shotgun. We get to see what selection she picks on the radio. Very important. Hold on. Give me a minute to scramble up the dial."

Ben blinked heavy and slow at me, which I took for a full-force two wink at his amusement of it all. I took a sharp breath as I clicked the old seat belt in place. This was new, but I could do this. We had a case to solve. I'd learn their ways, and they'd get used to mine. I'd never had to worry so much about fitting in. This team felt different, and they'd survived the years with Jackson, and now were faced at welcoming in a fresh body, only a day-old position filled. What if one of them felt they needed lead? What if they felt slighted or jealous? I glanced between them as Mike roared the truck to life. No. I wouldn't go there.

Instead, I turned the radio to soft jazz. Ben clapped. "Finally, I've found a woman who doesn't go to pop."

"There's nothing wrong with pop," said Jade. "It's better to dance, too."

"Not my kind of dancing." Ben caught my eye.

The heat of the truck or our eyes meeting caused my face to blush. I'd call it the temperature in the cab. I looked out the window, anywhere but getting lost in those eyes. 'Day one on the new job, Heather. Keep it together.'

"So, tell me everything you know about this case," I said.

"This one has haunted us the most," said Jade. "She just got her license."

Ben added, "We've worked every angle. Ex-boyfriend, family members, school enemies, drifters. It's two years cold, Heather. Not much we can say other than we never caught a lead."

We tumbled over a deeply potholed dirt road, making

me grip the door handle. "Now I see why you wanted to drive."

Mike grinned. "I always drive."

I let their banter drown around me as the soothing trumpet sounds of Louis Armstrong roped my mind tightly. When we came to a sudden halt, I burst out, "Jesus take the wheel!"

Mike laughed. "No need. We're getting out."

4

J ade pointed over at the water's edge. "Emma's body was found right about there."

The river lapped up against the old, wooden dock. A couple of splintering boards protruded from the frame and a few planks were missing. It didn't appear to be sound enough to walk across, but I wanted a closer look. What I thought I'd see, well, I didn't know. Maybe a clue from the watery depths, which would've been pretty much impossible at this point but at least it would have let me know me coming here and dragging my new team with me wasn't for nothing.

Ben said, "They strapped her in the chair in the boat. We figured they had killed her at another location and placed on the boat unless the killer took the time to clean up the blood."

"Straps weren't original to the boat. Hauling ties for big loads," answered Mike. "Tractor type grade. Typical for these parts. All the farmland. All the places someone could've gone on the property and cut without an owner knowing their old equipment even tampered with."

I asked, "No tracing to a manufacturer?"

"No," said Jade. "Went through that. Dead end."

Dead end. An end that left one thing for certain, a dead girl. An empty bed. A bleeding heart of a mother.

I kicked the stones and pebbles lightly pressed on the sand. "Any leads on whose boat it was? No offense, but the paperwork was sketchy. Sparse."

"You mean, pretty thin," sighed Ben. "Don't think we didn't do our part, Heather. We took that case on with all we had. We can tell you more than what's in the report. Jackson wasn't a paper pusher, if you know what I mean. He only put bare bones to get the folders stacked. We did the legwork."

"I didn't mean to imply you weren't doing your job." Even though his words could've been cold and defensive, they weren't. They were just matter-of-fact. It happened this way. We did our best.

"I get it," Ben smiled. "We're used to it, Heather. I understand your frustration. I can see it on your face."

I laughed, nervously. "I have a face."

"That you do," said Mike, winking at her. "It says, this is a mess. There's nothing here. Why did we come? What do we do next?"

"Well, I'm that easy to read. Let's you know how bad I suck at poker."

"Don't get them started talking cards. They'll try to rope you in," snipped Jade. "I'm still burnt from losing that hundred."

I brought them back to the line of questioning still burning my mind. "Any trace on the boat?"

Mike said, "Yeah, an old friend. Mercy Jensen's, down by Moss Point. Do you know that bait and tackle shop out on Straightway Road? Mercy owned that shop for forty years. He rents out canoes, boats, that sort of thing, but somehow, didn't have a record of a rental to the boat her body was found in. They stole it."

I said, "I'd like to see that boat."

Jade frowned. "We searched the boat, Heather. There was nothing there. Not a trace of evidence. No fibers, hair, DNA. The little blood that was there was Emma's. It was clean."

"All the same," I said. "Let me just spend some time here, and then we can head over to the Jensen 's place."

The location was a perfect place to dump a body. Isolated and covered with overgrown brush. It was off the main road, two miles deep, with only locals and old-timers probably knowing the site. I couldn't see an out-of-towner having access to the dock. No car could easily make it down the road, so the killer must have used a truck to bring the body down here if they killed her in another location like they originally assessed.

Jade grabbed my arm and gingerly followed me down the broken pier, worn and weathered with years of neglect. Her heels weren't field work worthy.

Mike called out, "Be careful, ladies. Not a safe place to be."

Jade said, "Thanks, Pops. We've got you to save us if we accidentally fall in."

My face turned a bright shade of red. "I can't swim. Might as well know it."

Jade gasped. "Really, Heather? You must learn! I have a pool at my apartment. Come over anytime. I can teach you how. Private lessons. I was on the dive team in college and lifeguarded throughout high school. I've got you."

I thanked her and blurted out, "I like you, Jade."

She laughed. "I like you, too. You know, when we were told Jackson was out and his replacement was starting in the morning, I was a little leery. Just having to start over, not knowing your personality or anything, you know. We'd heard some things about you."

Ben called out, "Only nice things. The rare kind."

"That's good to know," I said. I had worked hard at the job, never causing issues or stepping outside the lines. I kept mostly to myself, so the thought that people even knew me around the department did surprise me a little.

Mike said, "You know they call you Holy Roller."

Jade hushed him. "And we call you Pops."

"I'm fine with it." I shrugged. "There's one way to start a conversation about Jesus without me having to. People at least know where I stand."

"On the promises," said Mike. "That's a lady right there I'm glad we've got in our corner. Time we did some praying around here for these poor lost souls."

I said, "Back to the case. Emma was found around here in the early morning hours by a family coming out fishing?"

Jade frowned. "Yes, one of the child witnesses had to have counseling after coming upon the scene. A residential treatment facility. It was that bad."

I revisited the crime photos in my mind. They strapped her with heavy yellow ties, ten inches wide. Her jaw was broken, and the misshapen way her mouth hung screamed torture. Pain. Eyes wide open.

We made our way back to Mike and Ben. Jade stared off in the distance as if she were reliving it in her mind again, and I saw the sadness etched across her face.

I squinted against the sun, trying to follow her gaze, but it led across the river as if she were praying the killer would row his way around the bend any moment. "Can you tell me what else you know?"

Mike answered, "Someone had strangled her. Ligature

marks were more than likely made with a fishing wire or some kind of thin cording. Only a few spots of blood were left on the scene. We're pretty sure it was from after the killer left. He was meticulous. Wiped it clean."

"Which way was the boat facing?"

Mike said, "Towards the shore. Two ties, and anchored just out a little way but facing us."

"Strange," I said. "With the positioning of the body and the prop, it was clearly a premeditated, staged event. This wasn't random or an act of passion. So, when you walked here, you'd see her waiting for you. Not her back. Not facing the river. But facing the shoreline. Facing the family who found her. He wanted that attention. That shock. He wanted whoever found her to see his handiwork."

Jade leaned in closer. "You think?"

I said, "Why else would there have been two ties? When you tie down a boat, it would seem to be only one rope needed to keep it secured to the dock."

Mike said, "That's true. The line or the anchor should've done it."

"Call Forensics," I said. "Who's over the third-floor team?"

Jade said, "Dakota and Tina, mainly. They switch shifts."

"Have them come out here," I said. "See if you can get them both. Now. We'll wait."

Ben started, "But years . . ."

"Look behind you." I pointed to the tree line. My heart pounded. Questions exploded in my mind. The wind was picking up and a little howl whistled by my ears. I turned sharply but saw nothing behind us. Tricks. Games. It had begun.

Jade walked back towards the riverbank. "Oh, my God."

Ben was already calling it in. "But why? Why now?"

Mike said, "That son of a biscuit eater."

Jade giggled. "Here we go, already cleaning up the language with the Holy Roller present. About time. Heather, you're already making an impact."

We stood on the bank, facing the pines, oaks, and spruce, with their saplings crowding the tree's knees, fighting for the light. They painted the message only on the oaks. Every detail like that mattered. Why not pine? Why not evergreen? Why oak?

Jade said, "What is PS1:3?"

"It's an anniversary date," said Ben, brushing it off. "Pat and Sally. January 3rd. It's a tag."

Mike said, "That makes sense. Out here with it being so secluded. Maybe we've got a young folk lover's lane. It could be a courting spot."

I said, "And he shall be like a tree planted by the rivers of water, that bringeth forth his fruit in his season; his leaf also shall not wither, and whatsoever he doeth shall prosper."

Jade said, "What is that from?"

We didn't see any fresh tire tracks when we came in. No clear prints on the tree line. I answered, "Psalm 1:3. PS. Abbreviation for Psalm. It's a book in the Old Testament."

Mike said, "This might not be connected, Heather. It's just a verse. Somebody might've been making a video out here, some sermon illustration. The lengths that preachers go to these days is so commercialized. So fantastical."

I didn't want to disrupt the scene, so I pushed away the instincts I had to go closer and touch the bark. "Was this here? I saw no mention of this in the notes."

"No, it's fresh," said Ben. "It might just be spray paint."

Jade said, "We see red. We think of blood. It comes with the territory."

I agreed. "I think the murder itself was symbolic. Think

about it. The killer positioned the boat to be just off the shore, facing the tree line. Was there something written on the trees then?"

Mike said, "No. We would have seen it, I'm sure."

I prodded, "Any other signs? Any notes? Anything? Number? Letter? Anything? Whatever this is now, it's the one he wants us to see."

Ben questioned, "But why now? He has gotten away with the murder for two years. You'd think he'd want nothing to draw attention to the crime. That's why I think it's random. No one knew we were coming here. It would've been a message for no one to see. Why that? What would he have accomplished?"

"It's accomplishing something. It's not a lover's lane. It's not a tag from a boyfriend. It's a warning. Let's take some samples, get someone out here to help us case this out. It feels wrong. Whatever this is. It's wrong."

Mike sighed. "I agree. Whether it's red paint or blood, it has no business being in a place Mercy swore he'd never rent out again in honor of the Sanders' family. No one should come down here."

I said, "After we get word from Forensics, we'll take a trip to Mercy Jensen's. Can you call him, Mike? Just let him know out of courtesy we might stop by."

Mike had his number on speed dial. "Sure thing. He's been an old friend of my family for years. Used to come down to another fishing hole with my dad and Uncle Joe. We'd rent a cabin from him, too, out by the Falls."

Jade said, "I just texted Forensics, asking them to take a walk-in instead of the drive. We might get some tire tread. I'm thinking someone needed a ladder to get higher with the first line of the verse. They wouldn't have carried it in. So, we might get lucky with a tire match."

"Unless they took a boat in," I offered.

Mike said, "Prints could be on the cleats."

I asked, "Shoes?"

He fanned himself with his cowboy hat. "No, what they used to tie the boat down. Let's just stay put awhile. Should have brought my cooler and some sandwiches, had us a picnic while we were at it."

I surveyed the area. Such a peaceful place. Serene. No unsuspecting visitor would've ever known the gruesome story. She would've been here unnoticed until that family stumbled upon her. With that thought, it left more questions. So, why go to all of the trouble? The staging? Was it a ritual? A private party? Did he take video or pictures to keep as souvenirs of his work?

In the distance, the river took a turn toward the falls. The sound of the water lapping up against the dock, the lull of the cicada, and the chirping of the birds calling out for the noon feeding hour hurt more than soothed. This place, no place, deserved tragedy. This place deserved laughter from friends and family. Fish tales. Not the scene of a heinous crime and some maniac leaving behind a message. I knew it wasn't innocent. I knew it was connected, regardless of the questions that kept bouncing between them.

"Jesus preached on Simon's boat. He taught them a little way off the shore. The body was positioned there to send a message to the world. Not just a random thing, Mike. None of this is random. Look at the verse. He's prospering. The killer. He's grown bold because he's gotten away with it, yet he wants attention. He's reminding us."

"Of what? That he's a psycho?" asked Jade.

A chill ran down my arms, little goosebumps standing at attention. "That he's been busy and we've missed it. He wants us to see the light."

Ben said, "Are you saying he's killed again?"

I prayed I was wrong but knew within my spirit that what I suspected would be true. "And that's the blood of his last victim. I don't need a test to prove it. I know."

Jade waved and called out, "Over here."

Mike said, "Well, we're about to find out in a jiffy. Here comes Forensics now. It's Dakota and one of his assistants."

Dakota fought his way through the brambles. "You sure picked a hot one to do this, Ben. What's the rush?"

They broke through and came to stand by us and followed our eyes. Dakota gasped. He knew it, too. Not paint. Dried blood. Dark. Sadistic. Enough blood to know the other person wasn't alive.

I asked, "Can you get on that? Quick? Tell us paint or blood? Old or fresh? Watch your step. Any extra gloves in that kit?"

"I see," he said.

He pulled out a handful of gloves, and Ben and I took a set.

I followed in close behind them. No signs so far of anyone treading across the pebbled sand. Dakota slipped out a bottle of luminol and did a quick spray. His assistant followed suit with the UV light. Blue showed what I'd suspected from the first sight of it. I told him what I suspected and could tell by his facial expression that he was agreeing with me before the light hit the mark.

Ben sighed heavily. "You were right. We've got to test if it's animal or human."

I replied, "Either way, it's sacrificial."

Dakota pulled out another test. I recognized the precipitin kit to test the stain origin and knew we'd have our answers soon enough. "It's not a good sign. I agree."

Ben said he'd stay with the Forensics team, and I moved

from the area to let them have room to work. I made my way back to Jade and Mike.

Jade was busy making calls and getting more people we needed to investigate the area. "We're going to comb this place. The cadaver dogs will be here shortly."

"We won't find a body here, but I'm still glad you called in the dogs. It's worth a shot, and we can't leave anything unturned," I said. "But another crime scene here in this location would be too obvious. He's planted the message by the river, though. There's something about the verse." I held up the screenshot I'd taken of the verse earlier as a reference, even though I knew that one by heart. It was actually one of my favorites. Did he know? Was it a message for me? "Read that. Fruit in his season. He's gloating."

Mike cursed under his breath. "You're saying you think we have a serial?"

I said, "Two and time make a serial. It's some twisted murderer or evil somebody roaming this area."

Mike nodded. "We need to find out who's behind the message anyway, even if it's innocent. This is property that Mercy sealed up after Emma's body was found here, and I'm sure Mercy wouldn't want anyone back here even if it is a PS, I love you message."

"Nothing looks disturbed," said Jade. "No signs of a ritual or a mass gathering. I know sometimes the churches use the river for baptisms. What if it was that and we're overreacting?"

"We're not," said Ben, joining us. "It's human blood, estimated to be a day old."

I said, "He couldn't have gone far. He doesn't want to, anyhow. We've got to see if anyone's been reported missing. Jade, can you take care of that? Mike, call Mercy again. Tell him we can't stop by today, but we'd like him to take a drive out here."

Mike said, "He's old, and I don't think his nerves can take it."

"Ask him anyway. It's his land. He needs to know. Rather it be you to tell him than him reading it in the paper. Give him the option of coming down here or meeting us at the station later."

Mike stepped away from them to make the call. "Good point. On it."

Ben lowered his voice. "Heather, do you find it odd we came out here and this was waiting for us?"

"Very. He knew we'd come here, and he's telling us where the victim is."

"Where?" asked Jade, rejoining them. "You're saying this is a message that isn't about Emma Rose at all?"

"Emma Rose brought us here. Her murder is connected to this, no doubt. But this new lead . . . today . . . with me now assigned to the unit, I'm more certain now than ever that this case isn't a coincidence." That I'm not a coincidence.

Jade interrupted my train of thought. "No missing person reports came in over the last twenty-four hours, but I've told them to contact me right away at the first sign."

I called out to the handlers and dogs as they walked over. "Thanks to everyone for gathering. Okay, we've got to spread ourselves out. Look for anything out of the ordinary. Anything that isn't attached to grass and sand could be evidence. Call it out if you find anything. The dogs need to take the lead first. We may have a body here, people. We do know blood was left here. That's human blood you're looking at. Let's not waste a second. Let's go."

It was time for the hunt.

5

"**N**o new body recovered at the scene?" asked the Captain, after we all grudgingly came back to the office after a full day's search.

I spread out the images of the verse painted on the oaks. "Not a trace. Only this."

His face reddened. "I knew it was something more. I knew it."

Mike said, "What?"

"The cases Jackson let slip. We just don't get these kinds of murders here in Crystal Falls. Emma Rose's parents are relentless. They've never given up and are constantly pushing the case. That's why I asked you to bring it all back to life, but it's like this sicko knew it, too. Alley murders and an occasional burglary gone bad, sure. Having a young girl strapped to a boat? That's haunted me for so long. Did you look through the other files? Whatever Jackson did it's a crap job, anyway."

I flipped through but mainly focused on Emma's case. "Let me go grab the boxes."

His eyes narrowed, and I knew he was already making a

tick mark that I'd disobeyed him. 'Read the files before going all gung-ho,' I remembered him saying. Well, it was a little too late for that.

Ben and Mike both stood up. "We'll help."

When we were out of earshot I said, "He likes to blame Jackson for everything, doesn't he?"

Mike said, "Easier that way. He had it out for Jackson from the minute he transferred in from the state office. Said he was too high falutin' for our town. I think he knew more than he ever told us. Jackson was demoted coming from the state office. He left a trail of a mess there, and maybe Cap knew about it."

Ben added, "Not to mention Jackson was a jerk and never played by the rules. He was a shady somebody. Glad he's gone, myself."

"Me, too," said Mike. "Let's just say, we can get to serious detective work now. I liked how you handle that operation out there, Heather. You had them all in line. Jackson would've turned it into a line dancing show, probably texting the media for his shine in the spotlight."

"I left a good team for this," I said, realizing that sounded critical as if I were already judging them. Why did things always come out wrong?

Ben said, "I know Alex. We started on the force together, and Rodriguez, right? They are a cut-up crew. Good guys."

I smiled. "Yep, those two and Harris. I kept them straight. Wonder who is going to look out for them now?"

"You're the mother hen, are you?" added Mike.

"Maybe," I said, smiling up at him. "Holy Roller that I am."

Ben said, "Well, your office is cozy."

My little office, void of light and beckoning with its quiet lull of the air conditioning duct, was not meant to be occupied today. We were moving back out to the main area after all. Not how I expected to run the first day in a new job. Blood. A message. Cold cases. Questions. More questions than answers.

My spirit was ticking a strong rhythm. There was someone out there calling for us to save them, and the answers could be right in the boxes I'd abandoned to go out to the dock. But . . . if I wouldn't have followed that trail, we wouldn't have found the blood. Someone knew we would come. But how?

"We need a log of everyone on the visitor list to the station in the past day," I told Ben. He nodded and moved toward the front desk.

I turned to Jade when we made our way to the back table, set aside for the team to work. "Can you call all the local churches? Just check to see if they've had any baptisms down by that section of the river. They might've seen something suspicious—a person out of place, a sign."

Mike said, "I don't think there would be a church that would go to Mercy's land without him knowing, and he'd steer them clear of there, but it's worth a try."

Jade pulled up the online directory of churches within a thirty-mile radius. "On it."

I pulled the top off the first box. "How many cold cases did you guys rack up with Jackson?"

"Too many," said Mike. "We're good investigators, Heather. Don't think we didn't try."

"I didn't mean it to come across like that. I just want to know how many we need to scour through."

"What I remember, it's around sixteen cases in total," said Ben, after he popped open both boxes and checked the file headers.

I looked at the daunting task ahead of us and hated that

we couldn't be out driving around the countryside, catching this killer, but that wasn't really practical. Nothing could be gained by doing that.

Mike's wife called in, and he'd already given her the news. She knew it was going to be a long night. The casserole was on the way. Found out there wasn't a lot of take-out on the third floor but home-cooked delivery. I could get used to that, hadn't had that in years.

"Boss," said Jade. When no one looked up, she repeated. "Boss."

Ben nudged my arm. At first, I didn't recognize she was talking to me. I thought it was another nickname she had for Ben or Mike, other than the Pops for ol' Mike.

"Sorry, the first day is all . . ."

"The first day, and we caught a break. We just got a call from downstairs. A woman is reporting her daughter missing. She's seventeen."

I closed the file. "Another young one. Lord help us."

"Don't jump to conclusions. She could've run off with a boyfriend."

"Still. Let's go check it out. Mike, you come with me. Ben, can you try to categorize the cold case files into two piles? One for a possible connection to the Emma Rose murder and today's verse, and the other pile for random acts of violence."

"On what basis?"

"Your instincts," I said. "Let's start with that. Trust them."

He nodded and pulled out a handful of files. "I can do that."

Mike said, "We've got another interview on the way. Might as well get comfortable downstairs. I've got Mercy stopping in. He'll be here in about thirty. I'm headed by the break room for a coffee. Want one?"

I needed a whole pot of coffee. He could just bring the carafe. "Thanks. I need it. Heard you got French vanilla creamer. I'll take that, please."

"You're good for us," he said. "I'm glad it was you."

I murmured, "Well, thank you."

I didn't want to tell him how shaky I was or how much pressure the six-month order for results weighed on my spirit. I also didn't want to let him know how much I missed Alex and my team because it'd only been one day away. Rodriguez texted earlier that they busted the gang wide open and found over half a million worth of drugs. A pretty clean operation and I'd missed it. Mike, Jade, and Ben were nice and welcoming to me. That was a start. It just didn't feel the same. I felt missing in it all, as if I were outside of my body looking in at the whole unit. Moving and in motion but not in the moment. It was a strange sensation.

And now a verse. A missing girl.

"Ms. McCreedy?" I asked. It was easy to pick out the frantic mother. Her eyes screamed of another kind of missing.

Her voice broke as she grabbed my arm. "Please, help me find my daughter."

I leaned over to Sandy, who ran the front desk, "Can you call in Sara? Let her know what we're working with."

Sara was our on-staff psychiatrist. I didn't want Ms. McCreedy walking out of the station without at least spending some time with Dr. Clarke. She could follow up with her, too. This would be a tough night, and days to come would get harder. I prayed it would be over soon, and we could find her daughter safe and sound. Boyfriend troubles. Domestic issue. Nothing more.

Ms. McCreedy needed me to help steady her down the hall. "We'll just be going down aways. Let's get to a place where we can talk."

We settled into one of the empty rooms on the first floor used to question suspects. She stared at the glass window and asked, "Is anyone behind there?"

"No, ma'am. Mike's coming in with some coffee. He works with me. Would you like anything?"

"No, no. Just Katie."

I looked down at the initial report she filed with Sandy.

Name: Kathrine McCreedy

Age: 17

Hair: Blonde

Eye color: Blue eyes

Height: 5'1

Weight: 110 lbs

I stopped reading. "Can you tell me about the last time you saw Katie?"

"It was around nine o'clock a.m. yesterday. She was going on a weekend trip with her best friend, Brendi Veracruz. They're both going off to college in just a couple of months, so they begged me to let Katie go with Brendi's family for a river camping trip they had planned. Said it would only be two day. Since it was only a little way down the road, I relented. Katie texted me later in the day that they'd had s'mores and told campfire tales. This morning, I got a call from Brendi's mom. Katie wasn't in the tent. Nothing else was disturbed. All of her belongings were there, including her cell sitting on the portable charger."

I asked, "And why didn't you call it in this morning?"

"I drove down to the campsite, and we looked ourselves. My brother, Kurt, he's a park ranger, so he knows the area well. We thought she might've taken a morning run. She does that. It's her routine. Kurt said the police wouldn't take her disappearance seriously until it has been twenty-four hours, but I couldn't wait until tomorrow. It's getting dark. She's out there."

"We need pictures. Do you have a picture? Can you write the name of the Veracruz family members and their contact information? How about a list of her other friends? Can we get a full list of anyone that you might think of that would want to hurt her? Had she left anything in her room for you? A note? Maybe an indication she had plans after the weekend? A boyfriend, maybe?"

"No. No. None of that. No. I'm telling you she's missing. Taken. She's an angel. Full scholarship to State. Everyone loved Katie. She's truly the best daughter. Please, detective. I need you to find her. I can't live without . . ."

Mike interrupted her rise of emotion. "How about a boyfriend? Was she seeing anyone?"

The mom shook her head. "There was a guy once. His name was Charlie, but I don't think she was seeing him anymore. Maybe. I don't know. She didn't tell me much about guys. She knew I wouldn't approve. She needed to focus on her studies, not boys. That scholarship came with a lot of sacrifices. I had to keep a tight rein on her, and then the day I let her go is the day she disappears. Oh my God! She wouldn't have gone anywhere without her phone. Her phone was there. Right on the portable charger."

"You told us that," I soothed. "I'm so sorry you're dealing with this right now, but we need to retrace everything." I squeezed her hand and slid back the pen and paper. "Add the full name of Charlie, just in case. It wouldn't hurt if we talked to everyone who knew her. And could we get her medical records, too? We'd like to know all about her history."

Ms. McCreedy nodded.

Mike said, "Ma'am, tell us what she was wearing when you saw her last. Let us know any details about her that can help give us a fuller description. You said she likes to run. What else?" Mike got the mother talking, her voice in and out from frantic to calm. We took as many notes as we could gather from Ms. McCreedy, and as soon as Sara arrived, we passed her over to her care.

When she realized we would leave her, the moaning and mumbling began. My heart felt so heavy it was hard to focus. We had to find her. Fast. Ms. McCreedy didn't know about the blood we found on the Oaks. If she heard about it on the news, I knew where her mind would travel. A dangerous place of unknowing.

So far, we'd kept it out of the media's field of vision, but I couldn't guarantee how long that would last. They always had some way or another of finding out the big news, especially in a smaller town like Crystal Falls.

I stopped Mike in the hallway. "I need us to pray. Are you a praying man?"

"I am," he said. "Wow. No one has asked me that before. My wife, she's the rock. She'd love you, for sure."

"Let's pray right here. I can't go any further. Please, Mike. Just a minute before we go back."

We made it to the corner and didn't push the elevator button. Not yet. The hall was clear and my insides were on fire. We needed direction. Something. Anything. We needed to find this girl. I focused on her name. Not just a no-name figure out running through the woods who got lost. That wasn't the urgency I needed. I needed to focus on all of the dark things that could've taken place from the time she was abducted right from a sleeping bag, the last trip with a best friend before splitting apart and never being the same again.

A kidnapping. Blood. A moon in the distance. A man on that very moon looking down at the killer while we were behind closed concrete stacked walls.

Time was moving, and we were standing still.

Mercy...

...principle to...

It was moving, and...

6

_____

ercy Jensen arrived at the station as I reached
to press the elevator button. He called out to
Mike, and they embraced like old friends. His
age was wearing heavily on him. Mercy's sun-kissed face
held years of outdoor adventures and the deep wrinkled
lines coursed like flowing ripples across his weathered face.
His struggle to walk was noticeable as he leaned against the
whittled cane. Mike kept a slow pace beside him, and I fell
in step behind them. I listened to the small-town chatter
about how the fishing was popping down at the river and
what was up with the grandkids.

I had an overwhelming sense of nostalgia right in the
middle of the station. I missed my grandparents. They'd
lovingly taken me in when I couldn't go back home. I
finished out my middle and high school years with them in
Virginia, before heading off to college and losing track of
time. Occasional visits and a phone call here and there left
me aching to do better. I always wanted to do better at my
relationships, but it was hard to find the time. Or that was
the lie I always told myself.

As soon as we made it to the first empty interrogation room, Mercy fell into a chair a little too hard, and it rocked side to side.

"Too late for coffee, old-timer, but I'll get you a water," said Mike. He made his way out and was back quicker than I could even ask the first question. We'd just continued on with the small talk. I figured Mike needed to see for himself that I'd take care of a personal friend. I wouldn't start until he was present, anyway.

When Mike came back in, the tension in the room still didn't break. The more Mike kept on chit-chatting, I realized we'd be here all day and night because it was clear their friendship was one that had years of history. I didn't know Mike enough to get a good read on him, but I felt he would never get the questions started. Maybe couldn't bring himself to it. I took the lead and started with a recap of all Mercy could remember about the murder scene.

Mercy's admission startled me, and I couldn't help but feel suspicion rising. "You burned the boat? But why?"

"You think I wanted that death trap on my property? Rent it out to some innocent family and have the ghost of that girl haunting them? Burned it to nothing, that's what I did."

Mike said, "We checked it for prints and DNA. All of it was swept, Heather. It's been years."

I knew that, but still. I saw it as something else I needed to see. The pictures would have to suffice. The images of the Bible verse were spread out before him, and the sweat pooled on his forehead. Mercy took out his handkerchief and pressed it heavily against his face as if he could've wiped it clean off.

"Blood, you say? Lord save us all," he whispered. "This is blasphemy. I can't look at that anymore. Take it off."

I asked, "Do you know who has access to that part of your land?"

"I mean, y'all got down there, didn't you? I guess anyone under the sun with a decent truck. I don't repair the roads or send anyone to maintain that area. So, I'd say no one would know about that place unless . . . I closed off that piece of the property soon after that girl turned up dead. That's a resting place I can't disturb. My family stays away, too."

"Unless what," I asked. "Mercy, we really have no leads if I must be honest with you. This case has been sitting cold for a long time, and now we go out to just check out the crime scene and we see this? Something's happening. Right now. Something's not right. There's someone missing."

"Oh, God," he whispered. "Oh, God. Let it not be so."

Mike rubbed his friend's shoulder. "Look, Mercy. We just need to know if anything is out of place. You see anything, you call me. Anything. You hear something. Call me. We could have someone return there. It could be a meeting place for someone or a group."

"You mean like a Satanic cult or some mess on my land? I'm going to burn it, I say. I'm going to burn it all to the ground."

"Don't do that, Mercy," he said. "Leave it be. It might be a way we could find out who it is. Don't disturb it and best you did not mention this latest one to the family. We don't want the news of the blood all over town. That'll get ugly real quick around here. Someone asks to go down there, just call us. Let it be untouched."

I said, "We'll get some surveillance down there, Mercy. Don't mess with even a blade of grass. That place is sending us some kind of message and destroying it won't help our case."

It was a perfect place to hide the darkness. A deserted

area. A place for rituals. Yet, the message was planted there for us to see. Or was it? Was it for the police or the news or a private party? No one would scrawl that on the trees without an intended audience. That's the part I couldn't quite resolve.

Mercy said, "I'll keep people away like always."

I said, "They all know this? That it's off limits?"

"Everybody knows this. No one questions me," he said. "Why? Are you trying to say one of my people might've done this?" He looked at Mike with alarm. "Mike, tell this young lady that my people are good people. We ain't got a murdering bone in our bodies. This is a sick individual right here to use the Lord's words like this. Twisted."

"Let's just say someone wanted us to see this verse. They planted it there. They either knew we were back on the Emma Rose Sanders case and were taking a drive there, or someone has been frequenting that spot and it matters to them on a personal level. Hard to believe someone could read my mind because I was the one that had the idea of going down there to the dock to check out the cold case file I'd just been handed. I'm saying all this out loud to let you see how I don't think any of this is a coincidence."

Mike said, "We aren't pointing fingers at you or yours, but we do have two occurrences on your land, Mercy. We've got to go with this line of questioning. That's us doing our job. Understand. Just one more time. Any suspicious activity around your parts, Mercy? Any hearing of anything out of the way?"

He shook his head. "Nothing like this. We always got a church or two wanting to have some retreat at the cabin rental spot or out-of-town hikers wanting to go to the falls. Locals having their time for fishing or relaxing after a hard week at the glass plant. We've got no crazies around here like this."

I pointed at the pictures again. "We do. We'd like to look at your records. Can we get those sent over to us tonight?"

"You mean by the email? Oh, it's paper at my outpost, dear. I don't even keep a single record on a machine. Not about to let my personal information out there on that web or let that box crash on me and risk losing everything we've worked for."

"Well, can we get your written records? Your books? I'd like to see all the transactions, rentals, and sign-in registries. Whatever it is you've got, we'll take it. Even if you think it's not important, I want it."

"I can call my grandson, Mason. He'll bring it all over in the morning."

"No. Tonight," I said. "That blood tells me we've got a body somewhere. I'm thinking it could be somewhere close. I'm sorry but we can't wait until tomorrow, Mercy. We need the records tonight. Plans for tomorrow include searching your place again from top to bottom. We'll be back down there in the morning at first light, no doubt, but right now, we need those records."

Mike said, "Don't worry, Mercy. I'll call him and get him to gather everything. We really appreciate all of your help."

"One thing," I asked as Mike started to help Mercy stand. "Do you have any field cameras up? Hunting cameras?" Deer hunting wasn't in season, but it was worth a shot.

Mercy nodded. "My boy, Junior. He's got him some stands here and there set up with some feeding plots. I'm sure he's got a few cameras out. Showed us a coyote walking in the daylight hours."

"We need access to those videos. We just might catch

someone out of the way. Anything else you think of, please give us a call. We've got a mother in the next room over, worried sick about her missing daughter. We've got blood smeared on your trees. We need answers and we need them quickly. I know you'll do all you can to help us solve this."

"I sure will," he said. "Mike, call Junior. He can get you what you need, too. Tell him I said snap to it. He's probably in front of the screen watching the prelims. It's fight night so he'll be wanting to get it to you before the main event starts."

"Glad he'll have some motivation to hurry," I said, quietly, trying to hold the sarcasm in check. It should be obvious why he'd want to.

I stayed behind, pacing the room back and forth, my agitation rising, fighting against the fear of not finding this girl. I put my hand on the wall to steady myself and wanted to just reach through it, hug the mother, and let her know I would do all I could. I knew I didn't want to see the agony in her eyes again. Better to not face her until I had her daughter beside me.

Jade waved a sticky note at us when we made it back upstairs. "Results just came back. It's an O type of blood on the trees. Proteins show it's female and young. I hate this, Heather. Hate it."

I found the medical section of the report the mother finished filing for us before we left her. "She's an O. The missing girl. Her name is Katie. I need to get back out there."

Ben said, "It's too dark, and you know it. We can be right out there at six o'clock tomorrow morning. We need to get some sleep."

"Go ahead," I said. "Sleep all you want. I'm going back. Something tells me she's still alive."

"The spirit talking?" asked Mike.

"Something like that. Let's think about the message." I pinned up the blown-up pictures of the verse on the movable board. "Let's talk it out. Go."

Jade was the first to jump in. "So, they were by the river and the tree line. That's obvious. Check that off."

Ben said, "The fruit? There were no fruit trees."

"Plenty of leaves," added Mike. "I don't see it, Heather. What are we looking for?"

I held up my search screen on my phone. "There are 31,102 verses in the Bible. Why this one? Why this particular one? From Psalms? Why? There's something here. He's sending us to another location. He's playing with us."

Ben took the middle picture off the board and held it up for us. "So, something with the fruit? Let's just isolate that part of it."

That could be it. "Let's look up farmer's markets, road-side stands, fruit trees, orchards, grocery stores, anything dealing with produce. I say the bigger the better. If he is toying with us with this message, he wants the open space to play. He wants a grand stage, something like a farmer's market."

Mike frowned, pacing back and forth, with his boots clacking on the tile. "You think the girl is held at the county farmer's market? That's way too open. Someone would've seen her by now. It's summer, and it's in full swing there. A Saturday evening, too. It's packed with locals and out-of-towners. A girl held hostage there would be easy to spot."

This idea was growing. "Not if they didn't know where to look. Aren't the agricultural buildings along the back lot pretty much closed unless a festival rents it, a gun show comes through, or for the fair exhibits?"

Ben snapped his fingers around his head like a halo.

"She's right, Pops. I think she's on to something. The way your mind works, on all cylinders. Nice."

If they intended the message for us, I knew this killer would want a show. If it was a private affair, then this would be a dead-end, but we had to try. "He'd want the bigger arena. Not the roadside stand. He'd want the press pouring over that place, and he gave them plenty of room to set up on the scene. He'd want the very thought of him to live in the mind of any visitor driving up to the county market to think of him, and as they pulled into the gates, to shiver at what scene he left behind."

Jade hugged herself tightly, clearly got a chill without having to step foot on the grounds at the thought of it. "Are you thinking it's like the Marcus Pew case? A serial? We've got these cold cases, Heather, and never saw the patterns. Never saw a connection."

"Yes," I said. "I'm thinking he was tired of waiting for the police to piece it together. He's waited long enough and now he's pointing us again in the direction of his madness. If we take the stance that he left us this message and it's not a ritual sacrifice, then he wouldn't have left us this without planning something elaborate to go along with it. No revenge killing here. Jealous boyfriend. This is too much. I hate to know what we'll find."

The scene was already playing out in my mind in slow motion. He took that girl from the campsite while she slept. She wasn't out for a morning run or she would have taken her phone with her. Thinking about a teenager leaving a cell behind left the kidnapping thread more plausible. None of the Veracruz family heard a thing, and Brendi was sound asleep in the sleeping bag right next to her.

He was careful. Might have used a drug to make sure she didn't wake up or disturb the family. He surely left no trace at the campsite. They had scoured it over. Nothing but the blood two miles from the tent. "Let's gear up. I'm thinking we might have a showdown," and for the second time that day, I'd be securing on a vest with plans of heading out.

Whatever we found or didn't find tonight, I was sure of one thing. The killer would trip up sooner or later. They all do. And we'd be the one waiting for him when he did.

7

W e packed up one of the unmarked vans parked in the back lot. There was no way we'd go barreling into the farmer's market parking lot in the muffler popping Bronco. I'd organized a second team as a backup and felt warranted for the call. Just in case I was wrong about the larger convention buildings, Jade sent a list of the mom and pop stands for the patrol officers to survey. All hands were on deck for this one. I was sure the blood was no longer red on those trees, but a brown hue that would fade into the bark. He'd left it for us. For me. If this was true, and he knew I'd caught Pew, then why would he choose me? I'd been the one to get the closest to Marcus Pew. It was as if this killer was watching me. That was it. A stalker.

Not unheard of. The Marcus Pew case was national news. My name came with that story no matter how much we tried to seal up the night we brought him down. Was it a fan of Pew? Was it one of those sick, twisted wannabe followers of his out there doing his bidding? What if Pew was orchestrating all of this behind bars? It wouldn't be the first time a serial killer had tried that along with an escape. Pew was intelligent. This wouldn't be beneath him.

"He knew we were coming," I repeated what was circling in my head for the last three miles. "How did he know we'd be there?"

Ben said, "Maybe it was just a coincidence. He thought someone would see it, or maybe it wasn't even for anyone to see. Ever think about that? Maybe it was some kind of ritual for his gratification."

Mike said, "We know from profiles that killers will often go back to the crime scenes to circle back to relive their crime. That could be it. I was wondering if there was a leak in the office. I'd hate to think someone was helping him orchestrate this whole thing in our department or he somehow had us watched."

Jade said, "Don't you think that's a stretch? One of our guys working with a serial killer?"

I sighed. "I was thinking of a stalker, myself. Someone maybe under Marcus Pew."

"Probably would be, knowing that heathen. He is a madman for sure. He's like the Manson of our time and right here in Crystal Falls," said Jade. "Let's not be the first to be marked as the police department working with serials. Crystal Falls corruption going down in the books. Don't need to add a place like that to my budding resume."

I readjusted my vest. "I'm just thinking out loud. Don't mind me. I have a habit of doing that."

"We see," said Ben, smiling. "Keep at it, though. It's taken us this far."

Mike stretched his long legs. Being cramped up in the back of the van didn't seem to suit his frame. "So, you're thinking if the guy went back to Mercy's to paint a scene, it's like he's honoring it?"

I said, "Honoring it or commemorating it. More than likely it was closer to the anniversary date. What was the date of Emma Rose again?"

Jade pulled out her phone and started scrolling. "I'll check the database. Summer. June 24th."

Ben checked his watch. "We're getting close to that now. Another week out."

Mike asked, "Do you think that's it, Heather? He's saying it's summertime and wants to kill again? Like he's got the summer itch?"

"The season. That verse. We're hitting every fruit lead we can at the moment." That made me pause. "I know that sounded crazy when I just spoke that out loud."

Ben replied, "Kind of. Fruit lead of a fruit loop. Kind of funny, too, if you can have a sense of humor at a time like this."

"Better to have that than any other way," said Mike. "Required for longevity in this line of work."

It was my turn to pull out my app. I needed to check the verse and didn't want to depend on my memory alone.

I said, "I'm reading Psalm 1:3 again. Does anything else stand out? 'And he shall be like a tree planted by the rivers of water, that bringeth forth his fruit in his season; his leaf also shall not wither, and whatsoever he doeth shall prosper.'"

Jade said, "He thinks this is a way for his plans to prosper, or in his mind because he never got caught the first time. Maybe he's just an attention-seeking sociopath. He's gotten away with Emma Rose's murder. How many others? He is prospering."

I tucked my phone away. "In his season. He thinks it's his time. He's bearing the fruit of his toil. Of all he's planned up to this point, and it's all coming to fruition. The victim is the reward. 'His leaf also shall not wither.' We'll go that route next and break that line apart for any possible setting it could apply to."

Mike announced, "And we're here. What's the plan? Go all blazing, screaming, put your hands up, old school raid?"

The sign scrolled: Get your fresh flowers, food, and goods. Open 6 a.m.. The parking lot had a few cars parked sparsely here and there. Could've been left out for mechanical issues or a drop off point to take a ride with someone down by the river. A lot lamp flickered on and off in the night, giving me an uneasy rhythm. Giant moths and insects swarmed the lights, and I watched how eagerly they ran to their deaths. How many more victims ran toward the heat without knowing who they were running to?

The way the body was left in the crime scene photos should've screamed maniac when the investigation was first opened. I knew this fresh blood, the missing girl, and Emma Rose were all connected to the same criminal. So close I could almost taste the answer. If only I could've been assigned to the cases back then, but I was still a beat cop, not even with a chance of warming up an office chair when Emma Rose died.

I asked Jade to run the plates of the vehicles just to be sure before turning to Mike. "As for going in raging, that's not my style. Stealth, Mike. We need to give the girl a chance to be unharmed. He may strike at her when he senses we're close. Those boots with their clinking clank wheels on the back might not be the way to enter a building."

He acted wounded, holding his heart. "Now, she's talking about my spurs." He tipped his hat. "Next, she'll go after the symbolism of my black hat. Good guys wear black, too."

"I want you to stay by the van, Mike. Watch the exits. Be on the radio and take charge of the teams."

He mumbled, "It's the spurs, dog on it. She's got something against the cowboy in me."

I turned to Jade and Ben. "Both of you, with me. We're going in."

Jade put her hand on my arm. I could sense hesitation from her, even though she was trying her best to conceal it. I understood. "Do you really think she's in there?"

"It's worth a try," I said. "Let's find out."

The long row of agricultural buildings paralleled the lot, with narrow passages between each one. During the fair, large garage doors were lifted so visitors could move easily back and forth between the exhibits. Tonight, everything looked sealed tight, and chains with heavy locks were secured in place at the front entrances. The tin buildings ran to the back of the dirt arena used for tractor pulls, demolition derbies, or animal races. I'd worked at an international festival before, so I knew the layout. Anyone in the town would. They'd also know these buildings would be deserted. A perfect place to conceal a crime.

"We start here," I said.

If the message meant anything, Psalm 1:3, we needed to survey the first and the third barn. We moved through the first building by the back entrance. Funny how all the buildings from the front seemed completely secured, but with one twist of the back door, it was clear they were probably all left unlocked.

Squeaks of rats scurrying through the hay set off an alarm in my brain, and I felt the shiver go up and down my spine before I even made it in ten steps. The leftover smells of animals, no matter how long removed, weren't easily masked. Musty air from being closed up, along with dank mildew, add animal waste, mixed with a clear smell of overturned gasoline heightened my senses. Had someone deliberately wanted a fire to start with one of these barns to cover up something sinister? When one would catch a blaze, I was sure that it would be within a matter of minutes that the entire farmer's market would be consumed.

The concrete flooring wouldn't have worked with Mike's boots, and I was just about to imagine him with a pair of bedroom slippers on when I saw a light bounce on one of the window panes. My heart stopped. It wasn't a police issue light, but a larger beam.

I put my hand up to stop them. "Someone's out there."

We barreled down the long space, staying close to the market stands in case we needed to duck and hide. By the time we got out the back door and made it out to the edge of the first building, we didn't see or hear any movement. We'd lost him.

I called it in anyway. Mike and the others needed to know we weren't alone.

"Next one," I said.

We moved together. Jade had this cat-like slyness to her I immediately respected, and I felt trust in the team the more I recognized we all walked in one step, one accord as if we'd trained together and been on countless raids before, not just our first go. What a way to start a working relationship.

Ben pointed up ahead. We followed his direction and the flashlight was back, beaming haphazardly now as if it'd been left dangling by its wrist loop. That meant whoever was holding it had stopped in the last stall. Waiting. He would get a clear shot of us, but we didn't have any choice. We had to keep moving forward, but I lowered my position. Jade and Ben followed close behind. Jade's breath tickled my neck.

I heard it before we saw her, and my heart sighed. A

whimper. A voice so soft one would've thought an animal was mewing. Sounds meant breath. Breath meant life.

Thank God. We were not too late.

Jade flashed her eyes at me, narrowing them in recognition. I quickly nodded, and we moved forward.

The cries didn't grow louder but knowing that we were going to save her and get this maniac made my ears drum with another sound—my heart was racing and banging out of control.

Ben looked at me and waited for the signal. He swung open the stall door at the same time yelling, "Police. Hands in the air."

We moved in.

The girl, who I immediately recognized as Katherine McCreedy, was sitting on a stool, her neck bent awkwardly, eyes down at her lap, where her hands were poised in a praying position, silver duct tape keeping them in place. Heavy straps were crossed around her chest and legs and were connected to bolts sticking out of the floor.

The smell was copper penny strong. I checked for a pulse, and my heart sank. We were too late.

Jade called Mike to let him know to check the area, and close it off. There was someone just here, so close. They'd made their way out through the cracked window, now scampering out on the premises. The flashlight that was still swinging let us know he wasn't far.

Jade grabbed my arm. "What is that sound? Oh, my God. Is there someone else here? It sounds like a child."

It was looping over and over. Whimpering cries with a crackling noise in between. A dubbed recording. Why would that maniac leave sound effects running?

"We've got to cut that noise off," said Ben, as he walked

backward out of the stall. "Find the recording and cut it off. Please. Now."

"Let it play out. We don't have time to search for it, and anything we touch could compromise the crime scene. Let's move. Fast."

I motioned for Jade to follow me, but she stood transfixed. She was wearing it all over her face. The shock and sadness crept in, but we needed to push through it to find the killer. I didn't feel anymore when I came across a scene like this. I imagined it was fake, a dollhouse. Nothing more than smoke and mirrors. A design from a prop of a scary movie. A horror house I'd gone into once sponsored by our town fire department. I couldn't feel because it would impair how I functioned. I would only allow myself to move. Let the wave hit me when I was alone. Not at a time like this. Never in the moment.

I pulled her arm, and we ran out into the night air, so crisp and clean in contrast to what we'd just taken in. The sounds of the woods called to me. He was in there. Crouching low like a wild animal knowing he was being hunted. He wouldn't have made it to the open parking lot without the other officers seeing him. He wouldn't have chanced taking one of the cars, even if it wasn't his. I prayed one was. He had to transport the body here somehow. Then, we'd have a registration. A name.

"Mike, get the coroner. We've got a body. Bring in the dogs. We think the killer is hiding in the woods. It's way too dark for us to go searching alone. We need more backup. Helicopter. Everything we've got."

I lowered my gun, placing it back in the holster. "He's not coming out. He led us to the girl, but he's not ready to be caught yet."

Ben's anger was so hot, he was seething. "I'm going in

there. We're so close. It's almost like I can hear him breathing, taunting me."

"You can't," I warned. "It could be a trap."

I flicked my flashlight and walked closer, gun raised again, and hit the edge of the woods, just to be sure. They both followed. I knew we were grasping at air. This killer wasn't stupid. Far from it. He wouldn't stop and wait for us. Self-preservation. He needed to live another day to kill again or at least replay this in his mind in freedom.

Ben called out, "We're going to find you."

"Don't," I said. "If he is there, don't push him. That'll make it even more joyful for him."

Ben ignored me. "Go ahead. You think you're funny. Laugh. Just laugh. One time. I'll show you what's funny. Make a noise. I dare you."

I turned to him and watched how his jaw clenched, his eyes were like fire. Ben felt. He felt it all at the moment. I said, "He's gone, Ben. He will not give his position away. He's clearly too smart for that."

Jade said, "Let's get that chopper to beam into the woods. He'll at least know we are going all in to get him. Maybe it'll at least freak him out. Dogs and a chopper can play with one's head."

"I need us to still check the outposts. He could've ducked in any of these, gone out the other way. We've got to be sure." I called Mike again. "Did you see anything? Anything at all? We think he's either in the woods or in another one of these buildings, hiding out."

Mike's voice broke over the walkie, "Nothing, Heather. Teams are moving in on all the other ones, searching now. I keep getting the all-clear."

I said, "There are too many places to hide out here which could've been part of his plan all along. Have them search again. Everywhere. Even the outhouses. Every inch of this place from the lot back to the tree line. The dogs can take the woods."

Ben said, "I don't think he would've trapped himself in one of these buildings because he'd know that would lead to his capture. He's out there. Where do the woods lead? Private property? The river? It seems like everything leads to the river in this town. What's the nearest highway?"

Jade was already on that one, holding up a map of the area on her cell. "It runs to Purple Heart Road."

I said, "Then, let's call in two choppers. One to search-light the woods and the other to track the roads. I've got a friend over in Bender County. We can get his guys to set up a block, too. We're about to hit the line. As far as we know he's on foot so he couldn't have gotten too far."

Jade said, "Who's going to call Katie's mother? I . . ."

"I've got it, but it's not a call, Jade. We'll go by there in a few when we get a positive ID," I said, trying my best to keep the cool in my voice. Matter of fact. Unwavering. Business discussion. That's all.

Jade sighed. "Okay, sorry boss. This is so messed up."

"Don't be sorry. First body?"

"First one."

"Ben? Are you okay?" But that question wasn't one I should've asked. None of us were okay. I could just wear the mask a little better, I guessed. Let them think I was immune. I don't think anyone ever is. Unless they're the sociopath that did this.

He looked at me, with his blue eyes ringing with fire, and gritted his teeth. "Fine."

I whispered, trying to bring down the tension. "Let's just do one more circle, okay? Can we do that?"

I didn't have to ask them again. We were back out, the

three of us moving, with the slim hope we'd somehow catch him hiding under one of the truck beds or behind one of the abandoned water feeds. It was worth a check, even though everything in me told me he was gone, through the woods, and out of our reach. We couldn't just stand there with our feet puddled in the murk. Our bodies needed the movement, the alertness, the sharp knowing that all areas had to be searched and overturned just in case we could catch him. To stop him from hurting anyone ever again.

8

The frustration danced between us as we huddled in a circle by the van. Forensics brought out jewelry in bags. Jade took pictures of the victim's belongings. The clothes matched the description of what the mother said she packed with her. That meant we would have to make the trip to the mother soon. It didn't help that the media had shown up. We'd taped the area off the best we could to barricade them back, but their incessant chatter and yells with their questions mounted over us, adding to the pressure.

Captain McBride joined us. "So, Heather. Let me guess. You didn't catch him."

"No, sir," I said. First failure on the job. A major one.

Ben said, "He got away from all of us."

The captain paced back and forth, mumbling to himself as if he were preparing his notes. "I guess I have to go face the wolves. You need to be by my side for this one. I'm introducing you as lead and passing this disaster over to you. They can ask away. I don't need to hear it here and there. Come on."

I stood my ground. It's not that I didn't want to be in front of the cameras, well, it might've been that, but there wasn't a word I would spill about this case. "I'll just tell them it's an ongoing investigation and leave it at that. We don't know enough and the one thing I don't want to do is cause panic. We need time to work the case first before I make any statements."

"Tell them something, Heather. We've got a mother running up to the scene now."

"Oh no," I groaned. "That was fast."

"It's a small town."

I looked to my team with urgency as the captain took my arm as if I needed an escort to the arena of reporters. What a show this had turned out to be. Exactly what the killer wanted. He couldn't get a glimpse of that mother. I refused to give him that view.

"Shield the mother, Mike. Take her to the ambulance fast and see if we can get a positive ID. Regardless of the outcome, hurry her to the back of the van," I called out as the captain led me to the reporter zone. "Please, go easy, Captain. We have to get her out of sight of the cameras. Don't let that murderer have the satisfaction of watching it play out."

The team moved into action and followed the instructions. Captain McBride made his opening remarks, and then I was thrust into the circle of lights. I repeated the lines I gave to the Captain, but the questions kept coming.

I held my hand up to silence the eager crowd. It didn't take me long to read their faces. The eyes were like a window to the soul and no matter if their badge said News 5 or the Observer or Channel 11, that was only a cover for the battle raging within each one of them. He called them wolves. The reporters might've gotten it wrong a time or two in this town, but I realized at that moment they were clearly scared. Alert. Panic. Exhilaration. Story of their life. Worry. Fear. They had daughters, too. They went to church here. All of it mattered. It all flashed before me in a second.

"We'll hold a press conference when we find out more. In the meantime, go home. Keep your families safe. If you see anything suspicious, don't hesitate to call it in. That's what we're here for. Thank you. Goodnight."

My first taste of leadership in front of a camera. The captain whispered, "Well, done. Knew I had the right one to parade in front of the media. Jackson was a half-wit who could barely get his sentences out. You did that with a smile. Very nice."

I said, "Very sad I had to do it at all."

The captain took me to the side. "Tell me this. Do you think this is all connected to the Emma Rose Sanders case? Both young girls. Both strapped down?"

I thought he'd just walked on to the scene. "Did you go take a look?"

"I saw the forensic frames. I'll stick around here awhile. Tell me what I'm looking for."

"You're looking for anything religious. A letter. Note. Probably written in blood. I'm not going anywhere, either."

"Go home, Heather. You look terrible."

"Thanks."

"Don't go home. I take it back. Take Jade and Mike. Go talk to Ms. McCreedy. Then, go home."

We made it back to the van but by the captain's pivot, I could tell he didn't want to face the grieving mother any more than Jade did.

I said, "All due respect sir, I'm not going home."

"People can fill you in," he said, absentmindedly, staring off towards the woods.

"I've got a feeling it's connected. We'll see." I opened the sliding door of the van. Mike was already in the driver's seat. "Take us out of here, Mike. Let's get Ms. McCreedy home. We'll get someone to bring her car around later."

"Good idea," said Mike.

By the stone-glazed look of the mother, I knew she wasn't ready to talk here. How could you ever be ready to handle a conversation like this? She was staring through the windshield in the direction of the ambulance where her daughter lay lifeless on a stretcher. She would never see those pictures of the stall and never know the horror of it. I would see to that.

We pulled into the driveway of the small craftsman style home off the historic main street of Crystal Falls. Crepe Myrtles lined the property and ivy trailed the bay window. It was such a quaint house. Mike cut off the van, and I took the mother's hand. It was soft.

I whispered, "I'm sorry, Ms. McCreedy. Let's get you inside."

"She was my only," she whispered. "My light."

"I'm so sorry. We'll do everything we can to catch the man who did this." I never said I promise I'd catch him or if it's the last thing I'll do I'll catch him. I knew the truth. Sometimes murders were unsolved. The cold case files proved that to be true. Sometimes killers got away. It wasn't a way out of committing. I would do all I could do. But reality hit me hard. He was so close. Right at us, and he slipped away.

Ben said, "We didn't get a good look at him, but he was in that location. We might get a lucky break with some evidence. Hold tight, Ms. McCreedy. We'll look into every possible lead and not rest until we close it."

"She knew that Emma girl."

My head snapped up. "Emma Rose Sanders?"

Her voice was soft, playing in the feathers of memories. "Yes. They have been friends since middle school. Had a sleepover once and that darling little girl French braided Katie's hair. I used to pray for her parents, and think of how awful it must be to lose a child. An unfathomable hole. I'd hug Katie a little tighter every now and then when I'd think of it. I used to pray. I don't know if I can pray anymore."

I would never tell her that her daughter's hands were tied to be in the praying position. The image flashed before me, and I forced it aside. "Do you remember who else might've been there that night?"

She stumbled around in her fog. "You mean the sleepover?"

Jade was already taking out her phone to write any names we could collect. Anything. We needed anything and everything all at once. We'd take what we could. The mother rattled off some of the girls but couldn't remember the last names. She said she had photos on her computer and could send them over. Just as I knew moving helped me get through the pain, I couldn't have Ms. McCreedy still. She needed tasks. She needed to be busy to distract the mind from the pain, the same way we did. A way to deal in an impossible situation. I couldn't bear the thought of losing a child and never said I understood. That was beyond my comprehension. Instead, I only listened.

Ben took her gently by the arm and led her inside. He then broke away and hastened through the house. I knew what he was thinking. Maybe the killer cycled back. I'd be watching for everyone that asked a question. Anyone lurking around would be considered someone to keep a tail on. The whole town could be a suspect for all I knew.

Mike came in and nodded all clear, then started the tea

kettle. Jade and I fell in step beside the mother to sit beside her at the kitchen table.

Jade asked, "Would it be intrusive if I asked could I keep Katie's computer for a couple of days. That and her cell? We might pull some information that could be useful. If we retraced her last contacts, that could be a start."

Ms. McCreedy whispered, "Anything you want, dear. Take it if you think it would help."

Mike poured the tea and served us. Ben joined us, shaking his head. I knew that meant there was no sign of anyone in the house or anything disturbed. Ms. McCreedy had turned off the alarm system as we entered so that gave me a little peace of mind. In case he'd come back to get a kick out of witnessing her grief through a window, I'd put someone down the street.

Jade was fussing over and comforting Ms. MCcreedy the best she could.

I would let them be. "Ben, could you go with me to collect some of Katie's things?"

"Sure," he said.

When we made it up the stairs, I whispered, "Thank you for believing me."

"It's those strong instincts you've got, the puzzle solver in you."

"I hate puzzles," I said. "Never could stand them. Why ask what fills in a four-letter word for a sandwich? I could never take the not knowing. I always want to know."

"And you just actually created a new puzzle. S-u-b-s. Four letter word for sandwich. See, it's that mind of yours, sharp."

I sighed. "Unintentional. I hope there's something here we can see that solves this puzzle. Who was the killer? Did he know her? Had he been following her? To know she was at the river camping and snatch her right out of her sleep with no one hearing a thing? To get her instead of the Veracruz girl? Why? Why her? Is it her blood?"

"You think it has something to do with the blood? Not the typical scenario where a killer picks out a certain hair color or facial features or body type? Emma Rose and Katie were both brunettes. Teens. White. Petite. If we called a profiler in, they'd say that was all the connection we needed to see his type."

"It's the type. Type O. Universal blood. Let me call to check something fast." I dialed the station and sure enough, five minutes later, I found another lead. As random as any other person might've seen it, I saw it as a clear line to evil.

I ran down the stairs, holding Katie's book bag that I'd stuffed with her computer, notebooks, and some folders found on her desk. As much as I hated to leave Ms. McCreedy alone, we needed to get back to the office so I could get my hands on the files. Photos showed no husband in the picture. No boyfriends. The house was so empty. The clock ticked in the hallway. Soft sounds of sobbing came from the kitchen.

Everyone looked at me as I stood facing Ms. McCreedy, a line of questioning already forming in my head, but I knew it wasn't the time. When would be the time? I was thankful to know Jade had called Ms. McCreedy's sister to stay with her overnight.

Beams were already shining in the driveway, and she went to look out. "It's my sister, Clara."

I asked, "When was the last time Katie went to the doctor?"

Ms. McCreedy said, "Just last month. She had a physical for college she needed to turn in. Had to get her last shots. I worried about her getting meningitis on campus. Think of it now. Things I used to worry about. None of it mattered."

I asked, "Who's your family doctor?"

She said, "It's Dr. Davis, down by the corner offices on Main. He wouldn't hurt a fly. He's been our family physician since she was a baby!"

"I'm not accusing the doctor. Just—did anyone else know about her blood type?"

The mother shrugged, looking between all of us as if she were trying to figure out how to speak. "I guess her records show it. I'm sure her school records might've had it. Maybe down at the blood drive? She worked at the community center with the Methodist church, serving as a volunteer. Katie was accepted into the pre-nursing program, so she was always doing one thing or another at an internship or volunteering somewhere to build up her college resume. Please tell me what her blood type has to do with this?"

"I don't know if it does," I admitted. "I'm just wondering if that's what set Katie apart. I told you, Ms. McCreedy. I'll follow all thoughts out on this one until they don't lead to anything. And then, one might just lead to something . . . and that will lead to him."

As crazy as it sounded, I had a rising feeling that the type of blood was drawing the killer to his victims more than the physical attributes. For the life of me, I couldn't figure out why. If we could find the why then that would lead to the motive, and we might form a solid suspect list out of the haze.

Anything. Something. All of it. It had to add up. It couldn't be nothing because then we'd be lost.

The last words I said to her before we left broke my heart to speak aloud and probably broke a couple of rules, too. "I know you said you don't pray anymore. Can I ask you a favor? Can you pray for my team? Can you pray for me?"

The mother looked stunned, but at that moment I saw a small glimmer of light. "I will try," she whispered.

"So will we," I said as I squeezed her arm. The mother hugged Jade tightly before we left her to lock herself away with the longest night a parent should never have to face.

Jade didn't speak as we made it to the van, but I could hear her shaky breathing, puffing outrage, mixed with grief over a girl we never knew. I said, "You did good back there. You took care of her. That matters so much."

She spat fire. "I did nothing. I let that animal escape."

"And we'll find him," I said, turning from Jade and Ben, then giving Mike a long look before he cranked up the van. "And we'll take him down. What did you say back there, Ben? You wouldn't rest until you did. Then, let's not rest. We've got miles to go before we sleep."

9

B en talked out what he claimed was a pretty good system for organizing the files, a task I'd assigned him to do before the trip to the farmer's market.

"This stack seems like petty crimes gone wrong, wrong-place-wrong-time crime, and still some loose ends we need to tie up but seem to be like we could nail down a couple of suspects from estranged family or exes. These, on the other hand, I don't know, Heather. They got me somehow."

Mike asked, "Like where? Your heart? You're claiming to have one this month? Last month you said you were so heartbroken you'd never recover or feel a thing."

I guess the look on my face asked the question I was thinking. Jade answered my thoughts. "Bad breakup. This hairstylist in Silver City named Mindy. She did a number on Ben."

"She also gave terrible haircuts," grimaced Mike. "She messed up Maude's hair. Said she was making her look young again. I swear it looked like a mullet on a woman."

Jade hid her smile behind her palm, but her eyes

danced with joy from the memory. "So glad I didn't let her touch these locks."

I pulled up one of the rolling chairs and put it between Mike and Jade. We made a small semicircle facing Ben, who was still rearranging the files, contemplating his decisions. His nervous energy could be felt, and I wanted to reassure him it was going to be okay, but I didn't feel like holding a mothering class at the moment, so instead, I forced the issue to get his mind back on the files.

I said, "So, let's see what you've got. Class is in session. Ben's going to teach us a few things about instincts."

He held up the first file. "You asked me to look for connections. You want me to draw conclusions with spotty police work, at best, so we're going to need to start fresh just like what we did with the Emma Rose case. No offense guys, but what I saw about working that missing girl case was nothing like what we've experienced with Jackson. I'm not making excuses, but it was a different working environment. We needed you, Heather, years ago."

I hid my embarrassment at the praise and said, "I'm here now. You don't have to have a brown nose or try to flatter the student. I think it's supposed to work the other way around. Go on, Mr. Teach. We're all ears."

"These are young. Females. Missing persons for days, one for over a year before the body was recovered. We don't have much to go on. I've combed the files for Bible verses, notes, messages, but there is just nothing I can find. No memory of any verses standing out either, at any crime scenes. So, why this new thing?"

Jade asked, "So, you think he's developing a new angle? He's growing bolder? Leaving messages? Maybe. At first, it might have been to see if he could kill and get away with it. Now it could be for the show."

"Serials can change their MO. They can develop strategies that grow over time," I said. "But the boat straps, and the straps at Katie's stall, they're the same. Think back to anything connecting these two to past ones. Biblical references?"

Mike said, "I think I would've remembered verses, Heather. What is it about the blood type connection? The blood of the Passover lamb? You think it's that kind of religious symbolism?"

I nodded. "Could be. Or the blood of salvation. If they drained the blood from Katie to be used as the message on the trees, the killer transported it from one place to another. Imagine traveling with a bucket of blood in your vehicle, planning out your day. He then wasted it all on the trees? Has to be something."

Mike narrowed down the files. "If you're thinking about the blood type angle, these have O. Three of them. The rest is a collection of A and AB, one B."

I pulled those from Mike, flipping through the photos to see if anything hit me at first glance. "Then, we'll start with these three and then work the rest, just to make sure. I could be way off here guys. I'm not saying it's the thing. I'm saying it might be something. Anything we can use right now. Anything at all, let's go with it. I just don't want to waste time."

"Anything goes with coffee," said Mike. "I'm going to make us a fresh pot."

I asked, "What about the single serve?"

"I'm a pot man," he said out loud, then lowered his voice. "Now, I'm the one blurting out nonsense. That didn't come out right. I've never used substances in my life. I meant old-fashioned percolation. A glass carafe. Never mind."

I realized the time. "Maybe you should all head home.

Get some rest. We can get back at this in the morning. It's been some day."

I didn't have to tell any of them twice or force them to leave. They were already making their moves to gather up their things. I'd be staying. My office chair was going to be my bed for the next few days. There was no sleep for me. Even if I tried, I was sure I wouldn't be able to close my eyes.

"Some day, indeed," whispered Jade, reaching for her designer purse. "My man, Miles, he'll be pouring me a hot bath before I can get out of the parking lot."

Mike stretched out and grabbed his keys. "And my lady, Maude, she's always a-waiting up for me."

Ben was still pouring over the medical records. "I think I'll stay a bit if that's okay."

"I'm here," I said. "I'm not going anywhere. I just don't want you guys to . . ."

"I appreciate it," Ben said. "I think I want to go through this one more time."

"And I want to follow after you. Hand me the first three. From those, we can prioritize and work on them tomorrow. I can start posting on the board the similarities we find."

Mike said, "You don't have anyone waiting for you?"

At first, I didn't realize he was addressing me. I was busy at work in the files and figured they'd made their way out.

"Heather?"

I looked up at him. His tired eyes were also kind. "Yes, Pops?"

"No family here in town, do you?"

"No. Just me."

"Not to get personal, but anyone at home?"

"No."

"No pets?"

"No."

"Okay. Just wondering. Sorry to ask. I'll start the coffee brewing on my way out. Maude will get us a casserole tomorrow. We'll work straight through."

"It's okay," I said. "The old saying about being married to the job applies to me. No pets because I would be a neglectful owner spending as much time at the station as I do, and I couldn't handle the guilt. My parents passed years ago. My grandparents are in Virginia. I'm just here."

"And we're mighty glad you are," Mike said, giving us a salute before turning with clanking heels and headed out.

I opened the files and laid them side by side. My best way of work was talking out loud. Ben would just have to get used to it. "There's no sign of a struggle with her. Nothing under fingernails. No bruising. Toxicology shows a sedative."

"You think that's how he got them quietly. Drugged them and then moved them."

"Yes. Call down and see if they finished up the tox screen on Katie. Think about being pulled from a sleeping bag. The rustling noise. The unzipping. And that girl, Brendi, she slept through all of that? Maybe he got her with a shot, too. That means he has access to drugs."

"Every criminal I know has access to drugs. The black market makes it so easy these days to get whatever it is you need."

"Crying shame," I said. My phone beeped and it was Mike. He texted to remind us about the coffee. It was already out of my mind.

"Mike made us a coffee. Do you want to walk?"

"Sounds like a fine idea. I'll follow you."

Ben shuffled his feet when he walked. I watched as he didn't step on any of the lines, but picked up, stepped, shuffled in his rhythm. And that's when I noticed I focused way too much on the sounds of feet. Maybe it was because I had to be so aware of my brother's footsteps that might be closing in outside of my bedroom door, afraid he would kill me in my sleep. People thought Amityville Horror scared me when I was younger because we had an older, creepy looking house with a basement. It was because I had a house with that kind of brother.

This deranged, heartless soul torturing girls and draining their blood was not what I'd call a small-time criminal. Was he in a satanic cult? Were demons roaming free, right in our sight, in Crystal Falls? The coffee took me from my random thoughts to the facts. The jolt of the caffeine was what I needed to bring me back to reality.

"We've got these cases to go through, but we also have the tape. Do you remember the tape? Call up for the collection from the crime scene. I'm sure they've dusted everything for prints. We didn't get a close look inside the stall. Maybe something is on that tape."

"I can still hear her. The sound of the crying. I think that's going to stay with me."

I closed the files and leaned back. "I think they always stay with you. I think that's what makes us do what we do."

"True," he said. "I'll call for the recording."

"We'll need to listen to the tape and go back down there to the crime scene tomorrow," I said. "A text came through that forensics would stop by with something they found interesting."

And in less than ten minutes my anything-out-of-the-ordinary showed up in a collection of a bagged and tagged verse. I looked at the officer before he could go back down to the evidence room.

I held up the bag. "Where was this found?"

He frowned. "Sad story to that. It was folded up in her hand. Like a fortune cookie holding the slip."

I asked, "In the praying hands position?"

Ben went through the different crime scene photographs and pointed them out. "Here?"

"Yes, they said when they removed the ties and tape from her wrist in the coroner's office, the paper slipped right out and spiraled to the floor. They didn't catch it with their bare hands, let it sit there shaking a little on the floor. Said it quivered like a worm, trying to make it off hot concrete. As if it were alive."

I shivered. "Anything else?"

"No prints. This guy was cloaked up. Knew what he was doing. Left no trace of himself behind. No hair. No fibers. Nothing."

"He left this behind. This is something. Thanks for bringing it up. We'll have it sent back down when we're through."

"No problem," the officer said as he turned to Ben. "Have you heard about the Emma Rose case yet? I know that's what brought you down to the river."

"No. What?"

"Her uncle called into the station when he heard y'all were snooping around down there. Guess he couldn't hold it in any longer. It was eating him alive. He'd done it. He admitted to killing that poor girl. Said it was an accident, that she fell off the boat. But that doesn't mean a thing with the way she was found. Don't add up, I'm telling you. Thomas Riley was a good man."

"Thomas? Thomas Riley? The guy over the Parks and Rec center? Who serves on the town commission board?"

"The very one. He said he'd done it. Emma Rose's mother's very own brother. Imagine that. Having a family member that sick. Living right by you. Think they lived next door. Couldn't stand the thought of it."

I knew how it felt. I knew how awful it could get. Poor girl. I bet she didn't see it coming. I bet none of them did.

"Put that file away from the stack of possibilities," I said. "No use going that route since it's a closed deal. Someone else can take Emma Rose on for processing. We need to focus on Katie's case, and this."

I held up the verse. Ben took it for closer inspection. "He left us another clue, did he? Do you think it leads to another body?"

"I hate to say yes to that question, but I am telling you to go with your instincts, Ben. What does yours tell you?"

"Stuff I shouldn't ever have to say out loud."

I looked up the verse, Isaiah 43:2. "Let's see about some good old Bible study right now. What does this one mean? I think it's more than meets the eye," I said. "Let's not call Jade and Mike back in for a few more hours. Let them have the rest of the night. Go home, Ben. I'll need you fresh in the morning."

"Sorry, but is it fine that I stay?"

"Suit yourself," I said, as I typed in the verse. "You won't bother me. It'll give me someone to talk out loud to. If that's okay with you."

He took a sip of his coffee and settled in beside me. "I think I could get used to that. Talk away. So, what do you think it means?"

"I'm not sure," I said. "It's not a verse I readily recognize. Never heard a sermon on it. So, with it being obscure lets me know that this man knows his Bible."

"Seems like he doesn't know it at all."

I replied, "Said he knew it, didn't say he followed it. It means he's crafted some kind of warped ideology. Religious fanaticism, maybe. He might think he's following the word to the law, which also shows we're working with a distorted mind. An altered perception. He believes he's doing the work of the Lord. Wouldn't be the first serial killer who thought he heard voices from God."

"You think this is a serial killer?" The voice broke through their discussion and it started me. I hadn't heard the captain walk up.

"Yes, sir. I do."

"Then, we need to call this one in. I'm calling the State Bureau in the morning."

I didn't want all that heat everywhere. "And you think they're in to help us? Like they did with Marcus Pew?"

Captain leaned over and grabbed the baggy, squinting to read the small, typed print on the slip of paper. "Do you think you can handle this? Is that what I'm hearing you say?"

"I'm asking for a few days for us to try. If it's a local, then we're better with Mike and us working on it. The townspeople won't talk to outsiders. They'll clam right up even if they have something to share. I don't have solid proof it's a serial. As you know, that takes a three count. Right now, we've got one definite crime scene that wasn't an exboyfriend or drug deal gone bad. We've got a sick animal who drained a young girl's blood and smeared it on trees. There's something bigger here than just this one crime, and we need time. That's what I'm asking for."

"Time." He turned to Ben, rubbing his hands through his hair, and scrubbing his face to take away the tired if that could be how it was done. "You think the same thing? A serial murderer?"

"I think she's right," he said. "It's more than we're seeing."

"I give you that. Okay. I'll hold off on the phone call. Just do your thing, Heather. Do it as quickly as you can. I can't handle the town pressure for long. People will call it in for you if we find another victim on your watch."

"I understand. Thanks."

I tried to stay away from the politics beating behind the department as much as I could, made it seem like it didn't exist when I full well knew it was a driving force behind many decisions the captain made.

"All right, kids," he said. "Have at it. That Marcus Pew case finally persuaded me to put you up here with us on the third floor. Maybe you can tap into those talents you used with him. Have you ever considered this? Maybe Marcus Pew has a thought or two about the case."

"You want me to question a serial killer I put away for ten counts of murder about this case? You want him to know the verses, which as you know, could actually jeopardize the case more than help? He will tell the world or at least his fans. That'll feed his idolatry."

"I said it for you to consider. How many dog-on killers do we have to have in this town, anyway? People come here for the falls and the night catfishing. For a quiet life. Not for the crazies. Go if it helps, Heather. Do your thing. I don't want to see you in my office until you catch the monster. Is that understood?"

"Clear," I said and turned to my computer to find out all I could about the new evidence.

When he was out of earshot, Ben said, "You handled him well. Jackson would have started shaking in his boots."

I laughed. "What is it with cops and boots around here?"

"Country living. Fishing. Hunting. We live like that. I do think the captain is on to something. We wouldn't have two serial killers raised right up here in the falls, would we? Maybe it's something in the water."

"Maybe it's someone here for the water. The purification. The blood. They came here for both. Call down to IT. Get them to get us a list of every resident in town and the surrounding ones, from the county water, electric companies, whoever they have connections with. Every single last one. I want to know who might be new, maybe within the last three years. They came here for the falls. The water cleanses, but so does the blood."

"And you got that from the conversation we just had. This random talk led to this brilliant idea?"

"I told you it's the talking out that I need."

"I'm all ears," he said, as he picked up the phone to call in my request. "Look up that verse, and let's get to it."

"On it," I said. "You don't have to worry about a thing."

"Not with Heather Moody on the case," he said, jokingly, sounding as if it were a line from a third-grade mystery novel.

Heather Moody. Me. Lead Investigator. On another string of murders, I was sure led to another serial murderer. Catching Marcus Pew was easy, but I'd had a little inside help I wasn't ready to admit to yet. My spirit wasn't resting on this one, and something told me this time, I'd have a harder time to go.

ike and Jade walked in as if on cue. We were just talking about how now would be a good time to call them in after giving them time to rest. The plans I had for going back out to the farmer's market changed once we got the verse to analyze.

Ben smiled, a sleepy one that brought a softness to his face. "Telepathy, now? We were just about to call you both."

Mike said, "We left here knowing a six a.m. return was needed and agreed. Figured you'd both stay all night. We right?"

"Right as rain," I said. "We've got something."

Jade switched on her computer. "And you didn't call us sooner?"

I handed over a folder with the list we'd populated of newcomers to Crystal Falls. "Grab a highlighter, Mike. See if we can do some cross-checking with these names and anyone that has a prior."

Jade pointed to the board. "Both of you've been busy, I see."

She was right. We turned the moveable board from

roaming eyes. The open floor plan wasn't conducive to detective work, but I wasn't the one in Human Resources coming up with the grand office designs. We didn't need to show the connections we'd made to onlookers passing by, reporters stopping in to capture any news, or anyone else. I was still a little weirded out by the fact we made it to Emma Rose's crime scene to find the first message waiting for us. Who knew we would travel down that path?

I pushed my doubts away and caught them up to speed. We'd narrowed down three victims with O blood types. They took all females from places of comfort, no eyewitnesses, and no viable evidence. All were poised and positioned as if planning in the smallest of details was considered. Even with the similarities, hair color, small frames, and young, no one had their blood drained from their body like Katie. Which could've meant this was the first or the most creative. Serial killers creating their wicked art.

An art class we'd have to cancel before he killed again.

"I see the images of Katie's crime scene have been processed," said Mike.

Jade passed by the ones of the stall quickly and then rested in front of the small slip of paper with Is 43:2 typed on it, with the new verse blown up to readable size.

She read, "When thou passest through the waters, I will be with thee; and through the rivers, they shall not overflow thee: when thou walkest through the fire, thou shalt not be burned; neither shall the flame kindle upon thee. Isaiah 43:2"

Mike stood up and came closer. "He left this at the crime scene?"

"In her hands. He positioned her hands in prayer. Like

that." I pointed to the hands cupped innocently together. Such petite little hands. Sweet girl.

"Lord," called out Jade. "We need you."

"We do," I said. "Every second of every day. Mike, run the priors, but also check for church rosters. Deacons. Leaders. Someone in a position who seeks power. A serial killer feeds off of the power. It wouldn't be just a visitor or a regular member. Someone held in high regard. The praying hands. The verses. Jade, what did you find out from your searches yesterday?"

She shook her head, letting me know they were dead ends. "I've got a call into a professor at State. I once took a class with him as an elective but it focused on cult phenomena. I thought maybe he might know of any North Carolina cults out there in the wind that haven't found their way on the internet yet for anonymity. He's pretty much the closest expert I know. Did a documentary spot once."

I brought their attention back to the new verse. "I think we need to break this verse apart. I did some study on it last night, but as smart as I think this killer is, I don't think he's taking them on a deeper metaphorical representation. I think he's a literal reader. One that is surfacing the words and using them as destination spots to commit his crimes. See the verses. Both are again mentioning the river. His obsession with water must show his sins are conflicting with him, and he's seeking baptism and cleansing. He's seeking redemption in the blood. As much as he wants to stop. He won't. It's his way to salvation."

"Did I hear you think it's a possible serial case?"

Great. Just what we needed. The reporter from Channel 7, Dorothy Catrel.

Mike's voice bellowed even though he still maintained a smile. "This isn't a place for you, Dot. You know not to go snooping around the bullpen. Don't go to the press with any of what you might have heard. We're trying to catch a killer. We don't know what he is."

Dot twisted her hair in a knot, pulled out a small mirror, and checked her red lipstick. "But you do know he's a religious fanatic. Apparently with Detective Cain here, reading out that verse like she was reciting it in front of the church. You have an excellent voice and such a look, Detective. Ever consider television? We need a new meteorologist."

Jade rolled her eyes. "Enough with the flattery, Dot. It won't get you anywhere around here."

Ben laughed. "Speak for yourself. Flatter me, Dot. I've been trying to ask you out for months and didn't have the nerve."

As far as a reporter keeping her cool, she did not. Her face flushed hot. "Is that you asking?"

"It is."

"And we can talk about the case?"

"No," I said. "No one is talking about the case with any reporters. We're keeping this hush-hush for now."

Ben winked. "You're the one that's always showing up at the most convenient of times, Dot. Do you know of anything that could be useful? You probably know this town better than anyone on the force."

"Why thank you," she said. "I think I do. I should. I've been working this beat for ten years. Let's see. If you're looking for a church-going type that is a little cuckoo, too, you might want to check out that crazy group called the True Life Covenant of the Lambs."

Jade pulled up her database of churches. "That one isn't on the list."

"It wouldn't be," said Dot. "They call themselves a community organization. A nonprofit. They've got that as a cover I'm sure, and there's no telling what they're doing in that strange set of buildings out by Cooper's Landing. Your guess is as good as mine. From a helicopter ride over the river, it looks like some Jim Jones encampment if you ask me, and I know what happened when reporters started asking too many questions there. That won't happen to me."

I asked, "You think it's a cult?"

"True Life Covenant of the Lambs. Just the name itself sounds a little off. It's not like it's First Baptist. It's not registered."

Mike's voice didn't even try to mask any suspicions. "How do you know all of this?"

"Maybe we can ask you a few questions," I said. "Away from all this." I motioned for Mike. I'd already been in the room with him once before and established that he was my interrogation partner. I liked his style.

I leaned over Jade's desk, out of earshot. "Call that person you know. Ask about this True Life Covenant of the Lambs. See what you and Ben can find out."

Ben said, "Next move?"

"Get a quick fly-over ordered. Take a ride and get some shots. And while you're at it, how about getting some maps of Cooper's Landing. Let's get those on the board. This is the first out-of-the-way lead we may have."

Ben's face turned pale. "I could always help with the questioning. The thought of flying in a chopper before breakfast makes me feel a little sick."

Mike laughed. "You already asked a question and Dot pretty much said she'd use you for a story leak. Not an actual date response you should be after, Ben. What are we going to do with him?"

I smiled. "Seems like you've got an admirer, Dot. That might be a first."

"I'm not that much of a shark, Heather. I just do my job, and I do it well. I can't help that jealousy comes with that. Award-winning journalists pay a heavy price."

As soon as we settled into the room, I said, "The way you covered the Pew case was a disaster, Dot. You almost got me killed."

"And I'm sorry about that. Call it excitement. Call it jumping fast on a hot story that deserved the front-page news. I got an award for that."

"And I almost got a bullet for it."

Mike interrupted, "Ok, so let's see here, Dot. Tell us what else you might've seen that's off around town."

Dot took out her phone and turned on her recorder app. "I heard you say, point-blank serial killer. That's enough to get me with eyes and ears wide open from this day forward."

I squeezed her hand and moved the phone away. "Don't jeopardize this case, Dot, for the sake of your name going beside a tagline. Lives are at stake here."

"He is a serial. And I'll be the first to run it."

Mike said, "I could tell out there you knew more about this nonprofit organization than you were letting on. Who are the members? Everything. You are more than thorough when you smell a rat."

Dot's voice poured like syrup. "I'll tell you on one condition."

I didn't return the smile. She was just as bad as the rest of them. "Let me guess, you want inside details? Sorry. We can't do that. We can hold you for obstruction of justice. How about that condition? You tell us what you know, and we won't arrest you for withholding valuable information."

She held my gaze. "My condition is that you let me interview you and Pew."

I laughed. "You're out of your mind. You want to interview a serial killer, that's all. Go talk to him yourself. I'm sure he's open to it now that he's been locked away without his attention. Oh, wait, I forgot. He's been getting attention. Has little groupies that go see him on the regular. Interview them."

She shuddered and shook her head in disgust. "So far none of the women will speak to me. What draws a woman like that to visit and swoon over a murderer? Love letters? Really? He gets them by the mail bags. That's the question of the century."

Mike said, "What draws a moth to a flame? Some things will always remain a mystery. Now, tell us what you know."

Dot pulled out a notebook, almost the mirror image of Mike's. I smiled. Old school reporting and detective work. Jade would have the notes on her phone.

She pointed to one name she had scribbled across one page. "I don't want to say this name out loud."

Mike and I leaned over and peered at the page. He laughed, "Why? You think he's the boogie man?"

"I think these windows are proof enough that someone could be listening to me. You brought me here to discuss this when this whole department could be inside."

I asked, astonished. "Are you saying you think this is the cult leader? This is ridiculous."

She shrugged and closed the book. "Why not him? It's all pretty ridiculous, is it not?"

"It is," said Mike. "But what you're saying is sensationalism. You'd want it to be him just to get that story you've always wanted—that dream one where you brought down not only a cult but a powerful . . ."

"Stop," she said. "I have my reasons. I'm just telling you what I believe to be true."

I said, "And you know this how?"

She leaned in and whispered, "Believe me, Heather, I'm not making this up for a story. I'm not that awful. I promise. Sometimes you just have to have faith."

"Faith in you? I'm not convinced."

Dot stood up. "Then, I guess I'll leave you with this. Jesus said those blessed are they that have not seen, and yet have believed."

I eyed her closely as she made her way to the door. She was so manicured and polished. A perfect reporter persona, yet quoting bible verses?

Mike said, "Start talking like that, Dot, and you might give me a reason to add you to the suspect list."

"Do that," she said back with a plastered smile. "It would be an awesome story to be the one to clear my name while taking everyone else down with me."

Mike laughed. "And I thought you said you weren't awful."

She smiled sweetly, but her eyes were on fire. "I'm not. Unless I'm cornered. You don't want to see that. I'm willing to work with you and won't reveal until absolutely necessary. I get that interview with you and Pew. I'll set it up today. You promised." And with that, she sauntered out of the room.

"I didn't promise her anything," I said. "Did you hear me say I'd agree to an interview?"

"No, but she did give us a look at her names. Gave us more than what we had coming into this morning. We need to play her game a little, Heather. How would it hurt?"

I could stand right there and count a thousand reasons how it could hurt but then I'd be admitting that I felt something. That was more dangerous than sitting across the way from a killer I'd put away for life without ever having the possibility for parole. As Mike said, some questions would always remain a mystery. The name of this killer couldn't be one of them.

11

I needed the quiet of my office for a few minutes. Away from the ringing of phones, the station sounds, and the questions being thrown back and forth by my team. Good questions but circular, and my head was spinning with them. All leading back to Dot accusing the department and someone may be tracking my moves.

The silence welcomed me in and for the first time, I could feel my heart settling into a normal rhythm. The tying down of that girl on the boat couldn't have been that uncle. I'd read over the transcript of his confession and even though it was point blank—"I did it. I'm sorry," it didn't feel right. It was all too close and too far at the same time.

Usually, cases add up. A plus B equals C. Clear signs of struggle. Murder for money. For revenge. The murders of these teenage girls? No. It was more than that. It was from the mind of a twisted psychopath. Not that a criminal held the innocent mind or lived in an altered reality. But this. Warped times ten.

Captain and Dot both suggested I take a trip to the

prison to talk to Pew was another one. What was that all about? That was too coincidental. The text came in about thirty minutes after Dot exited the station. What was this? She had something going on with the captain? Was Dot somehow working in cahoots with the cops, and as much as he dogged the press? Maybe it was because he knew the guilt would spread across his face as soon as he stepped in front of the cameras.

The captain told me to go after the Emma Rose case. Now, he wanted me with Pew. And for her to write the mayor's name on that slip of paper, as if he could lead a cult with an active county role. That could've been some kind of political scheme to get him booted out. With us questioning him during an election year, that would be all Dot needed to twist the mighty pen to ruin his career. Mayor Aaron McColl wasn't the cult type. Scrawny. Tall. Like a scarecrow. Unassuming with no record. Not even a speeding ticket.

Yet, here I was with another Bible verse. The praying hands and the message let me know this was clearly a taunt. It meant the killer wanted us to follow him into his maze of darkness. It flashed before my vision. I didn't need to see the exact verse anymore. All I saw were the flames.

I called Alex, my old partner. I knew he was someone I could trust. "Do you still talk to Whitcomb?"

"Yeah, that's my boy. And hello to you, too. Busy on the third floor, I hear."

"Don't get me started. I need you to text me his direct number."

"You could've just texted me that. Let me guess, you wanted to hear my voice."

"Maybe," I said. "Ok. Yes." I wasn't going to lie. Where was my normalcy? My calm.

"Then, that means I can officially be thankful you moved one up from me. I was figuring I annoyed you or were avoiding me."

"Never," I said. "Well . . . let me take that back. Sometimes I get annoyed."

There was a pause that allowed my heart to quicken again. Just when I thought I had settled down, the pressure started rising when we hit a strained moment of silence. Why did things have to always be so awkward when people moved on?

He grumbled, "We miss you, Heather."

"Same," I said. Don't feel. Don't go down this path. Get the number. Talk about the case. Don't talk about anything but the killer. "Alex, between us, this is blowing up fast. I might need you guys as my backup."

I felt his concern in every syllable. "You don't trust your new team?"

"Not that at all. I fell right in step with them, but I think this is bigger than what we can handle alone. We already had to call in a unit last night. The captain said he didn't want me to come into his office until I caught this guy. I don't need permission to gather my reinforcements, my guys. I just need you to say yes when I need you."

"And you seriously think I'd say no?"

"Maybe," I paused. I had abandoned them. "I don't know."

"Never. Text. Call. Any day. Any time. I'm speaking for me and the guys. We've got you."

I could hear them all hollering around Alex in a chorus of agreement. I forgot that no conversation was ever private. "Thanks, guys. I'll owe you."

He chuckled. "Not sushi. Never that."

"One of these days, you'll all develop taste."

That led them to banter that could last an hour, and I didn't have time to join as they begged me to take a break and visit. I'd already admitted I needed to hear their voices but didn't want to see their faces out of guilt. Funny how I could be a coward in a closet when I'd just tried to chase down a murderer the night before.

The text came right after I hung up. Mark Whitcomb was the chief of the fire department, and I wanted to give him a courtesy heads up on what we were dealing with. And I needed to read the verse to him. I didn't know what made me think of involving him, but I felt led to do it. Maybe it was to let him be aware that if any call came in for any fire, even a yard fire out of control, to call me immediately. I wanted to speak to him personally on his cell, not on the department line, just in case Dot was right. If the mayor was a cult leader, he'd have an opportunity to have offices bugged. And if a fire was in his distorted mind, and that's how he'd strike next, that would be a place he'd possibly have targeted. It could be absolutely nothing. But it could also be something big. I needed to be cautious yet cover the basis at the same time and didn't want to take any loose chances. What a fine line I walked as the time ticked on.

I started the call without the typical back and forth pleasantries, even though I had no time for small talk or polite introductions.

"Can you step away from wherever you are at the moment and get to a secure location? A place away from ears, eyes, and anything that could catch this conversation."

"Hum...Sure," he said, hesitantly. I heard him shuffling away in the background and excusing himself. "What's this about?"

"We've got a killer in Crystal Falls. A body turned up last night that may be connected to a cold case file."

He sighed. "I saw that on the news. Poor thing. Going off to college, I heard, on a scholarship."

"Yes. And in her hands was a Bible verse. The second one we've recovered from crime scenes. When you get a moment look up Isaiah 43:2."

"And you're telling me this because . . ."

"It involves fire. I need you to be careful. I need you to watch your people. Please let me know if anything suspicious comes in."

His voice rose in alarm. "Are you saying one of my men or women could be the killer?"

"No. I'm saying fire was in the verse. The killer is going to set something on fire. Possibly today or very soon since we found it with the victim."

He raised his hands. "Oh my word. Are you saying we have another serial killer to deal with? How much do we have to take in Crystal Falls?"

"I'm saying it's a possibility, and I need you to be as discreet as possible on this. I don't want media outlets getting wind of this just yet, but I need you to be mindful we're dealing with something out of the realm of a typical homicide. I'm calling you to make you aware of what we found on the crime scene because it could involve you or your people facing a dangerous killer. It could very well come today, and I want you to be ready. We all need to be ready."

"We're always ready. Part of the job, but I'll also make sure my conceal carry people are packing during shifts."

I ended the call. This was a mess. A mess and a half. So many unanswered questions pinged in my brain, trying to make sense and connect the dots. Speaking of Dot. How could one reporter's words have this much of an effect on me? It could be any of them. Members of the cult, disciples of the mayor. People with power. The very chief himself held a position of authority. Did he want me on this case because he knew I might be able to crack it or because he wanted to catch me before I caught him? I did take down Marcus Pew. Is that why he got rid of Jackson? Planted crooked evidence on him to frame him out the door? Get me in this position to do the very same? Maybe the insider leak was the police captain.

I called Mike. "Get a patrol car 24/7 on the Mercy lands."

"That's a lot of land. Do you mean specifically around the area of the crime scene?"

"Yeah. See if you can locate a spot right off one of those side dirt roads where traffic can be seen easily but cops can stay hidden. If anyone sees us, they'll think we're setting up country speed traps."

"You think the killer will double back again?"

"Most serials will revisit their scenes. They like to relive it, and it's just a precaution. We've got fires and rivers in the verse. Don't want to make a mistake by thinking it can't be possible. He'll try to go down there and burn the place down."

Mike sighed. "You think he's got something against ol' Mercy? That can't be it. He's an old coot, ornery at times, but a heart of gold, that one has."

"I'm not saying it's that either. I'm just saying we can't be too careful. Maybe you and Ben should go visit the Mercy family. See what you can see without letting on you're looking too hard."

He whispered, "You can trust us, Heather. We'll call it a hunting expedition."

"And I appreciate that. Call my cell." I didn't want to tell him I wanted to keep it off the main lines.

"I'll do that," he said.

A hunting expedition. That was exactly what we're all on. The problem was, who was the prey? Was it a victim or was it me? Was he trying to get to me with these verses? Marcus Pew wasn't this methodical in his killing, yet he was brutal, targeting elders in their homes in broad daylight. He had a thirst for blood and money, but it was different somehow than how this new killer was operating. This killer was about something more. The narrative was playing out right before me but I couldn't catch the storyline. Not yet, anyway.

I made my way down the hall to the bullpen and saw them still at work on the verse. "Is it not a cult but vampirism? You think they're drinking the blood for power?"

Mike snickered. "And you're suggesting that's a thing."

"Sad, but it is," said Jade. "Let's not rule anything out. I got a return call from my old professor. He knew of that cult, by the way, the True Covenant one. He agreed to meet with us. Crazy it's right here under our noses and we didn't know it was a thing."

"How about we move down to my office," I asked.

Ben leaned forward. "Are you getting paranoid, Heather? Thinking Dot might be actually on to something?"

"Just don't want to take my chances. We've got to have some leverage in the case and keep some of this under wraps in case we do have some suspects come forward. This open floor plan doesn't lend itself to privacy."

"Understood," said Jade. "Let's take it all down." She wheeled the board down the hall, facing it to the wall instead of letting anyone catch it with a roaming eye who might be looking. Mike took two chairs with him, and Ben hopped in one of them for the ride.

"So, we're doing this," I said.

"You did say . . ." replied Jade.

"I did." I unlocked the door and let them into my little bit of heaven. "Then, I guess we've got a tight living quarters for the day."

Ben said optimistically, "What if we could catch him in a day? Some record."

I said, "Then, that would be an amazing day. I wish life were that easy, but I've learned otherwise."

When we were locked in my closet of an office, a sense of relief washed over me. I leaned against the door and told them about my suspicions. All of it. Even the questions I was now raising about Jackson and the captain. Didn't want to leave any secrets between us if we were to be a team. My instincts told me I could trust them. If I was wrong, then so be it. I had to jump. Sometimes I just needed a leap of faith.

Mike said incredulously, "So, you're thinking the phones are bugged? Or the station has recordings of what's been happening around here?"

Jade answered, "Well, the good news is, if we stick in this hole . . ."

I laughed, "Hobbit hole. I like to refer to it in a loving way."

She continued, "In this Hobbit hole, it would be easy to detect any equipment here out of place with the lack of furniture. I've swept it from corner to corner. No wires. Nothing."

Ben asked, "You really think someone in the department might work with a killer or this cult? This is crazy."

I sat down at my desk and cleared the top away for them to pile the folders across it. "What if Dot's suspicions are true and the mayor has something to do with this. You know how much he walks through, him and his assistant. They visit weekly. Someone knew we were going out to Emma Rose's crime scene. Tell me how they knew all that and had time to paint the blood."

"The log. I logged in where we went that day," said Mike. "That was micromanagement on the captain's part by making that rule a standard procedure when a team goes out to investigate. So, if it's not bugged, the mayor may have eyes. This is ridiculous. Mayor McColl? Really?"

I said, "And I called the fire chief to let him know to be on alert. Call Mercy, Mike. Let him know we've got eyes on the place, and just as a security measure, he might want to beef it up as well."

Ben said, "There are more ways we can keep eyes on a property. Deer cameras, remember. Let's set them up, and we'll know ourselves what's the deal on the land 24/7."

Mike said, "Sounds good. I'm sure we've got a man or two to spare that might want to set up some cameras. We're still waiting on the footage from Junior."

I'd forgotten about that. "Why is that taking so long, by the way? Did they have something to hide? We should've confiscated them ourselves. Send a couple of guys out for their logs, records, receipts—anything with a paper trail. And tell me more about the deer camera idea."

"Pops and I use deer cameras all the time. We've got an app that alerts us at any movement around our feed plots," said Ben. "If something's moving, we'll know it."

"Then, set everything up and give Jade access to the app. Do your thing. Whatever it is. I'm going to go back over the Emma Rose case and check the evidence room. I'm thinking there was a verse left there on the scene somewhere. Maybe a crime scene photo will pick up something that was missed."

"Easy," Jade said. "I can start working on the cameras. Let me go get my things. We can all crash in here. One cozy family."

My little office was about to be taken over. It had to be, though, unless they all wanted an alternate place to go outside of the department, this was the safest way. "Yeah, might as well move in here, guys. I know it's cramped but believe it's necessary. Even if it's just for a day. Get what you need."

Mike said, "Better go grab your deodorant, Ben. That's a necessity. You smell like a mummy warmed over in a microwave around lunchtime. And with you not going home last night, that meant no shower for you. Nope. No ventilation in here . . . just saying."

Ben defended himself but still sniffed to make sure. "I took a quick shower here, thank you. I have a change of clothes stashed in my locker."

As they left to collect their things, I walked up to the board. Visiting the crime scene of Emma Rose started this, I was sure. The captain requested I pick up that file. Said it haunted him because she was a child, but why her? There were more young victims. Why did he call out her name specifically when so many other unsolved files were carried to me in the boxes? And the uncle coming in to confess? Just the thought of it didn't sit right with me. Everyone was now sure it was a closed case, but not me. So, why was he taking the fall for this? He was confessing while we were out chasing, so that made him either an accomplice or someone who knew something that could be useful. The uncle would be another in the line of questioning. The job was never done.

When they all filed back in and rearranged the space to

give themselves some semblance of comfort, I said, "These three victims had O blood type. Let's look at their dates."

Ben leaned the chair back up against the wall. "Birthdays?"

I said, "Death days."

He pulled out the files that his instincts had told him were related. "We've got Tracy Harrington's murder on January 6th, 2013. Madeline Wells was on September 16th, 2012, and our last date we think is connected is Josyln Black, March 31, 2013."

"Hear that," I said, leaning forward to grab Jade's hand. "Hear it?"

Mike said, "What is she talking about? Here we go. Do we need to make sure we pad this office for you when we leave you in here?"

"September. January. March." I said, flicking Mike playfully on the arm. "Emma was in June. We are now in June."

"What does it mean?" asked Jade, as she pulled up her calendar on the screen to type in the dates specified.

I sang the nursery rhyme I was sure they knew from their childhood Sunday School days, "Summer, fall, winter, spring. We're all God's children, yes indeed. He sent His Son to rescue you and me. Blood of victory sets us free. Summer, fall, winter, spring. Living water sets us free."

Ben said, "And you look at us as if we know what you're talking about?"

"You've heard the song, right?"

"No," said Ben. "They don't play that on Z98.1. Sorry."

I paced in the small space, knowing I was on to something. "It's a song we'd sing in church all the time as a child."

Ben laughed. "Your mom let you sing a song about blood? No wonder you . . ."

"Stop," I said. "Seriously, guys. This is it. He's a seasonal killer and made his summer statement. He's now baiting us and preparing for the fall. What do they do in the fall of the year? They pull in the harvest and burn the fields. There will be a fire. I know it. But it's not today. It's going to happen in the fall."

"So, you're saying we should expect him to return in the fall?"

"Exactly."

"It's not just seasonal," said Jade. "Come here. This little booger is leaving us something more to work with."

She had five calendars up on her screen. I looked at the blocked out days. The three Ben called out all happened on a particular day. Not just a season, but right down to the day.

I asked, "Why the other two calendars?"

"That's Emma Rose. June 24th. And that's Katie's."

I said, "I knew Emma Rose was related."

"That could still be random," said Mike. "We got a confession."

"Those can be false. Those can also be forced. We need to take a trip to visit this uncle. Who's with me?"

Ben said, "I am. I'll take this one. You're used to my smell by now. Don't want to offend Mike any longer."

"Oh, please," said Mike. "I don't want to follow you around. Call Dot and let her know you'll be visiting Pew, too. I've already got it arranged with the warden. Took a few strings but got it. Give her a little for what she gave us. She might come across some more juice in the future that might come in handy. Let her think we're playing along."

I paused, thinking of what that might mean for me. "I don't like cameras, Mike."

I didn't want to see Pew ever again. What would he say? Would he tell?

Jade said, twirling my straight hair at the ends with her manicured nails. "You are beautiful, Heather. Work that camera for the case. I think Mike is right. Tell her off the record. Tell her something. Figure out a way to spin it while keeping her in the pocket."

Mike grabbed his keys. "Jade and I will organize the setup of the cameras on Mercy land. If what you say is true, hunting season starts in the fall. He may be out there plotting and planning. Scoping out the lay of the land and using the expanse of the Mercy property and the old man's inability to get around to surveillance it as another set up for a kill."

I took down anything that would be telling and stashed it in a folder, placing it in my bag. It would come with me. If there was an internal problem, I wouldn't leave anyone a crumb. "I believe it makes sense right now. It's the pattern I see. Thanks, guys. And Jade, get that professor to agree to a virtual conference meeting this afternoon and let's find another place to meet instead of my office. We can keep the cult idea quiet until we find out more about membership. If there's anything I do know, it's that you never know who you can trust until you do."

"That doesn't really make sense," said Ben.

"The instincts. You've got to trust them. That's the truth. But you also have to know that we can get it wrong, too. That's being humble. I would rather be prepared than sorry, and standing on prayers and instincts is all we have right now. We need evidence. And a place where we can safely filter through it all. Concrete proof we're dealing with what I think we are."

And with this case. This time. There was no room for a slip-up or letting this killer get away. We couldn't get it wrong. A life depended on it. And she was going about her summer, maybe attending concerts with friends, hanging out by the river where all the teens loved to go, possibly having the time of her life. A young girl with her feet on the steps of promise, about to dance in the fall towards a nightmare. No. We couldn't get this one wrong. I would see to that.

12

Mike was right. I owed Dot a heads up that I'd be going down to the prison after giving us two viable leads, especially alerting us to the organization called the True Covenant of the Lambs that regular church list roster checks wouldn't have recovered. The name by itself sent off warning signs to me and led me to believe it probably was far from a non-profit community outreach service. Even though I felt so conflicted about having her in on an interview, I let her know the time Mike arranged. I'd get there first, say what I needed to say to Pew, then only allow her certain questions to ask or just let her be present to get some shots. I didn't want to be in his presence for long. It was almost as if he wore darkness as a shroud and the residual effects of his evil could be touched in the air particles. I never wanted to face that again. That feeling.

One thing I was sure of, I couldn't allow a reporter to have control over a situation. They'd never know where the limits were. I understood we wanted to play nice, especially if Dot somehow had insider information that could be useful, but I wasn't about to let her expose key parts of this case just to get her fame at the expense of jeopardizing any leads. I would never let that happen.

Ben turned into the gates of Falls Correctional Facility. "Why the hesitation with the call to Dot? I heard how strained your voice was when talking to her. Polite but still with a hint of stress mixed in. Seems like you'd want to retell the story of how you captured Marcus Pew. I'd be proud of that."

I let the silence fall between us as we parked and walked into the gates. I tried to think of all the ways to tell him I hated being involved with the Pew case to begin with. When I tried to start the conversation, I lost my chance to respond since we were being processed and reviewed.

"I don't want to relive that, honestly," I said, as we made our way through the first round of maximum-security checks. "And what good does it do? Drawing attention to that madman? We shouldn't give him that glory."

"True," said Ben. "Calling in on him as if you were one of his new disciples, just to catch him right before the act of killing that runaway teen took a lot of courage. It could've backfired on you."

"Well, it didn't." I didn't want to say how close I'd come to death that night, and also how leaky mouths went to the press and almost blew my cover. History I wouldn't repeat.

Ben reluctantly gave up his gun at the last desk, and we were escorted in. "Have to say this is my first time on the other side. How many have you put away?"

"Serial killers? Just Pew."

"No. Criminals."

"It's not like keeping a tally boosts my level. I don't play this like a game and never took the time to count. I've been on the job for seven years. That's what I know of numbers. I know this because I'm counting down to retirement."

He chuckled. "Already thinking about an exit strategy. Think of the old days and the notches on belts of those captured or killed by the law. I could see Mike having one of those western belts with the shiny flag buckle. Might just get him one for his Christmas present this year. He'd appreciate it."

"And why did the chief call you Quick Hands? Anything to do with the ladies? Should I be concerned? He had a name for us all. I guess they like to nickname us. Give them something to do while sitting at their desk."

"I'm offended," he said, but his relaxed attitude and bright smile told me otherwise. "I'm a one-woman man when I actually have a woman in my sights I like. Haven't had much luck with the ladies as of late. Heartbreak after heartbreak."

"Yeah, you struck out with Dot. She is a beautiful woman. Sneaky. Conniving. Appears to be glued to that microphone in her hand. She'd probably ask for your interview over a seafood dinner to catch what it's like just to be a cop of cold case files."

He wagged his finger at me. "I like the way you can read people. You're as sharp as a shark's tooth."

"Never heard that one. How about sharp as a tack? My granddaddy used to say that all the time, and then my granny would threaten to leave one in one of his chairs unawares." I looked away, blinking. Where did that memory come from? I'd never once spoken about my private life in all the years at the force. I tried to push my grandparents out of my mind but a twinge of ache resided. Guilt that I hadn't reached out more started to surface. I couldn't get vulnerable before seeing Pew. Focus.

"That's a funny story. I can see them now, chasing each

other around with threats of a tack. You do take a bite outta crime, so I like the shark metaphor best."

I grinned. "Let's get team t-shirts made. I want to be the cookie-cutter shark. I always thought they were cute."

He laughed. "You're cute."

"Don't start," I said, pointing straight ahead to get his eyes focused off me. "We aren't flirting. Quick Hands. It does fit."

"Who said I was flirting? I was speaking about straight facts. You are cute."

"She is cute," said the guard as we continued down the hall. A couple of cellmates had other choice words that echoed out. I closed my ears to that.

"Guys, enough. You're getting them all riled up."

"You're doing that all on your own. I bet some of them haven't seen a lady in ages," said Ben.

"Focus, Ben. Tell me where Quick Hands comes from again?"

He winked at the guard. "She's a tough cookie. I can see the cookie-cutter shark fitting her nicely. The nickname comes from an earlier case in my career. I was like Quick Draw McGraw, and when I won the duel, I got named for these quick hands," he said, as he flashed them up in front of me, shaking them like they were on fire. "It makes Mike think I'm his sidekick or something like we've got our own wild West sitcom."

"So, mine isn't cool?"

He shrugged. "According to what you think is cool."

"And I took Holy Roller as a compliment. At least everyone knows where I stand," I said.

The officer started the drill, what was allowed and not allowed as we made our way into the inner hallway, taking us to death row inmates. The paint was peeling and the stench was more evident at this part of the prison. No proper ventilation. A musty smell of sweat, sickness, almost hung in the air like a misty cloud. It wasn't a comfortable feeling, walking by the most dangerous of criminals. It was almost as if I could feel their demons wanting to slip through bars and chase me.

I said, "How many visitors does Marcus Pew get on the regular?"

"Not many," said the officer. "I can get you the log if you'd like."

I smiled. Another reason to be here. Let us get more names of free roaming sociopaths to add to the kettle. "I would. Thank you. The visitor's list and his mail. I want that, too."

Ben grinned at me. "Even now you're thinking two steps ahead of me. I was wondering about the Braves game tonight, and you're thinking of visitors who might have ties to a murderer, out doing his beck and call."

"We are on the job. My mind never quits."

"Neither does that smile. It goes for days. I think I'm going to convince the guys to change your nickname from Holy Roller to Smiles A Lot, like a Care Bear, because when you smile, I think you'll always get what you want."

"Smiles can hide many truths, Ben. Remember that," I said, lowering my voice before we made it into the final lockdown room. "Pew will smile, too. Just the thought of walking through this door to face him again . . . Can you guys just give me a moment?" I felt faint. He'd talk. He'd say it all.

The officer asked, "Are you okay, ma'am?"

I closed my eyes and pushed back the sickness rising within me. "I just need a minute to pray."

"That's not allowed in here," said the officer, jokingly,

then took it back. I guess I gave him a look that made him apologize.

After praying, I looked at Ben, moving in closer. "We need to see if he knows anything. Tell me again this is a good idea."

"It is, Heather. Nothing can happen here. I'm with you."

"Thanks," I said, dryly, knowing Pew could cut me with all the words in the world and never need his weapon of choice—a blade—to inflict wounds.

We'd made it to an open room, surrounded by glass. Metal doors with small window slots lined the far wall, but someone would have to be over six feet to take a peek inside. I was thankful I was short for the first time in my life. Nothing behind those doors would pique my curiosity. Evil resided within. This area was reserved for guests and lawyers of those on death row. It was all gray. Steel. Stripping me bare of all emotions that were trying to rattle and stick to my bones.

When the officer unlocked the door, I immediately assessed the situation. I was first greeted by the clanking of chains. A sound that should've given me at least satisfaction in knowing I'd put him in them, but the sound of the metal scraping against the concrete floor only heightened my nerves. I was greeted by the low, grating sound of Pew's voice. One that could haunt any dream. It was the kind that brought nails down a chalkboard through my spirit.

"Hello there, sweet disciple. Come to pay Daddy a visit? Already brought me this recruit, this pretty lady right here, and, you there, boy, you could serve as a henchman. Nice of you to join the circle."

I looked between him and Dot, the surprise clearly on my face. She was earlier than what I'd arranged. That gave me no time to get out what I needed to say to Pew and ask him the questions I needed off the record.

"How long has this been going on?"

"Don't worry, I just got here. Set up and ready." Dot smiled radiantly. I realized by the red blinking light we were already rolling. I refused to let it break me, and in a second, I'd composed myself settling into the cold room.

Ghosts lived here. I often felt they did. The victims are always haunting their killers, never letting go.

I said, "Let me introduce you to Detective Caraway."

Marcus Pew cackled. The sound too familiar, as old memories from witch cartoons filled my mind. Not a place to conjure up pure childhood images with such a maniac three feet away. I hadn't seen him since the day I had to testify, and then, the last walk out of the courtroom after his conviction. Pew's face was sunken in, sallow and pale. A beard bristled across his face, trying to put on the appearance of a wise man. A self-proclaimed holy man with clear blue eyes, and behind them was the monster.

His smile revealed a missing tooth in the front. Probably was knocked out from his free-flowing mouth-offs. I'm sure the other prisoners couldn't take his voice.

He chided, "A lover? And I thought you only had eyes for me."

"I have eyes on you, for sure. Even here. Don't you forget it."

"I know you do, sweet girl. That's why I'm so taken with you. Smitten is a better word. I see how you're looking at her, boy. Keep your eyes off my sweet girl or I'll puh-luck them out and swallow them whole. I might get hot on this beauty queen right here before the night is over, though. Would that make you jealous?"

I looked to Dot as if to say she wanted this. She got it. "Can we cut the camera off for a minute?"

Marcus cut off Dot from speaking and talked over her as soon as she started. "Why? You don't want the world to know how much you truly love me? You don't want the truth about . . . "

"Cut the camera," I demanded. Once the light was off, I turned to Dot. "Show me your list of questions."

I could tell her nerves were shot by the tiny twitching of the nerve below her eye. She wasn't as strong as she was playing, and I knew Marcus Pew would call her bluff quicker than any other ever would. "I've got them all up here," she said, knocking her forehead with her finger.

"I agreed to this out of courtesy to you, but we need to be mindful that we have an ongoing investigation he could be part of. Don't ask anything about the new cases." Ben and I had rehearsed how we'd try to get a rise out of Marcus and maybe he'd spill anything he might know of the murders. This was my way in. Having two serial killers in Crystal Falls probably wouldn't be to his liking.

"New cases," he said, leaning in, his voice rising in a shrill of laughter as if I was telling him something inconceivable. "You mean to tell me someone's out there showing off? Let me guess? They want to be me. They want to be like their daddy."

"They aren't copycatting you if that's what you're asking," said Ben, acting as aloof as possible. His voice was steady. "They are brilliant. Your murders, how do I put it, they were boring. Base."

Marcus's eyes crossed as he lowered himself down into the seat, scowling. "Base?" "You mean, third base? Or home plate? I did what I wanted to every single one of them sweet things and . . . "

"And this one is way smarter than you, Marcus. He's out there having the time of his life and not getting caught. Don't forget you were taken down. That leaves you lacking. Lacking in many ways," I reminded him. "Never forget that."

"And that's why I'm here," said Dot. "How did that make you feel?"

I rolled my eyes in disgust. "You're asking Marcus Pew how he felt to be caught? That's your question. Of all the ones you could've asked? He doesn't feel, Dot. He's incapable of feeling."

"He's human," answered Dot, her hand slightly shaking. "He has feelings. Regrets. Remorse. You have that, don't you, Mr. Pew?"

"She calls Daddy, 'Mister.' You could learn some manners from her, sweet girl. Let me guess. You come here to see who's been paying me visits? You come here to see who's been writing me letters?"

Ben exchanged a quick look at me, and I knew the rumors about Marcus Pew were out there as if he could read minds. No. He was smart in his way, but not that.

I smiled. "You think you know what I'm here for, but you've got it all wrong."

"No, I don't. I saw that look," he said as he turned to the guard. "She already asked for my list, didn't she?"

The guard refused to even look at Pew and keeping his stone face was a blessing.

Marcus chuckled. "You know my fan mail exceeds the mailroom capacity. You know my disciples are far and wide and across the rolling sea. How can you number the stars? How can you quantify their beauty? They all shine for me. They are all mine."

"Thanks for the information. Now I know to ask for your fan mail. Hadn't thought of that. What else can you tell me?"

I said, coolly regaining my calm. Dot's presence beside me was making me a little uneasy, but at least the camera was still off. I could speak freely. "Anyone out there you want me to catch, too? Show them how they can't outdo you. I know you won't let that happen. Anyone out of the way around here showing off, like you so put it?"

"Oh, not as big as I'm going to show off. Let me take you to the next room over where we get our family pass."

I ignored his comments and wouldn't stoop low. "Any knowledge you have that will help us in this case, will make sure the murderer is caught and won't get your count. Not only that. You'll be seen as a hero. A very own Bundy, helping the authorities from prison. You know you want to have your name up there beside Ted. Isn't he one of your idols? I know you want to be the Legend of Crystal Falls. Surpass them all."

"Sounds like I could be as large as Bigfoot. Got parts that already are, and I can show you. The Legend of Crystal Falls, I like that, sweet girl. I might just call that my next book title. Got a deal in the works from some big-time publisher. Wanting the whole story about me and you. Think I'm going to tell them. All for a charity, you see. Can't give the dead man walking the money but can go all for the charity cases, feeding my disciples."

I slammed my fist on the round table and it shook it back and forth. I think it startled all of us, including me. "You know this very day that you're about to be overtaken out there. Someone is going to steal your light. You won't be shining bright any longer. You know what will happen next. Let me spell it out for you. Your fan mail will diminish."

His eyes lowered. I knew I was getting him. I pointed straight at his face and then circled the room. "Your disciples will turn from the dead man walking and follow the one out there—outside these walls—who can still devour. You're losing your fame and allowing it to happen. Don't talk to me. Don't tell us what you know. Just realize your day is coming. Alone in the cell. Where no one will ever remember your name."

He leaned forward, his shackles clanking against the metal chair as he raised his hands as far as he could in an extreme contortion. He was bolted down to the chair so he couldn't move far. "Oh, you'll never forget it. As long as you whisper—Marcus Pew—whisper it in your dreams, I'll be glorified. My power is infinite. The power of three will show itself soon, and you sweet girl, shall feel the redemption in your very soul."

"Don't count on it," I said. I'd never let him know that all the counseling in the world would never get him out of my head. He was there whether I liked it or not. He just wouldn't have the satisfaction of knowing it.

"I'd like to have the interview now," said Dot, motioning for the cameraman to resume his position.

I stood up, the chair making a loud scraping echo as I pushed back forcefully from the table. "I'm out. He's useless. Guard, take him away."

"But you said . . ." Dot stammered. "You said I could . . ."

"You were here with me. I asked the questions. I got nothing. Figured as much, this sorry sack of nothing, but did it to amuse you. Show you that sometimes what you ask for is not ever what you need."

Dot hastily got up. I knew by her reaction; she'd had enough herself even if she wouldn't have readily admitted it. She didn't have any other questions, any that warranted her to be alone with Marcus Pew. Spittle was dripping down his chin like a rabid dog and knew he'd worked himself up over knowing someone was out there about to steal his light. I'd studied Marcus Pew enough to know how much he craved the light, so our seeds were planted. Let them work their way. I could use those very words to pierce his soul, make him threatened enough that if he did know something he'd find a way to talk to me, and when he did, I was sure he'd tell me something I could use.

The guard was waiting for us at the door to escort us back out into the waiting area. Out of earshot of Pew, Dot was livid. Her red heels clicked and inmates mimicked the sound with the clanking of the bars. My head felt as if it would explode any minute, and as soon as my purse was handed over to me, I swallowed down a couple of headache pills with no water to push them down.

The guard handed me a folder. "Here's what you asked for," he said. "Digital shots of all the mail is included on the link. And I've left you something else in there, too."

I tried to smile and thank him but at this point, it was no use. My temples were throbbing. Ben did it for me, helping me out into the bright sunlight, where I immediately reached for my sunglasses to shield me from the blaring rays.

I held up my hand in protest as soon as Dot started in on her stream of insanity. "Don't start, Dot. I'm done talking with you for the day. I'm sure you got enough to air something."

"I did," she said, smiling, holding up her suit collar, where I noticed a small American flag camera was positioned at the perfect angle to catch shots. "I caught the whole thing right here."

I sighed heavily, playing into it. "You recorded that?"

"Yes, ma'am. With your permission of course before the meeting. I did go in there for the interview. I always get what I want. One way or the other."

Ben said, "Well, isn't she a doozy."

"A . . . a . . ." I let the words trail. I wouldn't let her deception get a rise out of me, especially when it played right into what Ben and I planned. We would discover if we had a confidant in Dot or was she just another loaded gun with a story to tell. "I will say this to you once. Listen to it well. You will not air that until after we solve these cases. If he does have someone out there, that was the bait we left him to drop into the lake and go fishing. Let it play its course. Understand why we said the things we did. It was rehearsed."

She said, "Oh, I saw through it all, meaning he probably did, too. But who knows. He's a narcissistic one, and you've left him with a lot to think about. Playing Bundy like that. Calling him a legend in the making. Nice, Heather. Nice on your feet."

I didn't need a critique of my performance from her, a snooping reporter only looking out for herself, not the American people, as she so often repeated as her tagline— Dot on the Spot . . . For the People.

I looked at Ben, who was still reiterating why she wouldn't talk, not yet. She finally promised him and relief swept over me. We'd see if she'd hold to it.

I gritted my teeth. "Thank you."

"No, thank you. Now I just have to find out who this publisher is that wants his story. I'm going to convince them he's a sham and not worth the time."

"You'd do that?"

"For you, honey? I'd do anything," she said, with a sugary, maple syrup drawl. "And for my benefit, too. I want to be the first."

"You're almost as bad as him," I blurted out. "Sorry. I

didn't mean that, Dot. My head hurts. This isn't a good day. I didn't mean to say that."

"Apology accepted. Go get some rest, Heather. I'll check in on the investigation later. I want to know personally what you find out about that particular name I slipped you. In confidence, of course."

"Of course," I said. "That I will do."

Dot turned to her cameraman and with a signal he was off to load up the van, leaving her alone. "Look. I'm sorry I set that up back there that way. I wanted to see if I could get anything."

"It's okay, really," said Ben. "We just need your cooperation. Don't go letting out that there might be a serial in Crystal Falls again. That would put the people in a panic, and we don't have solid proof of that yet. We've got one fresh murder. That doesn't equal a serial killer. False reporting will be the end of you, too."

She said quietly, "I understand. I am for the people, Heather. For you. I'm not out to get you or the team or stand in the way. I'm going to like working with you, way better than that Jackson fellow. He was a jerk and a half."

"And I'm sorry I jumped," I said. "Really. Just not a good day. No excuse though. Know we will do all we can to catch the killer."

"Remember to be careful," she warned as she walked away. "I think big things are at play here. Big things."

"Agreed," said Ben. "And that Pew is a snake, ain't he? I can't tell if he knows anything or if he's just some psychopath looking for attention."

"He knows something," I said. "All evil is connected. One source fuels them, and they answer to that source. He might not know a name or a description. He might not have a face or a clear picture of who the killer is. But he shares the evil. That is a language they all speak. It's a common pulse of darkness and despair. One that I don't ever want to know fluently but must get close to again to snatch it from this world."

"And that's what you tried to do when you went after Marcus Pew undercover? Know their evil language? Thinking that would catch Pew? Maybe we should try it again. It worked that time."

"If you're asking me if I should go undercover in that cult, the answer is no. No way. I'm too public now. They'll smell me a mile away. Marcus Pew was too caught up in his delusion of grandeur to sniff out my spirit. A cult will see through it because they know I took him down. It's not like my work is a secret around these parts anymore. The sensational trial saw to that."

"True," he said as he started the car and pulled out onto Highway 74. "Well, if we can't go undercover, then we just need to bring the cult to us. You've got a list of names. We accomplished at least one thing on this trip into the bowels of hell."

"It was more than just the names. We planted the suggestion inside Marcus Pew's twisted mind that he's about to be overtaken. He wants his name in a book. He wants it all, and he'll fear he's losing and he'll strike. I'll look at the names when I can focus. My headache . . ." I let the words trail away as I rolled down the window for fresh air. I couldn't get sick on the ride back. I had too much work to do.

He switched off the radio, and I was thankful for the gesture. "Get those a lot?"

"Since I was a child," I said. "Manage them with meds, rest, and extra vitamins. It'll pass soon. I might rest a little."

The station was only a few miles away but closing my eyes for even a little bit would make it better.

"I'll go get you some caffeine and lunch. Heather, I'm sure you need food. Let me take care of it." He was already calling Mike and taking orders.

Thankfully, he didn't say you—take care of you. I wasn't able to lift my head, so I wouldn't have been able to argue with him, and I was in no mood to fight. I'd already had harsh words with Dot I regretted. At least I apologized. It was nice to clear the air between us and start over. I'd send her an email requesting her number. We'd keep our lines private, and I'd thank her again for being quiet and not running the interview until we knew this whole nightmare was over. Better to follow up and remind her of the promise she made to Ben and follow Mike's lead, keeping her thinking she could be on our side was the best way to handle the situation. She'd given us her word, and we'd have nothing to do but believe her. I could have faith in Jesus, but not people. Jesus was easy to trust. Man . . . not so much. Not from all I'd lived and seen.

13

Thankfully, it didn't take but around an hour for my headache to ease off. They left me alone in my closet long enough for a short nap. They were busy at the table in the bullpen when I stepped out to let them know I was better. As soon as Jade caught my eye, she started gathering the folders up, snatching one from Mike and told them to meet me back in the office.

Her eyes danced, telling it all. She had something.

"Cameras showed Mercy Jr. roaming, which we kinda figured, a couple of the Mercy grandkids taking their girl-friends out kayaking, and this." She handed me an enlarged, grainy photo. It was someone cloaked and out of place, carrying a sheetrock bucket.

"Look at that costume," Mike said. "Looks like they are in some medieval church play."

The robe was concealing, and the hood cast a shadow over whoever was lurking. This wasn't the typical hunter, poacher, or fisherman. This was a fashion statement that screamed ritual and gave me the cult vibes.

When we were safely behind my closed door, I added

the image to the board. "I wish we caught his face. Any other signs?"

Ben said, "The True Covenant of the Lambs has a registered board of trustees, required for non-profits, but probably something none of the members have on their public resumes. Dot was right. This is big. Big names. Ones you'll recognize without having to pull up an internet search."

"Are you kidding me," I said. "So, if it's public record, why hasn't any other investigator or reporter ever checked in on this group?"

Mike said, "Since they're registered as a community organization, but are keeping their matters private, they've snuck under the radar. I had never heard of them until Dot gave us the tip, and I was born and raised here. But to have the mayor, his assistant, one of our officers who retired last year, and prominent business owners where their family names have graced signs in this community for generations just throws me for a loop, I tell you. One big roller coaster loop that's making me pure sick to be on."

After sweeping the office one more time and finding it clear of any devices, Jade set up the private conference line and began rearranging the chairs for the call with the expert she knew. "We've got Professor David Gates waiting. I think he might be able to give us some insight."

I let Jade take over this one, rolling her chair center. She did all the small talk and the round of introductions, then started her line of questioning.

After all of her initial questions and further details about his background, she got to the point. "We've got the name of a possible cult we'd like your input on. Can you tell us what you know of the True Covenant of the Lambs?"

"Sorry. Never heard of that one on this side of the map.

Heard of them, though, just not in Crystal Falls, North Carolina. If there's a cult here, I'd know."

"Yes, right here. I've got pictures of their buildings purchased under the guise of being a non-profit. We speak these words with proof. An informant passed the possibility to us, and we'd like your take on it, with the utmost privacy around the issue, please."

He nodded. "I've worked with the FBI and the SBI on a few cases in the past and understand the importance of the veil of secrecy on my end. But I'll tell you, frankly. If there's a cult that is established in your area, and I've not caught wind of them, then that only means one thing . . ."

"That they're up to no good and pretty deceptive at hiding it," I answered.

He said, "Exactly."

While Jade was sharing her screen and displaying photos of the Cooper's Landing area, the professor rambled on about how the seclusion of the property and the barbed wire fencing was a clear indicator they might be up to something secretive, wanting to keep others out or insiders facing a realization each day that beyond the electric fence lay the real danger, when it was clearly lurking within. A tactic to entice fear in members and total control of physical space.

"Does anything about this stand out to you?" I held up the picture taken of the cloaked figure from the deer cameras and told the professor about the Bible verse written in human blood. "I'm sure inside that sheetrock bucket was the victim's blood."

He confirmed what we'd already said. Blood ritual, sacrifice, and symbolism of blood was a highly used form of ritualistic behavior, showing this cult wasn't about organic foods or sustainable living practices in a commune, but more than likely being commanded by a messiah figure or religious leader to carry out these things. A charismatic leader who quite possibly used mind control over the members into believing the leader was some type of god or close to God.

Mike said, "You mean, like receiving direct messages from a higher power? That's some Manson sh ... mess, right there."

I narrowed my eyes. "We've got some pretty well-known people in our town registered to this organization."

"Typical. There have been people of notoriety to fall for cult leaders, and honestly, they want that. The leader would want not only the power, money, and connection, but the feeling that comes with that dominion over someone that appears worthy to others, magnifying their own worth in the community."

Professor Gates continued with his lecture, and it was clear he was one we needed to call on when we had a cult question. Jade was brilliant.

"It usually is the case that the messiah type leader would not be the one to carry out the crime directly but would have followers who would murder for them. You need access to the inner circle. The loose ties or new recruits may not be as invested and might fear this type of behavior or action. Don't go for the big names. They'll make waves. Try to find some young ones. Someone who has a weakness, maybe a record, and would be nervous to be questioned."

After we shared the rest of the crime scene photos with him, he drew references to Koresh, Jones, and like Mike, Manson. I knew enough about those charismatic leaders just from their coverage and countless documentaries.

Jade said, "What we need is a member list. How could we get that from what appears to be an open organization with a bare-bones website just keeping up appearances?"

"Find out who's been giving donations," said Professor

Gates. "Consider them as an active believer to support the prophet or the cult's mission. Tithing is common, not just in mainstream religions. Without manipulation and exploitation, you may not have a cult. It may be very well what they claim to be. It's hard to convince a member they're a practicing cult member. I wouldn't use that word lightly. You'll get closed doors and mockery. Tread lightly if you want to walk far."

Jade was already drawing up a new window on her laptop. I knew she could easily get their financial statements and history. That would be a good place to start.

We thanked the professor.

He said, "I'll keep seeing if anything turns up on my end about this and will keep my ears open. I may take a flight around there soon to see the place for myself."

That was another good idea without a police presence. Maybe Jade could go and take some pictures. Or Dot. I'd think about that angle after we touched back in with him. "If there's anything else you can tell us, please don't hesitate to reach out."

We all did our thanks and goodbyes, then waited for Jade to send us the list of names. The silence hung heavily over all of us in the room. The realization that we were dealing with a cult, with names from the board members posted and highlighted on the board gave me the shivers. Was that the inner circle? If anyone walked in and saw those names listed beside a robed figure carrying a sheetrock bucket of blood . . . and it not be true? And it is a false lead? It could ruin all of our careers in one swoop. The captain included.

I walked over to the board and snatched the handwritten list down, tearing it into small pieces. "Don't mention the names. To no one. Let's do our digging first."

"We aren't mentioning anything about this case to anyone," said Mike. "You can trust us, Heather."

I wanted to say I hoped so, but then that would mean I had doubts, and I didn't with them. They were solid. I knew it. "Jade, what do you have? I see your eyes all aglow like sparklers."

"The donor list. It's not as long as I'd feared. Seems like we've got something to work with. How about one of us volunteers down there? Look, they have a contact form for interests."

"Hm . . . no," I said, quickly. "No undercover." The Marcus Pew visit reminded me just how dangerous that would be.

"But that might answer at least if it's a cult. We could pick up on the signs."

"Please, stop that train of thought," I said. "We won't go there. Not yet. And when we do, we are flashing our badges. Listen to Professor Gates. He said we could quickly close doors, and we want them wide open to be able to investigate. So, let's do our own way of digging without breaking the soil and see what we can find. We cross these names with the ones we've got from Pew's visitors and disciples, along with anyone on the Mercy logs. We might be looking for another guru-type figure like Pew was."

Crystal Falls. Population: 21,703. Two serial killers with religious MOs. Maybe Pew was the key to this. I retraced the steps I took to uncover the true identity of Marcus Pew. How low I would go to get that very name to repeat in my head in the middle of the night. I wouldn't send Jade, Mike, or Ben out to dance with devils. We'd get this done another way.

I said, "Ben, you think you can take a drive downtown to that spiritual bookstore called Simon Says Faith, and look around. Maybe ask a few questions? Let's stir it up a little in

Crystal Falls. With our visit today with Pew, and then planting more questions in the right places, we might get us some movement."

Ben said, "Dot is probably about to piece together the news story for the five o'clock. That'll fuel some fires out there."

I grabbed my purse. "She promised she wouldn't. Maybe she'll keep it. But just in case, maybe we should visit the mayor before he goes home to his young wife. Jade, I need you for this one. Ben, you and Mike take the downtown shops. Don't you need to pick up a present for Maude, Mike? Maybe go down to Hen's Fashion, too. If Hen is on the board, just seeing y'all in the dress shop might raise suspicion we're on to them or maybe not. They'll think they've gotten away with this and might laugh in your faces. Just keep your eyes fresh and pamper Maude while you're at it."

Mike's voice rose in surprise, "Do you want to let them know we're suspecting something? We can play that one up, me and my sidekick here."

Ben leaned over and said, "Old Rhinestone Cowboy thinks I'm his sidekick when he's mine. Love how he always thinks he's the man in charge."

I said, "I think we can trip them up. Get them nervous. It can play out two ways. They either call a meeting or they run deeper into the inner circle of secrecy. Either way, we'll catch them on the run. People change when they think they're being watched. Change leads to fear. Fear leads to failure."

"Inevitable downfall," said Jade. "I like how this one operates. But the mayor? I don't know, Heather. That's going to the top. Don't you think we need to run that visit by the captain?"

I reminded them, "He told me not to come into his office

until I caught the killer. We don't have him yet, so technically, we can do as we please. No need to ask permission when I can always ask for forgiveness later."

"Ok, just know we could open up a murder hornet nest."

"That's what I'm trying to do," I said. "Let's poke at the hive and see who's the first to defend and attack. That'll raise suspicions more, don't you think? Defense mechanisms are a sign of a cover-up."

Ben said, "We've got a few lucrative ideas for the t-shirt business. Maybe we can do that exit strategy earlier than you're counting down, Heather. Murder hornets. Cookie-cutter sharks taking bites out of crime."

Jade asked, "What is he talking about?"

Ben said, "Oh, never mind me. Just thinking of a gift shop idea and making my Christmas list out for everyone."

Jade said, "In June?"

"Never too early to spoil the ones I love," he said, with a wink.

"You're incorrigible," replied Jade.

"But you didn't deny that you love me," he said.

"You want me to spell it out for you. L-O-V-E is what I feel for you all."

"Love bears all things," I said.

Mike continued, getting one more jab at Ben. "And bares Ben's mouth. That's how we've put up with him for so long."

Ben said, "What we've had to put up with around here before she arrived on the scene is not worth speaking of. See how easy this is when we've got the right one at the helm. You're making me believe again, Heather."

I asked, "In the force? In God? In good old-fashioned police work? In crime scene investigations?"

Ben said, "In the goodness of people. It's almost like I'd forgotten."

"Me, too," said Jade. "Let's go, boss. I'm ready for this visit with the mayor."

Ben laughed. "Take it easy there, Jade. Watch her work. She'll be nice one second, all smiling, and then slamming her fist down on tables in a rage of fury. Don't say I didn't warn you."

Mike asked, "What in the world went down at the prison?"

"Nothing," I smiled, sweetly. "Just playing the good-cop-bad-cop stereotype."

"Yeah, all in one person. Dr. Jekyll and Mr. Hyde, that one is."

"I love that book," I said. "One of my favorites."

Mike said, "Don't get Ben talking about books. He'll never do his job."

"And you read?" Before I could stop myself, I'd said it out loud. How embarrassing. As if he couldn't?

He smiled, clearly picking up on my reddening cheeks. "Don't take me just for my pretty boy charm. This brain of mine has a thirst for knowledge."

Mike said, "And a thirst for Bill's milkshakes. That'll be our last stop on our downtown shopping trip. Are we using company funds to buy Maude this present, or can I put it on Ben's tab?"

As they walked out of the office, Ben said, "That reminds me, you owe me twenty bucks from that last Braves/Yankees bet."

I could still hear their light banter down the hallway when Jade and I locked up the office tight. I stood by the door with second thoughts. Should I take anything else down off the board? Should we conceal our cameras in the office to see if we'd have people scoping out the evidence we were putting together? The names were shredded. We had our things with us. Best to leave it unlocked. Let them see what we were working on. See how we were getting closer than anyone else ever did.

"I thought you were going to secure it," said Jade. "Wasn't that the purpose of cramming everything in there?"

"On the surface, yes. Let them think we have something cooking," I said. "I've got the good stuff in my bag."

"You've got all kinds of tactics about you. Glad Jackson's gone."

I took the wheel this time, saying a quick prayer of thankfulness that my headache had disappeared. "Was he that bad to work for?"

"The way he'd dodged the genuine detective work made me suspicious. Like he might've been in on something bad himself. Bribes. Payoffs. I was actually thinking his name would appear on the donor list. Surprised it wasn't there. He was probably more of the one collecting the money than freely giving it away."

Her accusation shocked me. "Was he religious?"

Jade applied a new layer of lipstick and was checking herself out in the car mirror. "Jackson? No. Bonafide atheist and spoke of it more than once. But again, that could've been a ploy to make people believe him to be that way. He was cocky and easily one of the most deceptive people I've ever met in all my days."

"Cocky and narcissistic doesn't necessarily mean cult member or murderer."

"No, you're right. But there was this creepy vibe he'd have about him. Just creepy. Hard to put your finger on it, you know. Like you just know he's not right."

"I've met a few of those in my time," I said, remembering

how I first felt when I'd come into contact with Marcus Pew for the first time.

"I'm sorry about your parents."

"Wait, what?" I said, blinking myself back to the reality of what she'd just said.

"I'm sorry about them. My mom died of cancer when I was twelve, and my dad did all the raising. He was a cop, too. Guess growing up in the bullpen and having a homicide detective as a tutor bred me for this line of work."

"And having my parents killed led me to mine? Is that what you're saying?" I shuffled in my seat. I thought I could get to know Jade more on the drive but didn't think it was going to turn this personal, this quick. I'd never talked to anyone about my past, except the staff psychologist they required me to visit after the Pew case. That was part of my clearance after I killed one of Pew's closest advisors the night of his arrest.

"Sorry to bring it up."

"It's okay. It was tragic," I said. The word didn't even begin to describe it.

"Did you always know you wanted to be a cop?"

"It was before their murder," I said. Didn't want to tell her it was the day I was chased by the very one who took my parent's life that I realized I wanted to be a detective. I wouldn't speak his name to her. Out loud. Ever again.

Jade changed the subject. "So, tell me about you and Alex."

"Wait? Do we go from one deep conversation to the rumor mill? Jade, I haven't had a friend for so long. Is this how small talk goes?"

She laughed. "Sorry. I just heard that Alex and you might've . . ."

"No. Alex is my friend. He was my partner. Truth is, I do

miss him," I said. "But we had nothing going on. Was that a rumor?" I'd been so caught up I hadn't checked on the guys, but they haven't reached out to me, either. Exactly what I feared and thought it'd be when I was moved up a floor.

"You know office talk," she said. "That's why I keep my personal life separate from my work. I've got a fine broker. He's a financial genius. Safe. Handsome. Boring. Just the way I like them."

"Boring would be nice," I said. "Too much action in my life already."

Jade said, "I'm sorry again that I brought that up, about your parents, I mean. I won't pry. I was just . . . prying. Sorry."

"I promise, it's fine. So, let me tell you how this might go down. We may walk into that murder hornet nest of a city hall and, just by our presence, create the buzz needed to get back to an organization that might be behind this. Or we might create a dangerous chain of events."

Jade said, "I've never shied away from a threat if that's what you are hinting at."

I needed to change the subject. "I was thankful you were with me for Katie's mom. Sometimes I think I lack the softer touch. I'm going to work on that."

"You've got it," said Jane. "You're just all business more. Don't think that was easy for me."

"I know it wasn't, but you were good at it."

"Thanks. You're good at redirecting."

I laughed. "Thanks. I will try. Now, I've also been told I'm good at smiling. Let's both do a lot of that."

"So, that's why I'm here. In case the mayor needs a little softening up?"

"You're here because I want you to get an eye on his tech. I won't know what to look for. See if he has anything in his office that doesn't belong. We might be able to obtain a warrant if we find something."

She grinned, looking as if this was the permission she'd wanted her whole life. "You want me to spy on city hall?"

"Could be useful," I said. "Think of the names on that list. And, I need you to tell me about that creepy feeling you get, and if it comes back. Have you ever spoken directly with the mayor or his assistant?"

"No, I can't say I have. I know them but don't rub elbows with the elite in this town."

"Me either." I paused, checking my text. After saying I hadn't heard from the guys, it was like they could read my mind.t Alex sent a stream of texts asking about my day and if I'd catch a bite later. I let him know I wasn't sure. I hated to make promises I couldn't keep.

"Then, we might be in for a treat. Lookie who's coming to meet us—Sebastian Lackey, his assistant. We got an escort."

"How lovely," I said, turning my full attention to the face of the man walking towards us. He might not have let off the creepy vibe that Jade described earlier, but he was oily. Slick as his hair greased back in a smooth 'v' design. Tailored suit and manicured hands. A quick glance let me know he was of old money. The man you didn't want to cross but would love to have on your side if you were going places. The mayor must've been hungry for such an assistant as this. One who could help him get a state seat, no doubt.

Power. Connections. Names. All of it, every piece of evidence, note, and verse floated in front of me as we took the steps into the historic halls of the city building, constructed in 1833. I thought of how a serial killer could thrive under such an umbrella of protection. I also thought of a saying my granny once said as we looked up across a crisp, clear Virginia sky, readying ourselves to go out to a church meeting. She stuffed her clear, plastic rain bonnet in her purse. "Rain can come any day here, you know. Let's be ready for the pour."

I would be ready. Ready for the downpour. Ready for whatever was ahead. There was no other choice. If it was the mayor, the Spirit could do the talking around here. I prayed for insight on the case as our feet hit the marbled tile.

With every click of Jade's heels and shuffle of Sebastian Lackey's polished loafers, I took in the way the light crept through the tall windows, shining across the patterned floor.

"It's never this easy, is it," I said. "Never this black and white."

Sebastian said, "Excuse me?"

"Nothing. Just admiring the architecture," I replied, stepping in behind them, catching his swagger as he kept in line with Jade, giving us the two-cent tour.

14

T he mayor stood by his ornamental fireplace in his too-rich-for-his-britches office. It was in the middle of the summer, yet the flames roared, and he held the poker like a sword. He set it down in the brass holder with flair. So, he was a showman. Just like Pew. I made a note of that, along with the ceramic lamb he had resting as the centerpiece of the mantle. Nothing was a coincidence. I was sure that was just the sign I needed. Not like I needed much of one. His name was on the donor list.

His southern drawl was immaculate and deep, sweet as the tea served at Bill's. "All right if I take me a gander at why two detectives are paying me a visit."

"You may," I said, holding my position by the large cushioned chairs he'd motioned us to sit in. He was standing. So would I.

"You're here looking for a favor. They always come with favors. What are you offering in return?"

"We're not here for favors, and this isn't a social call. I need you to be the first to know in case they air a story tonight that shouldn't be. It might cause an uproar in this town and out of respect for you and the good things you've done for Crystal Falls, you should be aware of an ensuing panic."

The mayor rested his arm on the mantle, relaxing a little. "So, you're here to warn me? How nice. Polite. What did you say your name was again?"

I could hear him say little girl in his mind as if he'd spoken it aloud. It was the degrading way he said it that was unnerving.

"Detective Moody." I paused, wondering if I should push this viper. He was a slippery one. The captain would have my badge if I kept this up much longer. "Listen, we might have a serial killer in Crystal Falls again."

"Again. Like that Pew wasn't enough for us and the world. Wait," he paused, squinting his eyes at me, which was ridiculous because I was sure he had predatory eyes that could see very well. "You're the one that brought in Pew. I remember those eyes of yours. They were the haunting kind caught on film. The kind that screams pain and strength all at the same time. Haunting eyes. Anyone ever told you that?"

"You'd be the first," I said. "No one knows we're here. We just thought that maybe you should be aware. Hold off the press if they make it to City Hall. Stand behind a tight lip."

"Any leads," he asked, with that lilt at the end dragging away. His stance changed, and I watched his shoulders tense with it.

"A few. That's what led us here to you." I said, without hesitation. Let me get him sweating by that blessed fire in a room already clearly at one hundred degrees. If it was him, the killer, I will say he was practicing for the afterlife.

Jade took out her phone and acted as if she had to take a call, leaving me to directly speak to the mayor while she got a better eye on the room. I moved in closer to him so he could see he didn't intimidate me.

"And my services are at your disposal. What can I do to assist in this dastardly case?"

"You can tell me what the lamb means," I said, in a hushed tone.

His assistant cleared his throat. "Water? Would you like water or tea? Coffee?"

"No, thank you. I'm fine."

The mayor said, "Go fetch me a lemonade down at Bill's, if you don't mind, Sebastian. Leave me time to school this young detective."

He did it again. The way he spoke grated my nerves. Reminded me of Pew. "I would appreciate your insight into the symbolic nature of it."

The mayor laughed and straightened his vest. "You want a Sunday school lesson, or are you here for something more?"

"More. I know you're giving money to the True Covenant of the Lambs. Why?"

His face turned a reddish hue, but could've been from the heat or, rather, what I suspected—that he knew he'd been caught. "It's my business what charities I support. I rarely know where the money goes. Here and there. Everywhere. All in the name of the Lord's work. Are you a believer?"

He pointed at my cross around my neck. The look in his eyes gave me chills.

"Very much so," I said, fumbling the cross through my fingers. "Who writes those hefty checks of yours? Maybe they're doing it without your knowledge? Maybe you have nothing to do with this? Maybe you do? What is it you have to gain? That's my real question."

"I have all to gain. It is my mission to support those who are called to do the Lord's will. The organizations in Crystal Falls deserve a fair place to assemble without scrutiny from nosy haunting eyes."

"The lamb. The sacrificial lamb? Religious symbolism, though, right?"

"I'm sure you know this," the mayor spoke in a lower tone, condescending and dark. "What game are you playing here? Because I can play better than you. Anything you have to say, just directly say it."

"I just wanted to know more about the True Covenant of the Lambs. I'm looking into it for a connection to a recent case. You might have heard of it. The Katherine McCreedy case. There was bloodletting. Between us, and you may even hear it from Mercy, but there was blood smeared down on the oaks on Mercy lands. The victim's body was mutilated and drained of blood."

He said, "Poor sheep led to the slaughter."

I held up my phone and showed him the image of her slumped over and strapped in the stall. His reaction let me know he'd never seen an actual crime scene photo before. He would have stared harder at it if he had been relishing in the thought of the replay. Lost in the scene. He wasn't the killer, but he might know who was.

He turned from me, positioning the lamb as if having it turn the other way from me. Like it didn't need to see the truth. But evil existed, and it could be breathing in this very room.

"I don't know anything about that," he said.

"If you learn something, let us know."

"I'll be calling Captain McBride over this."

"Do that. I'm sure he'll thank me as I've come to tell you as a courtesy before this entire community gets wind of the psychotic maniac loose on our quiet streets. He'll be thanking me. Maybe give me that raise I deserve. Here's my card so you get my name right."

"I won't forget your name," he said, not taking the card.

Jade came back smiling. "What's going on? Sorry, that was a call I couldn't miss. Everything all right?"

The mayor drawled back into his rehearsed voice. "Everything is just fine, sweetheart. You two carry on now. I've got more pressing matters to attend to."

"Thank you for your time," I smiled, just as sweetly as I could. "We might talk again soon."

He nodded. "I'm counting on it."

When we made it out in the massive hall, bustling with an afternoon court session break, we passed his assistant carrying a lemonade and a bag of food from Bill's. He nodded pleasantries, but it was almost as if he'd overheard what was being said by the glaring look he gave us.

"Well isn't that odd," said Jade, recognizing it, too. "Out of earshot but ever so close."

"So close it's almost like he was burning in the flames right along with Mayor McCall."

Jade agreed. "Just like that. Well, I got to see the folders on his computer. He had one labeled lamb. If we get a search warrant, we would want that for sure. I have some shots of the room, too. The mayor doesn't mind his photo being taken."

"You did all that by standing near his desk?"

"I did. He was too engrossed in your private little soiree. Nice distraction."

"Good instincts." That girl was on fire, and I was so glad she was on the team.

"I'm ready to crack open his files. Wonder if the lamb alone could get us a way for a judge to jump on a warrant."

"I wish it worked that way. Wonder if there's a judge in town that might be willing to take a risk." I started the ignition to let the car cool. Too much heat in that office left me a little dizzy. Maybe the effects of the headache, too.

Three steps closer. Jade's laughter caught in midair and hung for seconds around us. She'd just joked about duping city hall like she was some super spy, and the world exploded right in front of us. The car let out a small stuttering pop, then with no other warning, burst into flames. We were blasted back by the force and everything blared loud.

The sounds. My ears were ringing. Nearby car alarms. Screams. Debris spiraling. People falling. Brakes squealing.

Black smoke billowed as we lay in stunned silence, staring up at my burning car. Jade's eyes were wide with understanding. That wasn't random. That was meant for us. No doubt. We were walking targets and still exposed on the lawn.

I said, "I think we need to call the captain."

And then the world went dark.

15

My Granny's voice met me in whispers.

"What a dear friend we have in Lord Jesus," she sang softly, continuing with the hymn and a mixture of others about open arms and walking in a valley. She never played it by the lyrics but was remixing before it was a popular trend.

"Granny?"

"Sugar," she replied, her pet name for me. "We got to talk about this career choice of yours. Might need to reconsider under the circumstances. Come on back home with me and your Granddaddy."

Tears stung my eyes. My head hurt. Was it a migraine? Why was everything in such an in-and-out fog? Her voice crashed against me like waves, carrying me out into the depths. I felt my body going under and then returned to the surface where her voice would meet me again.

"Sugar. Sugar," she sang. "You are our one sweet girl, and I think I love ya." But that wasn't my grandmother's voice. It was the voice of Marcus Pew.

My eyes snapped open, and I knew I called out. What

sound it was, I didn't quite register it, just the movement of it vibrated my throat, and I felt the rush of people by my side.

Mike stood over me, and I saw the black cowboy hat on his head, yet it looked as if he were a caricature drawn at the fair. "We're here, Heather. It's all right. We're here."

I groaned, fell back on the pillow, then winced with the pain. "Why am I in the hospital?"

Ben asked, "You don't remember? There was an explosion at city hall. A remote bomb. The FBI is helping us with determining if it was an act of terrorism, protest, or directed at the force."

"You mean at me? Where's Jade?"

Mike looked away. "She's gone."

"She's released? Thank God. I think I might have a concussion, but I'm good to leave. Was my Granny here or was I dreaming? I'm so glad Jade wasn't hurt."

Ben squeezed my arm. "Jade is gone, Heather. Gone."

I blinked back the tears. "She's dead?"

"Yes," said Mike. "She died right after the explosion."

"But we weren't in the car? How could that be?"

"The blast. The shrapnel. It doesn't matter how. It is." Ben wiped his face and turned away.

I pushed through the pain. My chest felt like it would explode with it all. "Have you called her guy? The broker?"

Ben's voice shook. "Yes, and we called her father." Ben's hair was disheveled, shaggier than normal. His clothes were all in disarray. It looked as if he hadn't slept in a week.

"How long have I been out?"

Maude put her arm around Mike and said in her sugary, kind voice, "Two days."

"Get me out of here, Mike. Don't let me stay here. Please. I can't stay here."

"We've been taking shifts, Heather. We haven't left your side. We don't want you to worry. You're safe."

"I need to get out of here," I said, pushing out the tubes from my nose and sitting up. "I need to see Pew."

"You want to see Marcus Pew? Why? Do you think he did this? He's locked away tight, Heather. You're still recovering. You're not thinking straight."

"It's Pew or the mayor," I said, in a frantic whisper. "He was so shady. Oh my. And that assistant. He went out. Lemonade. He planted the bomb. That lamb. That lamb told me everything I needed to. And those eyes. Get the surveillance tapes of the parking lot."

"Already did that," said Ben. "Even with a concussion, she's asking the right questions."

"Always working," said a voice from the doorway. It was the captain, and by the looks of it, he wasn't pleased. "Can you leave us?"

"Sure, sir," said Mike.

I looked at Ben. "Please stay."

"Caraway. Out."

Ben gave me a reassuring look. "I'll be right outside. We aren't leaving."

Mike twisted the blinds open before stepping out of the room. Maude fixed my covers and patted me. She whispered. "Don't worry."

The captain closed the door behind him, but Mike pushed it back open again. The captain glared but then took a few steps in. "I'm sorry to have to do this Heather, but I don't think you're in any condition to continue with the cases I gave you. Alex and the . . ."

"Sir, you can't take me off the case. I'm close. This proves I'm close."

"It proves you were at the wrong place at the wrong time. The mayor? Really? I got an earful from him, I swear."

"I went to warn him," I said.

"He told me you'd pull that crap. You went there accusing him of killing Katherine McCreedy. Without evidence? Accusing a politician in this town without any proof?"

"We had a lead. A tip."

"To the mayor? It's an election year. Whoever told you that just wanted to jeopardize his long-standing, clean career. Tell me about your informant."

"Sorry, sir. I can't do that," I said. "I did go to warn him. The accusations didn't fly. I'm sure he has a recording of the entire meeting somewhere hidden away. I did ask him about his connections with the True Covenant of the Lambs."

"The what? Do you still have a brain blast or whatever that doctor warned us about? Seriously? What are you talking about?"

Ben walked in then. "She's talking about the cult that's been operating right under our very noses in this town. The same very cult that the mayor has been financially support-ing. Monthly checks like clockwork, at the beginning of every month. Appears he takes his tithing duties seriously."

"A cult? Here in Crystal Falls? I think you all need to take some time off. Losing Jade is tough. You'll all report to a round of counseling sessions as soon as you get back to the station, and then I'll reassign you all as soon as this smoke clears."

"We aren't leaving the case, sir," I said. "With all due respect, I can't. For Jade. And I can't leave Ben and Mike. We're a team."

The Captain said, "I know it's hard. I've lost a partner

before. You stay in this long enough, and you're bound to lose somebody."

Mike said, "And did your captain kick you off the job?"

Captain sighed. "No."

"Then, don't be that other guy," said Ben. "Be the one that goes down fighting with us. We're going to get whoever did this. They'll pay. Let it be our team who cracks it. I know the FBI is ruling out terrorism. We'll cooperate. But don't take Heather off as lead. We need her."

Ben and Mike came closer to my bedside. Maude rubbed my arm. It wasn't my Granny after all, but Mike's wife, comforting me. Wonder if she was singing the hymn or was that a dream, too?

The captain sighed. "When you're cleared for release, take a couple of extra days. Wait until after the funeral. Give Jade that."

"She wouldn't want us waiting," said Mike. "That woman would want us to bring whoever did this to justice."

"So would her father," said Ben. "I think we deserve to give Chief Cain answers."

"Be careful with Cain. He's been retired going on for about seven years now, but he'll be wanting to join in, if I know him. He doesn't need to be involved in this."

Maude said, "I wouldn't blame him. If it were Mike's girl, he'd do the same."

Mike's hands trembled as he held them tight against his chest. "Jade was like my little girl. Not too far from Maddy's age. They were just a few grades apart."

"So sad," said Maude. "So sad. Heather, what can we get you?"

The captain made his way out as Ben and Mike started fussing over what they thought I'd need from my apartment.

"Do you think you guys can handle it?" I asked. "How

about letting Maude pack me a bag. I wouldn't feel comfortable with you two putting your hands in my drawers."

Ben announced, "Then, that'll be Mike going with Maude. I'll stay here with you."

I saw the fear on his face. "You believe I'm in danger, don't you? You know I was targeted."

He stared directly at me, his eyes never wavering. "Yes."

"Mike, you and Alex go. Call Alex. I'm sure he wouldn't mind. Just in case."

"Alex and Rodriguez are outside covering the two lots," said Ben. They're off duty but signed up for an extra watch.

"Then Harris. You need someone to go with you to my place. Maude, before you guys enter, click my alarm fob, it's in my purse. You can undo it right from the outside of the door and know if anyone's been inside. It's loud enough to hear through the door. I've got it programmed to say the last entry date and time."

Mike said, "Any food while we're out?"

Ben said, "For me or her? Because I think I can't eat."

"What? Ben at a loss of appetite? Jade would get a kick out of riding you about that," I said.

We looked at one another, and a heavy silence fell over us.

"Remember when she said she loved us," said Ben. "Nice she got to tell us. Makes not saying goodbye a little more bearable."

"She loved with all she had," said Mike. "That poor guy. Miles is his name. Hate he had to lose her. Said he'd been carrying around an engagement ring in his pocket for the past year, so nervous to ask her because he felt he wasn't good enough for her."

"And she did love him," I said. "Let him know she was

just talking about how much she loved his fine self today. Say it like that when you talk to him. He'd like it."

Mike and Maude left, and the silence still hovered. Ben paced the room at first, checked the windows, opened and closed the bathroom door, then closed up the blinds of the long window with a view leading out to the hallway.

After his round, he pulled a chair up to my bedside and flipped on the television. It was set to Wheel of Fortune. "We can do some puzzles together before the 7:30 Braves game."

"Do I get a say so? I think that TV right up there constitutes my TV at the moment. My bill. My TV. My remote."

"Are we arguing about this? Please? You know you love Wheel of Fortune."

I sighed, the pain settling deep in places that medicine couldn't fix. "How did you know?"

He called out a vowel and slapped his knee when he fell short. "Because you are a walking puzzle. A mystery."

"I'm far from that," I said. "I'm as boring as they come." I thought of my last conversations with Jade. All of the words we spoke hit my heart like a thunderbolt.

"Do you need to rest? I can cut it off. Do you need me to get the nurse?"

I shook my head. Stupid tears. I was feeling. Don't feel, I commanded my brain, but it was too sloshy to hear me. Don't feel, please don't.

"Some things I won't ever forget."

Ben leaned back in the chair and cut off the TV. "I don't think we're meant to."

"It would be better if we could."

"Maybe not," he said. "I think it's better that I remember. Makes me know how lucky I was to know her."

"Maybe," I said. I didn't want to tell him I felt that. I felt it all. Felt. Everything.

"We're going to be ok," he said. "Mike and I will look after you."

"The puzzle was Forever and Ever Amen. It's an old country song."

"No way," said Ben, as he lunged for the remote and flicked the TV back on just in time to hear the contestant call out the puzzle. "No fair."

The clicking of the wheel brought back sweet memories of me, Granny, and Grandaddy, having our spin at the fortune or dreaming we'd win that dream vacation trip to Hawaii when they'd place that card over the lucky spot on the wheel. I would call them. Tonight. Let them know I loved them. Say it. Tell it out loud. Even if it hurts. I would someday fall in love. I would love even if they did not return it. I'd feel it. I'd let it in. Love bears all things. Because just like Jade, my life could be taken like that. In a moment. Gone. Yet, I'd been gone for so long that meant I'd first have to let life in. It could start with a phone call.

en joked at Mike as soon as they walked into my room, "So, that took you long enough," and would've continued with his tirade until he read the look on their faces.

I sat up in bed. "Wait. What is it? What happened now?"

Maude put the bag she packed me beside the recliner and sat down at the chair closest to me. She didn't make eye contact. Whatever it was, it wasn't good news.

Mike pulled out his phone and flashed it in front of Ben. Ben said a few choice words under his breath.

"What is it? Let me see," I demanded. "Y'all can't leave me in the dark about anything. My head is clear. Proof of it when I could answer every puzzle except the final round. Those were always the stumpers anyway."

Mike said, "Someone broke in. Did you have a lot of furniture before today because, if so, that explains why the place was pretty empty?"

"I'm a minimalist," I said. "Not a collector."

Mike said, "You didn't have a couch, Heather. That's not being a collector. That's comfort."

Maude said, "Leave the poor girl alone. She's been through enough, already. Just because you have to have your exact lazy spot on the couch in front of a television, doesn't mean it's the life for everyone."

Ben said, "Wait? She doesn't have a couch?"

"No," said Mike. "That's what I'm trying to say. That place looked like she'd just moved in. How long have you lived there?"

"I live pretty much at the office. Why bother spending money on things I don't need," I said. "And I know this tactic well. You're diverting from the facts. How did you know someone broke in?"

Ben said, "Show her. She will find out eventually. I can vouch for her sharp cookie-cutter mind. It's back. A few hours of my company can heal the world."

"Oh, my Lord," said Mike. "Do you hear this guy?"

"Show me, please," I said, trying my best not to lose my patience.

"I don't like any of this," said Mike. "Any of it, I tell you."

I asked, "He left another verse, didn't he?"

Maude said, "It wasn't in blood."

"Can you show me?" I asked again. Blood or not. Someone was in my space. Invading my private life and showing they had the upper hand, yet again.

"Here it is," said Mike, and he passed me his phone.

Ben took it from me when he saw my eyes try to register the words. He read, "'And when I passed by thee, and saw thee polluted in thine own blood, I said unto thee when thou wast in thy blood, Live; yea, I said unto thee when thou wast in thy blood, Live. Ezekiel 16:6.'"

I said, "That proves the bomb was intentional. I knew it anyway. But to claim they knew my life would be spared or brought me to life and killed Jade as if she were the sacrifice, and they chose me to be the one to live. Do you know what I'm getting at? Passing by me and saying live . . . there has to be a witness somewhere. That lets you know it's cult-related."

Ben said, "The cops on the scene said it was so chaotic. People were jetting after it, not sticking around, so the witnesses were few, and what they did see was just the explosion. Nothing else registered with anyone as being suspicious. Too much shock that our town could even have a bombing in the first place."

Mike said, "Jade's phone was damaged in the blast. She had something on there, didn't she?"

"Yeah. She'd taken pictures of the mayor's office, checked into his computer files and everything, right when I was talking to him. That lady was a genius."

Ben asked, "What else can you remember? I know you're tired, but if you can replay the mayor's visit, that might be helpful. Mike, let's take it down now while it's as fresh as we can get it."

Mike turned to Maude and said, "Honey, you want to be our recorder?"

"Sure thing, darling." She pulled a shopping list pad out of her purse. "First time he's ever let me in on a case. He knows how much I loved Jade. He knows I won't be able to let this one go, and might have something to contribute. It makes me feel not so lost. Poor thing."

I went over the day as best as I could. I told them about how I felt the way the mayor stood by the fireplace was odd. "Wait, the fire. What was that verse? They knew I'd go to the mayor? He knew I had the verse and that's why he started the fire in his office. It was like he was flaunting right in front of me, and I missed the connection. Then, the car burst into flames. Let me see the verse the killer left in Katie's hands again."

Maude asked, "Do you think he is involved? And to think I voted for that nutjob."

Ben read the verse again, "When thou passest through the waters, I will be with thee; and through the rivers, they shall not overflow thee: when thou walkest through the fire, thou shalt not be burned; neither shall the flame kindle upon thee."

I sat in stunned silence for a moment, letting it all register and make sense, if it ever could. "It was a set up to prove I would live. The whole thing. To show a prophecy would come true. They'd planned a fire. And they planned for me to live."

"So, you're saying the fireplace in the mayor's office was like a taunt?"

"It was ninety-five degrees outside. That was some kind of sign as if they're playing with prophecy. Let's just say he didn't know about the bomb. He was playing with that fire as if he were an actor in some dramatic play. No one outside of our case knows about that verse. We didn't let that one get released to the press."

"What do you mean by prophecy?" asked Maude. "Like you think the cult leader spoke about you not getting burned from the fire to his members?"

"Exactly that. And the mayor does contribute to the True Covenant of the Lambs." I hadn't told them everything. "The lamb. On his mantle. He turned it at the end of our conversation. Why would he do that?"

Ben asked, "You think it was a sign?"

The more I thought about it, the more I knew we needed to get back into that office. We could easily request a search warrant now, saying it was to sweep the entire area, and not let them in on my thoughts about me being the target.

"He turned the ceramic figure facing the wall. Maybe that was a kill order."

Mike said, "Maybe he was just rearranging a ceramic lamb. Weird, but still possible."

I kept going. "Let's draw attention away from me and put it all on the mayor. Let's say he might've been the one targeted, an election year, and all of that. That might get him a police escort, and we can monitor him. We might be able to get back into his office. I want to see that lamb."

Ben said, "You think the inner circle has mementos or symbols of lambs?"

"Very well could," I said. "Did you see anything at Hen's like that?"

Maude said, "When did you go to Hen's?"

Mike said, "I got you a present, sweetheart. It's in the trunk of my car."

"For what occasion?"

"For being sweet on you. Do I need a reason to buy my gal a gift?"

She turned to me and said, "You sent him there to scope out the place, didn't you?"

"Yes." I laughed. "How did you know?"

"That man hasn't bought me a random present in about . . ."

Mike interrupted her, "Here we go. Don't get her started, Heather. We'd be talking all night. Let's get back to Hen's. We thought Hen got the signal we weren't there for a gift. He made a couple of calls while we were circling the racks. I knew it was about our presence. I could feel it. Tried to make small talk with the old fellow, but he sent his daughter in to help us with picking out something for Maude. Like I need help choosing jewelry for my wife."

"You actually do," said Maude. "I know how you shop."

"A pin. That's it. Did the mayor have on a tie pin? That's very common. I wouldn't have noticed it even if he did. Dot had on a flag pin when we were with Pew, and she recorded our meeting. That's how that Sebastian guy knew everything."

Ben said, "Wait? Who's Sebastian? I'm trying to follow you here, Heather. You're always two steps ahead."

"When we passed the mayor's assistant, the look he gave us was chilling. As if he'd heard all we talked about yet he had a bag from Bill's."

Ben asked, "Do you think the office was bugged, too?"

"Yes. I do. I think we were being recorded, and somehow that lamb was a sign. The mayor might've not been as preoccupied with me as we'd thought. He might've known all along that Jade was up to her magic."

Ben said, "And he killed her for what she had on that phone? Could be a motive. To protect his name."

"That. And to carry out the plan of the True Covenant of the Lambs. And on my wall, back to that. If that wasn't blood, what was used for the writing of the verse? Ketchup?"

"Lipstick," said Mike.

"I don't wear a lot of makeup, Mike. I don't own red lipstick." I turned to Ben. "Where are Jade's things? After the ..."

"Collection. Down in the evidence room. Her dad is coming in from Missouri, so we were just holding them for him at the station."

"She had red lipstick," I said.

"Of course, she did," said Ben. "A rainbow of colors."

"Tell them to run her purse for prints. They took her lipstick from the scene, right out of her bag."

Mike said, "They were that close?"

"I bet they were," I said and shivered. "Watch the tapes closely. If they didn't get the lipstick there, they took it from the station."

Maude leaned in and whispered, "Do you think it's a cop?"

"I think it's someone that can blend in. Someone that knows our moves. I'd hate to think it was someone close to us but at this point, I don't think we should rule out that possibility."

Mike said, "But to kill one of our own? Heather, that's just crazy."

"It's all crazy. Prints from Jade's belongings might pull us a suspect, at least. I think someone walking around wearing gloves in the middle of summer would constitute suspicious activity, easily spotted."

Mike said, "I hate to even think this way, considering someone close or someone that we know could do a thing like that to Jade. If it is someone that knows what we might do next, as far as the crime scene, I would think they'd be too smart to leave any evidence behind. But still, let me call it in. Just in case."

I stopped him. "Don't call it in. Do it yourself. Stand by and get the results. Watch the hands that touch it."

There was someone else I needed to see. It might not have been a coincidence that we'd made a trip to the prison and interrupted Marcus Pew's spotlight he felt he still had on him. He was sure he was still the light and savior to his disciples, and when I teased him about the new serial killer, he might've planned this spur of the moment attack on me to prove he still had his mojo, even behind prison bars.

I wouldn't put anything past Pew, especially if he felt he was being threatened. I grabbed my phone and called the warden. "This is Detective Moody, again. I'd like to let you know I'd like to visit Marcus Pew tomorrow."

When the warden told me what happened, I almost dropped my phone and looked at Mike and Ben, then back again.

"Okay," I said. "Hold on one second." Still trying to process what he'd said. Maybe I didn't hear it right. My ears were ringing. Maybe I didn't hear anything at all. I handed the phone to Ben. "Can you ask him to repeat that, just in case I got it wrong?"

Ben took my phone and talked for a few minutes to the warden. The look on his face told it all. When he hung up, he turned to me and confirmed that what I'd heard was true.

"He was found hanging in his cell. Marcus Pew is dead."

17

I didn't attend funerals. Not since we lay my parents to rest on an early Sunday morning in May. Today I had to make a choice when I knew I didn't have one. I had to show up for Jade. For Mike and Ben. To pay respects to her father. I was the last to walk beside her. I can say laughter left her lips at that last moment. I can tell how much I valued her as a cop and was just getting to know her as a friend.

Hiding away in my empty apartment was not an option. I had a lot of black in my closet and found it easier to keep to the basics in my wardrobe. Jade would've been all color and patterns. To know her lipstick stains had been removed from my wall after forensics did their work left me with a chill. It was as if I could still see the message there. Live. Live.

I lived to see another sunrise. I lived to call my grandparents and made plans to come and visit them once all of this was put behind me. Someone stole all of Jade's plans. My thoughts landed on a ring in a box with her name on it. Her boyfriend must be beyond devastated. No words matched these days. That's why I never showed up for them. The silence was awkward. So were the words. My presence would have to be enough.

The ceremony was far from small. It was as if the entire town showed up to pay her respect. The flashing lights of the police cars, fire department, and rescue services from not only our town but around the state showed up in a line formation all through the lanes of the graveyard and paraded through Crystal Falls. They piled purple and bright yellow flowers in every spot imaginable. Jade's picture of her in her rookie uniform stared out at us as if to say she chose this life. She knew the risks. His Eye Is on the Sparrow was sung by someone that knew Jade, and the soul-filled tune even had the birds circling in the sky in a patterned salute. The morning air wasn't sticky hot yet with humidity, but a warm breeze danced through the air.

Her father stood tall but the sight of him made my heart quiver. As much as he tried to appear fortress-like, the tiny tremors in his shoulders let me know the truth about his struggle. I wanted to tell him I was so sorry that Jade didn't live. I was sorry. I was sorry I had to be there to remind him it could've been me. But no words would come. He told me he'd see me tomorrow. I was expecting that after what the chief said.

"First thing. Six o'clock a.m.," was my reply. I couldn't deny him access to the case. I'd already thought it through. What the captain didn't know wouldn't hurt him. Having extra eyes would be a help.

"Just the way I like it," he said. "Never could sleep late, anyway. The routine sticks with you long after retirement sets in."

Mike said, "We could use your experience on this one, Cain. Just let it be between us. Captain already said . . ."

"Captain doesn't have a say. I say," he said, as he gave a slight grin. "There's nothing in this world that's going to come between me and this killer."

"Justice," said Ben. "Let it be justice. Don't take it into your own hands. Trust me. We all want to, but for the sake of Jade, let's do it right."

"You mean, you won't give me a minute alone with him? Just a minute. That's all I need," Mr. Cain said, his eyes narrowing.

"Not even a minute," said Mike. "Help us catch him. That'll be enough, won't it?"

Mr. Cain's jaw worked with the mounting tension. "I doubt it. I doubt it will ever be enough, even if I get that minute."

"The lipstick tube came back clean," said Mike, as we walked away from the graveside, knowing we were all dedicated to going back to the station.

Maude welcomed Mr. Cain to stay with them over the next few days while he helped us and sorted out Jade's business. We'd been told we had to take a few days off. And I was sure we were about to get that reminder.

The captain stepped into our circle, and we clipped our talk short. "Before you can leave the graveyard, you're already talking about the case. Can't you give it a day?"

I said, "You asked us to wait out of respect for Jade. We waited. We're going in, sir."

We all shook Mr. Cain's hand and separated from the captain. He could throw his weight if he wanted and call us down, but we couldn't let that happen. I saw Mike whisper to Mr. Cain and knew he was cooking something up. Sure enough, Mr. Cain took Captain McBride by the arm, saying he'd like to catch up with him. Cain gave us a wink before carrying him away to stand under a line of Cypress trees lining the iron gate.

I asked, "You figured we'd find nothing on the lipstick case, Mike. But what about belongings? Any trace?"

"Zero," said Ben. "The surveillance cameras weren't much help either. Everyone was scrambling, crawling, and dashing about. It was chaos, just like the cops on the scene reported. Nothing really useful for us. I did get us this," he said, as soon as we got into the Bronco.

Ben unzipped his gym bag and pulled out something wrapped in a towel. I gasped when I saw it. "How did you get to the mayor's office without anyone seeing you take this?"

"I walked in. Its city hall. It's not like they keep a tight watch over the place, and with everything that's happened, it was an easy in."

"Break it," I said.

Ben said, "Wait? What?"

"Break that creepy lamb. Let's see if it holds any recording device. If so, they've already caught us now on tape. They've got us, Ben. They've got you. We need to break it."

"She's right," said Mike. "I've got a tool bag behind the seat. Grab the hammer."

"If you say so," said Ben. He put the lamb on top of the towel and set it on the floorboard behind Mike's seat. "Here we go." He pounded on the lamb until it shattered.

I leaned over the back. "What's inside?"

"There's nothing here," Ben said. "It felt good to smash something, though."

Mike frowned. "What if it was a family heirloom? What if it was his grandfather's ceramic lamb, and we just took part in destroying the family token?"

I was still convinced the mayor was a crooked man.

"Then his family is in the True Covenant of the Lambs. That man isn't innocent. He might not have bugged the lamb, but there's something in that office. Wait, it makes sense, Ben. Think about it. He turned the lamb, so he had to have a camera on us. He set the stage. The fireplace was his platform and as soon as he was ready to send out the kill order, he turned the lamb. The camera was across the room capturing it. Sending it out to someone to follow an order."

Ben asked, "Was this the lamb you saw? The one on the mantle board?"

"It looks the same. Eerie looking thing." I shook my head in disbelief. "But then, that just means he knew we were coming. He switched it out."

Mike moved the rearview mirror but couldn't focus for long. "What is it, Ben?"

Ben held up a broken piece of the lamb. "This is crazy." He leaned back, slumping into the seat. "Heather, pull out your phone. Type this in. 1 J 5:8."

I said, "'And there are three that bear witness in earth, the Spirit, and the water, and the blood: and these three agree in one.'"

Mike banged his hand on the steering wheel. "You mean we might have three of these fools running around? Someone is acting as spirit, blood, and water?"

"Either all three as one or three to become one?" I said aloud. "Or what if Marcus Pew was killed to become the spirit. I still can't believe he's dead. He didn't seem the type to take his own life. He loved his life way too much. Do you think he was unstable, Ben?"

"Some questions, Heather. The guy was a sociopath. Insane. There's no reason to think he was stable, period."

"You know what I mean," I said. "I think it just comes at a strange time. We have the car bombing and Pew hangs himself? He might've sent out the order for the bomb because he wanted to get back at me. I might've reminded him way too much of his downfall. His demise. Or, he sacrificed himself by becoming some kind of spirit to this cult."

Mike said, "I'm going to quit thinking all the stuff you say is nonsense. None of this is impossible. I swear, I raised my kids in this town. Thank God they came out unscathed by this underground mess. It's a mess. That's what it is."

Ben said, "I don't think it's nonsense, either. Why have this verse in the lamb and it all connected with the river and the blood? Cooper's Landing backs up to the falls. They've got themselves a perfect compound by the river. They are now taking blood. We've got a dark web weaving. You know how you're walking and you're absentminded, you're thinking of other things. You're preoccupied with the world. And then the next thing you know you're feeling this sticky thread on your face. It startles you and then you start to jump. Do you think a spider might've landed on you? You shake your clothes, you shive ..."

"You scream," said Mike. "I don't like spiders."

I said, "The spider has to make the web. They have to catch their prey. It's the same here. They've cast a web and now we know the signs. They've set it openly right before us, but we've never had eyes to see. They just don't know how vigilant we are. How alert. We'll see the web before we crash into it. We'll destroy it right where it hangs."

"So, every time we see a lamb figurine, I pop it with a hammer? I like this plan," said Ben. "It'll help me deal with my anger."

"No, we don't go smashing up the world, and we don't go undercover either. We weren't born into the religion, and everyone knows we're now working the case. Pew was born into this. He was a religious guru in his own right but could've been a worker for the larger cell with his influential group of members he was charged to control. His sheep. A separate pasture but all on the same farm."

Mike said, "When you say there may be three leaders, then that would be us assuming to take the verse literally. Don't we know there could be so many underlying, hidden meanings associated with the way someone reads a verse?"

"No. They don't think that deeply. Every single verse so far has just been surface-level. It's not some deep metaphorical meaning or parable. We need to expose this fast because the car bomb lets me know they will relax."

Ben said, "I might have to disagree with you on this one. Don't you think that heightens their plans? Like they will keep striking back while it's hot?"

"They've killed Jade. They've done their worst. They think we'll take that as a warning and back off."

Mike laughed. "Then they are dumber than I thought."

"They'll take this time to call and nurture their members and pull out the verses to show their prophetic power. If we've figured out the space between the killings as seasonal, they won't strike again until autumn. Especially with Pew dead. Their spirit has to have time to shine and work. They won't take away from that time to exploit that whole dogma if it is part of their ritual."

Ben asked, "When you were undercover with Pew, do you remember seeing any lambs? Any symbolism that can connect the two?"

"Not that I can remember."

Mike said, "So if the three would be working to become one, that could mean they've tried to pull off three separate working parts. Like separate identities under the same roof until their transformation or enlightenment or whatever it is they believe."

Ben said, "Their spaceship trip to the moon."

Mike said, "Resurrection is typically a common theme to believers, right? Isn't that something we need to think about?"

"Yes, Mike. You're right. And who just died? Jade. Pew."

Ben said, "Wait? Jade? You can't mean she was involved . . ."

I cut him off. "No! No. I didn't mean Jade had anything to do with the cult. Just the opposite. Jade was innocent. She could've been symbolic of that innocence or the taking of a life that held a position of power. Like they could do whatever they wanted at this point, kill anyone without repercussions, or work right under us without ever the worry of being caught. Jade was innocent. Think about the innocent bloodshed. That's symbolic of Christ. We need to watch the graveyard. Someone might come for her body. But it could be Pew. Pew died on her same date, right?"

Mike said, "If those psycho's think Jade and Pew's souls somehow met up in the afterlife? No way in heaven could that happen."

"Cults don't believe in rational thought. That's what makes them a fringe in society and against the mainstream. They could be sitting there thinking about the very thing you suggest. Pew and Jade both dying on the same day can't be a coincidence. That was a planned attack. And honestly, they didn't care which one died. Me or Jade. It was either of us to go that day or both of us. They needed an innocent. One who was out to destroy them. We both fit that description."

"If you're right about this, there's no telling how far this group will go."

"Exactly," I said. "We need someone to watch their

burial sites. We might just have a grave digger come around tonight."

Ben said, "You don't think ..."

The phone rang on the dash holder. "It's Maude, hold on." Mike took the call and then said, "Mercy is looking for me. Said he'd meet me down at the station."

"Mercy? Did Maude say what for?"

"Said he's got to confess."

"Confess?" I said. "Mike, you think Mercy did something? You said he was a good person."

"That he is. For sure. Whatever he's confessing, I'm thinking his hand was forced. He doesn't have an evil bone in his old body. I've known that family for years."

"I think sometimes all we know is to not know."

Ben said, "Is that a Wheel of Fortune puzzle?"

I turned to Ben. "I never thanked you for staying with me. For both of you sticking by me when all of that . . . when . . ."

My voice cracked, and I left it there between us as we pulled into the station. Mike gave me a knowing look and Ben started joking about duty and honor and giving a welcome speech. I let them finish out all the things I couldn't say. I could feel it, but I couldn't speak it. I guess I would have to take it how it came. The feeling was a start.

18

Mike tried to calm his friend down, but it was hard to do. "Confessing you've planted a row of trees doesn't mean you are guilty of anything, Mercy. Have you been sleeping since we found that blood on your land? You need some sleep, man. I'm calling your daughter."

"Don't," he cried. "I have to protect them. No one can know I'm here."

I didn't want to give him the false hope that it was safe to be in the interrogation room with us because I knew that wasn't necessarily the case. Someone might know of our goings-on. Right now, Ben was in the surveillance room, recording the session. That way no one could sneak in and listen at least.

"What do you know about the oaks?" I took a swig of steaming coffee. This was going to be a long day.

"I knew they were evil, and I didn't tell anyone. I'd cut them all down if I didn't fear they'd haunt me even more."

"Here we go," said Mike. "You've got some supernatural story to tell? Trees can't be evil. They're just trees."

Mercy protested as desperation stuck on every word, "They are evil. They had that blood on them, didn't they? They witnessed that poor girl dead on that boat. Right there facing them trees."

"Slow down," I said. "Mercy, start at the beginning. Tell me what you know."

"When I was a boy this man came driving up in an old Ford truck. It was green. That's all I remember. He gets out and goes to my father. He says he wants to buy the land. He wants it all the way to Cooper's Landing. My daddy wasn't about to sell anything to that strange man. Later he told Momma how he gave him the heebie-jeebies. Besides, he loved this town. This land. You know it as well as I do, Mike. He was building something good. Something to pass along to me."

Mike nodded. "Good people, Heather, the whole lot of them."

"Well, I climbed on the bed of the truck when the man was trying to negotiate with Daddy, telling him it was in his best interest to cooperate. I was just a young thing, but I remember the voice. It took a chill over me in the middle of a warm day. I was out of school so thinking it had to be summer or some break. Easter. Around Easter. It was. That's right. Easter because Momma was still in her Sunday best."

Mike said, "Mercy, did you know the man?"

"No. Never seen him before or since. But I remember he had these baskets of wool in the truck bed. I remember hearing his cold voice and feeling the warm wool and thinking about the poor animals he'd sheared. Did he hurt them? I was worried about the animals. He wasn't a good man. Can't tell you why I know, I just do."

I asked, "What about the trees, Mercy?"

"He wanted the land to plant trees. My daddy was

confused. He said we had enough trees God already provided. The man went on to say they needed specific oaks planted. They needed it by the river. It would be a sign of baptism. He handed my daddy an envelope. You should've seen his face change. Like the light of the Lord shone on him."

"Money?" I asked.

"Must've been a wad because my daddy was then paying more attention. The man said Daddy could take the money if he could plant a line of oaks. He pulled out a map and handed him another envelope out of his satchel."

Mike said, "The seeds."

"I didn't think about it. Lost the memory until the other morning I was in the Word. I saw the verse and remembered it. It all came back. The oaks. Daddy let me help him plant them. Said we were doing a service. A good thing by creating a new habitat for some roaming animals that didn't have a home."

I asked, "What was the verse that brought it back?"

Mercy didn't have to pull out his phone to check it. He looked at me with a pained expression that let me know his guilt was real. "They will be called oaks of righteousness, a planting of the LORD for the display of his splendor. Isaiah 61:3. That man said that very quote, and I remember my dad saying how impressed he was that he knew the Word without looking. Even Satan himself knew the scripture."

"What happened to that girl wasn't your fault," said Mike. "I've told you that. Time and again, Mercy. It's not your fault."

"But it is. I planted the audience. The oaks. I gave the murderer a place to display his evil works."

I tried to console him as well. There was no need for this elder to carry around the guilt that wasn't a burden for him to bear. "And you say this happened when you were a boy. You planted trees with your father. You are innocent, Mercy. Please don't let this eat at you."

"My father took blood money. Blood . . ." his voice trailed.

"Your father didn't know," I said. "Please, Mercy. You have to let this go. It's not on you or your family."

"I've cursed them, I tell you," he pleaded. "I need to break the curse. What can you do to stop it from spreading? From reaching my kin?"

Mike said, "There is no curse. What it does show is that this was planned for many years. Way before our time, Heather."

I asked, "Anything else you can remember of the man? Anything stand out to you? Think back, Mercy."

"I can remember his voice to this very day."

I understood that. That's how I felt when I heard Marcus Pew. Some evil ran so deep it even resided even in the lilt, the pronunciation, the tone of the simplest word.

"Anything else," asked Mike. "Any scars? Tattoos?"

"Wait," said Mercy. "His arm. It had a weird drawing on it. My daddy had that tattoo of a woman he met. Well, she was once a naked woman tattoo when he was in the Navy, and my momma made him cover her up with a bikini. Remember that, Mike. Lord, her telling that in church on Sunday would make my daddy blush hot."

Mike passed him a notepad. "Can you draw it?"

He chuckled. "Candy is the artist in the family. I don't have the skills and can't draw a lick."

"Just try," I said. "Do you remember it?"

He took a minute, positioning the paper this way and that, and then scribbled an uneven star with three circles intertwined over it, like a Venn diagram, meeting all at the center.

"It was like that, I think. Something like that."

"And three will become one," I whispered. "Thanks, Mercy. You've been such a big help. We've got a lot to go on. An old green Ford truck. A tattoo. Years of planning."

Mercy cried, "How many lives? How many lives were taken by this monster?"

I tried to calm him. "I'm sorry, Mercy. I don't have all the answers. I know for sure, you're a good person just like Mike has always said. You've done nothing but help us at every turn, and we thank you for that. Now, go home. Take care of yourself. Let us work the case."

"But I know the one who does have the answers," he said, slowly rising to his feet. "The man upstairs."

Mike said, "I'm assuming you aren't talking about the captain?"

Mercy patted his friend on the shoulder. "The one of my very ship. Sorry to be so down in my self-pity. I'm glad I got all that out to you. Have to say, confession is good for the soul. I don't even have to stop by the church on my way home."

Mike put his arm around his shoulder. "It's not your fault, Mercy. Now, get some rest."

"I might sleep for days if I can just get my mind from motor-boatin' on and on," he said. "Any information from those cameras?"

I told him about the one suspicious character we caught but couldn't identify. I also thought of how Ben needed to get those new cameras they planted to send signals to their computers and phone. Jade had it tapped to go to her app. Jade. How in the world could we ever get someone with her skill?

When we made it back upstairs, I was surprised to see Mr. Cain staring at the board in my office. Maude must have dropped him off, along with a pile of Tupperware containers filled with food and lined up around the circle table we'd barely maneuvered into the space to give us some working room.

I asked, "Sir, how did you get in here?"

"A locked door doesn't stop me," he said, chuckling. "I'm not messing with anything. Just surveying the land. And don't worry, Chief Lee knows I'm here."

That reminded me. "I was just thinking about those deer cameras. They were hooked up to go to Jade's cell to alert us of any movement on the property. The perpetrators may be back, or the oak trees have already served their purpose. Still, to be safe, we need to get back down there, Ben. Figure out how to get them to send us the signals instead."

"Jade was our genius behind a computer," said Ben. "I'm sure you know how talented your daughter was."

"Talented. Of course, I knew. Who do you think taught her? She learned from the best."

I smiled. "So, you know your way around locked doors and computers?"

"And safes. I can crack those, too. And how about taking control over a server without being noticed and . . ."

I put my hand up and laughed. "Enough. You're hired. We can't pay you. I don't have the authority to do that, but when can you start?"

"I'm standing here, aren't I. Today. Right now."

"Then, let's get to it," I said, setting down my bag and turning on my computer. "There's much work to be done."

19

C hange was an inevitable part of life and the job. Nothing was ever secured or promised and even when I felt like everything was falling into place for me, I knew it was just a facade. Mr. Cain dove right into all the work of the case and watched with eagerness as we tried to show him the connections, no matter how loose they were, to how the mayor and Pew must have been involved. The timeline of the unsolved murder cases was reviewed.

I handed over the files to Cain. "These are the ones we've been focusing on since the summer of 2012 with Mercy lands. We now know why this was probably the first one."

Mike filled Cain in with the story Mercy brought to us. "These trees were the witness to the first crime. This uncle claimed he did it. He confessed and is being held down at County until trial."

Ben said, "I think we need to go pay him a visit."

"I'm with you," said Cain.

"No," I warned. "Not that kind of work. That'll put you out in the light. Remember in your unofficial interview you said you could do things without being noticed. Break codes. Safes. Servers. We need you here out of sight. If they did target Jade because they thought she was the threat, then that means they can't know you have the same skill as her. They'll go after you, too. We need you, Cain."

"Secrecy. Covert operation. You got it, boss. Long as I'm in the loop, I can be the silent thread no one ever sees."

"The one that holds us all together," I said. "Stay here and do me a favor. Get Jade's phone working. Find out what she had on there from the mayor's office. Next, get those cameras online. We need to see if the killer will go back to Mercy's land." I turned to Mike and said, "Don't eat all of Maude's food while we're gone. Save me some of that, will you?"

He patted his stomach. "I'll just get a little. What else do you want me to do, Heather? I need to keep busy."

"Finish up the Mercy logs, the donor lists, the mail and prison logs, and cross-reference all of them for any similarities. That's a huge undertaking, Mike. Sorry to leave you with all that. And, call down to the prison, and let them know we have reason to believe there will be a grave robbing."

"I told you to keep me busy," he said, then paused and looked around the office as if he expected a quick comeback. It didn't arrive. Jade would have had a nice one for him.

Recognizing where his thoughts fell, Ben said, "I know, Mike."

"Heather, y'all stay safe out there, okay. I can't have y'all in any danger and go off . . ."

"Don't," I said, quietly. "We'll do our best, Mike. That's all I can promise you. I can say that since I've been working with this team, I've felt things . . . things I've never been able to say outright or even allow myself to feel."

"That was Jade's influence," said Cain. "She could always get to the heart of the matter."

"And you are a boss like no other," said Ben. "I can print you one of those certificates off the internet to prove it. We can frame it. This closet of hers needs some decorations. Some touch."

"You should see her apartment," said Mike, starting in on me again.

"Hey, hey," I said. "No ganging up on me now. The less on the walls the less I have to pack when I find my dream home. Now get to work, the both of you, or Cain, you're fired."

He laughed. "You technically can't fire me. I'm not officially on the payroll."

"Great answer. I was just testing you," I said with a smile. "You passed with flying colors."

I could hear them rambling on about me as I walked down the hall, then circled back and closed the door. Whatever was spoken in that room needed to stay within its confines.

It felt so good to be out in the open air and away from all the eyes. Everyone kept telling us how sorry they were about Jade. It was hard. Sorry didn't cut it. It was a necessary word to say, one that was expected, but still hard to hear anyway, especially when it felt so close.

"Tell me about that home," Ben prodded, as we pulled out of the station drive.

"He's not locked at a home, but at the county correctional facility," I corrected him.

"Not the suspect—the dream home."

"Oh, I was just kidding back there." In reality, I knew I wasn't. My grandparents lived on a nice twenty-acre farm, and I wanted a plot of land like that of my own one day with my own gun range in the back so I wouldn't have to wait in the lines at Trader Hick's where all the cops and gun enthusiasts in town had to share.

"You don't talk much about your life with people, do you, Heather?"

"Why should I? I don't know much about yours. You are one good detective, I can give you that. Your name is Benjamin Caraway, named from the tribe of Israel. You love joking around. You want a t-shirt company, and you love to eat at Bill's, your favorite restaurant, but it's more of a stop in the diner, so not a place to hold down a quiet conversation with friends. You hang out with Mike because Maude adores you and sees more of you than most women in town, and you don't cut your hair because it reminds you that once this is all over you'll still be able to go surfing, the way you used to do down at the Outer Banks when you were a teenager."

"Oh, now. She speaks and tells it all. Can you please tell me how you know all these things about me?"

"Sticker on your car. OBX means one thing. Your cologne of choice usually smells like Bill's hot dog chili, so I'm sure you're frequenting that place more than anyone else in Crystal Falls, and you've got a soft spot for elders. That's why you are the way you are with Mike and Maude. You want what they have and just haven't found it yet."

"Who's to say I haven't," he said as he pulled into the park. "I might just have my eye on someone right this very minute."

I looked out the windshield and pointed. "The guard doesn't look like your type. Oh, look over there. That's a possibility but I can already say that woman is here to get her jailbird boyfriend out on bond with that outfit on, looking like she stepped out of some greaser movie, and wait . . ."

"Here we go again," said Ben. "You said wait. I know what that means. You're getting another missing piece to this puzzle."

"It's a woman who's going to try to get Pew out."

"Pew is dead," I said. "The warden confirmed it."

"There was a body in a death row cell. That's what we know. We don't have a coroner's report. We don't have DNA proof it's actually Marcus Pew. I want to see his body. See him not breathing. I bet one of his disciples helped him orchestrate the greatest escape there ever was."

"And you think that just because that half-dressed woman walked by the car?"

"Exactly," I said. "Come on. Let's hurry up and take care of this while we're here. I've got to look this uncle in the eye, and then we need to head over to the coroner's office. I want proof in my hands or I swear, I won't believe a word of it."

I couldn't believe I'd let that slide. I was in the hospital when I heard the news, and heavily medicated at first. The pain medicine had to wear off. Then, we've lived in mourning for Jade. Her funeral. My mind was so . . . is so . . .

"Don't let me lose my focus again," I whispered.

"So, the way you focus is for us to just have random conversations and then you get these brilliant epiphanies?"

"You do come in handy," I said, jabbing him on the arm.

"I'd like to call myself your muse, not your handyman, but I could be that, too. I was raised by a single mom and took over all the guy mechanical, fixer-upper duties at a young age. Years of experience."

I wanted to say that might've explained why he was so nice to me. He realized I was broken and had an intrinsic need to want to fix things stemming from the safety that provided him at a younger age, to not have to depend on anyone else but be the one in charge, but that wasn't a conversation lightly thrown around at the entrance of a medium-security facility. The maximum facility at the Falls was where the hardened criminals were kept. Those of Pew's caliber. This was a place I could spiral deeper into my thoughts if I allowed the prison name to register too long in my vision. I turned my eyes quickly from the entrance sign and posted rules. Just don't stare at anything too long. It will be like he doesn't exist and is walking behind this barbed wire.

"I don't think I can stay here long," I said. "Let's go in and out. We need to follow that lead to the potential girlfriend of Pew's."

"What girlfriend? I think you're chasing ghosts," said Ben.

I let his words hit me and knew he was so close to the truth of it but so far away from ever knowing just how close I was unless I was the one to let him in. I'd never told anyone the story of my past. I'd never told a soul about Rory, my parents' death, or the way all that ended. Jade was the closest that ever came to ask me about it, and it had taken me years to lock it all in a box and try to hide it in my mind. That's the funny thing about boxes. Over time they want to be opened. Seemed like I was going to have to go there to get to the other side of this. If it gave me something, anything, I'd have to try. I could always wrap another box away. Another day for that. I was an expert at hiding things away.

I flashed my badge. The startled look on the front desk attendants' face was priceless after she ran it through the system. "Hello, Ms. Moody. Are you here for Pew? He's got you on his shortlist of approved visitors."

"No," I said quickly. "We're here to question Thomas Riley. I called ahead."

"Oh, sorry. I just took over the shift. I'll buzz you in." With a couple of clicks, two passes pushed through the partition cutout, and a check through, we were in and escorted down to where Thomas Riley was allowed visitors.

As soon as Ben could, he asked, "Pew? I don't understand."

"Please, don't ask me."

"If it involves this case, I have to. Heather, why did they say you were here to see Pew. Marcus Pew wasn't locked away here."

"It's not that Pew. He's dead. Or he's escaped with a disciple, just like I said. I'm seriously not talking with you about this, Ben. Please drop it."

"Not before this day is out," he said, as Emma Rose's uncle was escorted into the room, shackled and positioned in front of us.

"So, why did you confess to a murder you didn't commit," I said. I wanted to start this out straight on and get out of here. Just knowing he could be in the next room brought waves of nausea to my stomach. I knew this place would affect me, but I didn't know how strong until my feet rubbed along the tile. The same tile that might have felt his scruffy boots.

"I killed that girl. I did it," he said.

"What girl was that?" asked Ben.

"Emma, that's what girl was that. I killed little Emma."

I said, "I know for a fact you didn't kill your niece, Mr. Riley. Who put you up to this?"

He wrung his hands together, clearly nervous as could be. "I'll pay for that crime I did. I'll pay. Let me pay." He whispered, "I want to pay. Let me pay."

I sighed, knowing this was a lost cause. His eyes were a blank void. "You want to go to trial for killing your sister's child? You did not do this crime. You might've committed others. I'm not saying that, but I don't think it was you."

Ben was in the moment with me. This interview was unrehearsed. "He might've done it, Heather. Look at those wild eyes. It's the look of a madman."

"It's the look of a lost man. There's a huge difference." I leaned forward. "We can help you, Mr. Riley. Did Marcus Pew force you to confess to this heinous crime?"

He frantically shook his head.

"Did someone else with power force you to confess to Emma Rose's murder? Power of three?"

His head jerked up, and he turned stone cold. Like an ice sculpture.

I had no choice but to ask him, even with the guards present and the beady eyes I was sure were watching me from the cameras in the corner of the room. I was sure they could pick up my audio, but just in case, I spoke louder. "So, are you a member of the True Covenant of the Lambs?"

"Like a lamb to the slaughter so he opened not his mouth," he spat out.

"You just opened your mouth," said Ben. "Didn't you see that, Heather? His mouth went up and down, and a sound came out. He opened it surely as I'm standing here today. Confounded and contradictory."

I crossed my arms, leaned back, and smiled. Finally, we had a break. I could see the evil coursing through him, his posture, his eyes, the way he threw back his head in this glee of the knowing, yet somehow felt he didn't do the crime. Now, to get him to talk. To give us the names. The plans. Whatever it was this cult believed to be the truth so maybe we had time to piece this together before they struck again.

20

We'd spent all afternoon trying to get Thomas Riley to talk, but he stonewalled the entire interview. There was a fine line between his walk with insanity based on his posturing.

I could read his body language and pick up on his glances and glistening, narrowed eyes. And to think eyes weren't the window to the soul. Truly, they were. To know he was part of the cult gave me another way to draw out the circle of influence. Find out who Thomas was connected to, draw out suspect names, comb through his past dealings. The question remained as to what they might've had on him to use as a condition for him to confess to a crime of his family member.

It's not like I wasn't aware that families weren't immune from attacks by their closest relatives. I was the first who would've raised their hand to that conversation. But something told me he didn't do it. He might've been capable of a lot of things, but not murder. Unlike Pew. If it wasn't our stop in by the coroner's office to satisfy my curiosity and reviewing the autopsy tapes, I would've never believed Pew could kill himself.

We followed up with Emma Rose's mother after he refused to talk. She said she knew her brother was up to some no good business, but she thought it was just petty crime—stealing stereo systems, and a couple of breaking and entering charges from his past. Nothing like murder.

I still didn't think he'd killed his niece but was covering up for someone inside the cult. Someone had something on him, and to absolve himself of his sins, I guess he was put to the test. Bring an innocent for slaughter. Maybe that's why they killed Jade. Someone needed to bring an innocent lamb to the slaughter and claim they'd made a sacrifice. To prove they were worthy of the cult way—an initiation of sorts.

I knew the lamb reference wasn't just a weird coincidence. The tattoo wasn't on his arm. We checked his records for any tattoos. The one that Mercy spoke of still nagged at me. If the man from many years ago wore the tattoo of the organization or cult, then he could've been marked as a leader. Someone would have to know about the strange symbols.

That's what led us to Dot. We couldn't meet in a populated place downtown to discuss it, and I wanted us off the phones doing it. Ben and I took a walk down to the falls, a beautiful landmark of our town, to meet Dot in the open.

"I loved this place," I said.

"It's still here," he laughed. "You act as if it were past tense, wiped off the map."

"I mean, I used to come down here a lot." I didn't want to tell him all about the plans I'd had once I moved to Crystal Falls. To live normally on my own without ghosts around every corner, to be out more, to do more. After a while, it all lost its appeal. The job became more demanding and filled in the empty spaces. Doing all of those things alone only reminded me I was.

I hated what that walk through that prison did to me. It had my emotions so raw and out of sorts. I leaned against the railing and took in the sight of the cascading water. Clear your mind of it. The hot summer humidity wore on Ben's face already. He was red with sweat.

I said, "You need to work out more."

"I'm very happy with this firm and trim body. I haven't had many complaints," he said.

I rolled my eyes. He was incorrigible. "Why can't life be this simple? The water runs. It has a purpose. It goes after it with full passion, letting nothing stand in its way. If so, it finds a way to divert and move on, always moving forward, never looking back."

"You're talking about you, right? You want to leave the memories behind but keep turning that way?"

I didn't answer. He was right. Every time I traveled down that path, it wasn't a refreshing stream of love running over my heart but a pain that would feel like needles stabbing against my heart. Best to be like water. Keep rushing forward.

"Can we talk about Pew now?" he asked, leaning over the railing to catch sight of the fish set out on their purpose.

I felt like it could swallow me whole if I stayed in that conversation. Thankfully, I didn't have to.

Dot came into view, with her tight jogging outfit on. She smiled sweetly at Ben, trying to get his attention, but all he did was look at me.

I said, "Thanks for meeting us. We want you to run a story, but we need a promise from you: you won't add to it or go digging for more about it, yet. It could be critical to the case."

She panted, taking a swig of water from her backpack, and then took out a pad and pencil to take notes.

"Wait, let me draw it," said Ben. "Give me that a second." He grabbed the notepad and began to draw out the tattoo sketch Mercy described.

It was just as scribble as what Mercy tried to do, but at least it was distinguishable. I showed the drawing to Dot. "Run it as a mystery. Who knows the symbol? What does it mean? Use that kind of jargon. Add my direct line for information."

"The viewers do love to be couch cops. I think this will be an edition that'll get some attention."

"Thanks, Dot. And thanks for not running that Pew interview."

"No point now. He's dead," said Ben.

"He's what?" asked Dot. "No way."

I said, "Yes. He hung himself in his cell. I'm as shocked as you, Dot."

"He seemed like he was going to ride that fame as long as he could, until his moment of execution. I did contact that publisher. He was right. They had offered a huge six-figure deal and agreed to give it to some charitable organization in his name."

Ben smirked. "Let me guess, The True Covenant of the Lambs?"

"Exactly," replied Dot. "I told you that place was no good."

Ben asked, "Ever done an exposé on them, or do you think that might be too dangerous?"

"I wouldn't mind a little danger. Think I just have the topic for my next series. I can run Pew's murderous rampage as a recap, cover his death, and then talk about this book deal discovery. That'll be a way in without looking as if I'm trying to bring them down, but maybe I can get into their good graces and learn more."

I asked, "Do you still have that recording device?"

She winked. "Which one? Darling, I'm crazy about spy gear. If you saw my briefcase, I think you'd be impressed."

"I bet," I said, grinning back. "Get as much as you can about The True Covenant of the Lambs while you're there. I mean get everything. Layout, internal names, faces, anything, and everything you spot, grab it on film. Send a couple of crew members with you for additional angles, maybe? That'll give us more footage. I'm sure that won't look suspicious. We can't request a search warrant yet. Nothing has turned up shady. If I go to the judge saying I needed to get into the compound because a lamb was in the Mayor's office, they'd laugh me out of the court and think I'd lost my mind."

"Trust me. I know how to get it all," said Dot. "Don't worry. I'll share it. You'll have open access to the files before editing."

"Thanks, Dot. I owe you."

"Maybe a one-on-one interview about Pew one day, then? Just the two of us?"

"Maybe," I said. "We'll see. Just know I'm so thankful you're helping us with this. I can't believe I'm telling that to a member of the press."

"We're not all sharks," she said.

"Let me guess," said Ben. "You'd be a cookie-cutter shark if you had to pick one?"

She frowned, putting her earbuds back in. "No. A tiger shark. They are the most aggressive off the coast of the

Carolinas. Let me be that—a little more aggressive to get the edge."

Ben laughed. "See. Shark identification tells a lot about the true nature of people. It should be on some survey we give out like a personality test. What's your ice cream flavor of choice, and what kind of shark would you be if you could? Two vital questions in life worth answering."

She ran off, giving us a slight wave, and we turned back to the view. "That was interesting," I said. "Wonder why she's trying to help us?"

"Not all people are out to get you," said Ben.

"I need proof of that."

"Always looking for evidence. How about just trust? Isn't that what your faith is supposed to stand on."

He had a point. I needed to let my guard down around him and Mike. They were my partners. I needed to trust them. Dot seemed genuine on this whole thing, and I'm sure it was for some ulterior motive, like capturing the big headlines before her competitors. If it worked, then I needed to trust it.

We didn't talk on the way home, but the silence was comforting. Ben escorted me inside my apartment, which I told him was completely unnecessary, but he insisted. Maybe it was to get me in my place to ask the question he'd been impatient about all day.

And just like I predicted, he started soon after he swept the place. "Who is this Pew? He had a brother? I checked the records, and he had no living relatives. That's why no one came to claim him at the morgue."

We'd also stopped by the county morgue office and spoke with the medical examiner assigned to his paperwork. I held the death certificate in my hands. The surveillance from the prison hallway leading to Pew's cell didn't show any movement around the approximate time of death. It wouldn't have surprised me if another inmate somehow got to him, or even a guard who'd had enough of Pew. Pew could do that to the best of people. Get them to break. What he could do to the worst of them was without boundaries.

"Heather, who was the Pew at County, and why was your name on his visitor request list?"

I said, "Marcus Pew had no brothers or sisters. He was an only, corrupted child."

"A cousin? A relative, then?"

I grabbed a couple of waters from the fridge and passed him one. He wasn't going to stop. I understood his concern, though. If it involved Jade, then he wanted to know. He deserved to know. It was just so hard.

"The Pew in County is my brother."

"Your kin to Marcus Pew? But you never said."

"I'm not. Listen, my brother changed his last name. He didn't want Moody anymore. He wanted Pew."

Ben didn't hide his confusion. "Why in the world would he have done that?"

"Because he idolizes Marcus Pew. He wanted to be like him."

"Your brother wanted to be like a serial killer?"

"Yes."

"I don't remember any of this in any reports or the news? Did you keep all this quiet? How in the world with the sharks swimming around every juicy bit of news?"

"With the last names, it slipped through, I guess. His psychosis did me a favor, for once."

"So, you have a brother that's locally incarcerated, changed his name like a fanboy of serial killers, and have no other family here?"

I shifted uncomfortably. I'd slipped about my grandparents to him when I mentioned how Granny picked at Grandaddy and couldn't believe I even did that. Something about Ben made me let my guard down, and I didn't like it. That meant he could get in. Some doors were meant to be locked. That was the only way I could guarantee their protection.

"No family here."

"That explains it then."

"Explains what?"

"Why you don't have anything in this place. Is that why you keep nothing here? So if you have to run, you take nothing with you but clothes? It is pretty bare. Mike wasn't wrong about that." He walked around the empty den with his arms outstretched. "You can get up and move anytime you want. I get it. Where are your grandparents? I heard you calling out to them when you were at the hospital."

"Across the state line," I said, knowing it was cryptic, but better that way. It could've been multiple states he'd have to work through if he ever wanted to hurt them. Wait, what was I thinking. Ben wouldn't hurt my grandparents. My life was out of hand.

Ben said, "About your brother? Are you still scared he'll try to contact you or come after you? Is that a reason to run?"

"He's not getting out if that's what you want to know. He's serving a life sentence without the possibility of parole. They transferred him, just didn't put him in a maximum facility because they didn't want him close to Pew. Thought he might try to get closer to him and stir up more trouble than he's worth. Now, I might petition for his transfer."

"Life. That's some pretty serious time."

I moved toward the door, signaling to him it was about

time for him to leave. One good thing about having no furniture. I didn't have to worry about asking someone to get comfortable. "Can we change the subject?"

"I want to know more about you, Heather."

"That's not about me. That's about my brother. I am not that, nor do I ever want to talk about that. Get to know me in a different way, Ben. Trust me when I tell you this isn't the way. I'd rather you just leave. I'll see you tomorrow at the office. Bright and early, okay. Good work, today. But I think we're done here."

I knew all he'd have to do was search the records now and find access to the reports, the files, the case notes. If he wanted to know that badly, he could do his own snooping without me having to say a word. It was my story to tell. And I didn't feel like telling it. Never would.

"I'm sorry," he said. "I don't want to make a mess of things."

"Things are already a mess. Let's just not complicate it any more than it already is."

"I understand," he said.

The silence between us screamed more, but I couldn't meet it in the middle. He stood staring at me. The look he gave me made me lose my breath. There was a sweetness there that I felt like if I touched it, I would melt into it. I was losing focus again. This wasn't supposed to happen, yet it was, and I had to find a way to stop it.

"Please," I whispered. He knew it, too. He knew he'd pushed me too hard and was the gentleman by bowing out while we still had a working relationship.

He left without saying another word. I leaned against the door and locked everything up tight. There was no way I'd find peace in this place anymore, knowing Jade's lipstick was on my wall. At the same time, I knew that would give the killer the upper hand over me and my emotions. At all costs, I couldn't let him win. I could just build another box. Put that memory in there, too, and seal it away. How crowded could my mind get with the stacked boxes I'd created over the years? One more couldn't hurt. Just one more. Maybe even make a box for what could be with Ben. If circumstances were different. If I were different, I might love. I knew that. But loving was vulnerable and led to dangerous territory. Better to not go there. Someone was bound to get hurt.

21

June turned into September and the days were fast approaching shorter daylight. Every strike happened during the night, so that meant my nerves were completely on fire with worry. Schools were back in session and the leaves crunched and swirled under children's feet on their walks in the brisk morning. We took extra patrols without complaint, but that was all we could do. Make rounds. Watch. Wait. That was a nightmare for me. The unknowing in the middle of the normal, when everyone skated a surface I was sure would crack and pull us under at any moment.

Friday night lights lit the stadium, and we had more cops on duty watching the high schools than any of the other areas in town, and it wasn't for rivalry pranks, but in anticipation for another young female kidnapping that may come in the fall. After all the late-night reviews and over-time working files, we came to hard conclusions that four murders may be connected, and the bombing made five. All revolved around a season and setting that could only be described as Biblical. There may not have been any recovery of verses at all the crime scenes, but there was something about the cases that left me with that nagging pull without evidence of a verse.

We already knew that just because Emma Rose Sanders' case was closed, with the uncle confessing, that didn't mean it was over. We felt like this was the first spring killing to honor whatever cult practice had been put into motion by a leader or disciples. Thomas Riley never spoke again, except saying one word in court. Guilty. Not even Dot could get anything out of him and, usually, killers craved the spotlight and attention. He sat licking the table on our last visit and catching imaginary flies. I knew he was beyond us. Whether he was playing us or seriously in a state of psychosis, he would not be of any use to us anymore. So, Emma Rose was known as the first in the line of killings that started us on the path to connect more to her same torturer.

The first unsolved case was Madeline Wells, fifteen, who was found strapped to the floor of a dilapidated barn on the outskirts of Crystal Falls as if she were some animal, held down and mutilated with a threshing tool. It was the fall of the year when the fields would be in full swing, so her body was meant to be found. Care was taken. A blanket was spread over her to cover her as if it were a modesty issue. The barn setting alone screamed the Book of Ruth to me. No one else had any other ways of explaining it away. Why was she there? It wasn't a relative of the landowners, just like Emma Rose had no connection to Mercy. We also found her last fall tied with heavy industrial straps, like Emma in the boat and Katie in the stall at the farmer's market.

The second case, Tracy Harrington, nineteen, was in winter and fit a possible link. It was the only winter killing that had odd crime scene familiarities, such as the straps, for one. But it was the positioning of the body that stood out to me the most, as if he wanted her eyes to take in what was on the cavern walls. Yet there was no message there by any of the crime scene photos we reviewed. I thought he might've used it as a personal projector screen, distorting images for her to view before she died. She was strapped down, laying on her side. Poor thing. She was a local swim champion, well known in the community, and had racked up a couple of state medals. I wondered if he had been watching her at the meets, and I could just see him blending in with the crowd, picking off who it was that he was going to kidnap next. She was taken out of her bedroom.

All the girls were taken at night. The most vulnerable time. When you are out for the count, in dreamland, feeling safe in pajamas and snuggled up, late-night texting with a boyfriend, then drifting off to sleep. Never knowing it would be your last night.

There were also thirty-three references to caves in the Bible that I knew of, so I was sure there was something in his sick, twisted mind he was doing to serve his purpose. There were so many clues Jackson might've missed with his lazy investigating, and we were convinced he either just didn't care enough or was in fact, a part of The True Covenant of the Lambs and served as an insider powerplay on the police force.

Mike handed me a coffee as soon as my phone rang, making me jump just enough to slosh it out of the sides and on my hand. "Sorry," I mumbled.

"Hey, Dot," I said, waving at Ben to get his attention. He and Cain were working on the final handwritten logs from the Mercy lands. Everything was a dead end. So frustrating!

"Well, I'm sorry it took so long, but I can show y'all everything I collected. It's a doozy."

I breathed a sigh of relief. Maybe this was the break we

needed. We'd exhausted every possible lead, and I knew time was running out. "Wait? You finally got in?"

"Yeah, yeah, I know. Rub it in. It took a while and a few interviews for them to start to loosen up around me. They are a well-rehearsed group, let's just say that until we meet somewhere safe. Gaining their trust wasn't easy, Heather. They are a tight-lipped lot until you put on the play about helping them increase their revenue by adding donation links and such. That finally got me through the doors. You won't believe some of it. Some of it I think can't be real."

"Let me try to set us up a place to go over everything. Would you be willing to take a road trip? There's someone I think we could go see that might provide us some insight."

"A getaway with my favorite detective? Is Ben going to be there?"

I'm glad she couldn't see my face. Ben just held up his hands in protest. He was close enough to hear Dot's loud voice through the receiver. "Maybe," I said. "I'll text you a location when I get it all set up."

"Sure thing," she said. "I'll be going shopping in the meantime."

We hung up, and I just stared at Ben. He shrugged. "I haven't talked to Dot since our last visit at the falls if that's what you're asking."

My face turned red. It wasn't my business if he had. I pushed the folders all together and stuffed them in my bag. It was the case. It was all getting to me. I didn't care who he spoke to. What was wrong with me?

I asked, "Did y'all keep that contact's information that Jade knew? The professor?"

Mike went through a box. "I'm sure it's in here some-where. I know we wrote his name down. He is at State, so all we have to do is just search for it. Can't have too many reli-gion professors on staff."

Cain was already on it and pulled up the list of profes-sors. I just needed his face and before the third one could pop up, we found him. "Thanks, Cain. Glad Captain finally put you on the payroll."

He laughed. "That's what you call it? It's chump change if you ask me. But what am I talking about? I would have worked this case for free."

"You think you could give him a call, Cain. Let him know your Jade's father. She was one of his star students, and Jade said he was her favorite professor. He may agree to see us and help us sort through all that Dot recovered. I'd like his eyes on it when we get it, and we need to show him these other cases we have. He's an expert on cults and us trying to sift through it alone will be a waste of time. I know fall lasts four months but knowing we are in September just lets me know the clock has already started ticking. Preparations are being made."

"Working the Pew case gave you a lot of experience with cults," said Mike. "If we can't get the professor to agree to help us, we've got all we need in you."

I smiled, but the self-doubt rushed in. "I appreciate the vote of confidence, Mike. I do. But I think we are so caught up in all of this right now we may be missing something right in front of our faces. Like that caught up. We need an objective viewpoint. I think we can ..."

Cain said, "He's in. He has a house on Lake Gaskins. I told him the meeting needed to be an out-of-the-way place. Here's the address. We've got it for the weekend." He held up his phone and showed a map image of tons of acreage, one road in and out, which could easily be secured, and a beautiful, picturesque lake house that looked as if it could fit us all easily without bumping into one another unless we wanted to.

"Tomorrow? That's perfect. Let me text Alex and let him know I can't do football duty with him."

It was Ben's turn to pick at me. "I know you don't want to miss cheerleading duty with the quarterback by your side."

"Whatever," I said, rolling my eyes. "The stadium duty is a lot easier than all this. Sometimes it's good to just be around smiling faces, cheering, and laughter, even if it's just over a ball being tossed around."

Mike stood up and crossed his arms. "Don't judge my football, too, boss lady. You can pick at my boots, my spurs, and my new shiny belt buckle, thanks to Ben, but don't go after my pigskin dreams. I can still make it on that Ravens team, I believe."

"And you act like we aren't smiling, cheering, laughing faces," said Ben. "We aren't all bad to work with, are we?"

I looked between them and immediately knew it came out wrong. "I didn't mean it that way. Honestly, I don't know what I mean anymore. Guys, we need a break. I need a break. Going to a house at a lake might just do us all some good."

Mike said, "You mean we can have some team-building exercises, like fishing expeditions together and tree-hugging?"

"Forget the tree-hugging. I remember this one time the office had to do this ropes course retreat. It was ghastly," said Cain. "They expected me to do a trust fall."

"Let's do one right now," said Mike. "Come on, old-timer. Me and you. I'll catch you."

"Let's don't," said Cain, curtly. "How about we go take some time to pack up and meet back here. We can leave our cars at the station and take one of the vans. I'm taking a surveillance rig with me. We'll have that place secured."

Ben asked, "Can I take Heidi with me?"

"We don't need any distractions," said Mike. "That'll be a no. Besides, I think I might be allergic."

"You want to take a girl with you on our working trip?" I said, trying not to make my voice rise. What had slowly been happening between us, whatever it was, was starting to affect my reactions. Not good.

"She is a girl. A sweet girl. See," he said, holding out his phone.

"It's okay," I said. "Not interested."

"She's my border collie."

"Oh," I said, grabbing the phone and smiling. I needed to see a dog picture. I'd missed Grannie's dog. His name was Bob Barker Moody and would often be called by his full name if he were being mischievous.

He continued to flip through the pictures on his phone as if the cuteness would convince me to allow her to come along. "Please. Please. Please, Mom?"

I asked, "Didn't you hear Mike? He said he's allergic."

"You didn't show a single side effect at the poker game at my house last week other than losing. If that is one."

Mike faked pain. "That's it, Cain. See, I knew it was something other than my bad luck. It was my allergies. Watered my eyes, and I couldn't see the cards."

"So, you're not allergic," I said.

"No," said Mike. "Just if he gets to take Heidi, I get to take Maude."

"Wait, what is this? Some vacation time? We all want to take kayaks, too. Maybe let's get our bait while we're at it and do that fishing you speak of," I chided. "Guys, we are going there to talk to a professor. To work."

Ben smirked. "All work and no play . . ."

"Don't," I said. "Ben, if you're taking Heidi, you'll need to drive separately. And if Maude goes, you know you can't drive company vehicles."

"So, then I get to take the Bronco out. Another excuse to live it up this weekend."

"You sound like a car commercial," said Cain. "Okay. My idea is out. I'll take the van with all of the equipment. I've got tons of family calls I need to make and catch up on. Let me follow all of you."

I said, "Maude won't mind a ride-along, will she?"

"This is the first vacation I've had with Maude in three years. I took her on one of them Caribbean cruises, and she hasn't let me live down not taking her anywhere else. Let her think we are having us time on the weekend, Heather."

"You can ride with me," said Ben. "Heidi surely won't mind. She might lick half of your face off before we get to the lake house, but other than that, we'd like the company."

"Are you sure?"

"He offered," said Mike. "You guys, really . . ." Mike walked away mumbling under his breath, already heading out with a bright-eyed smile on his face, as if he were excited to finally get away from the office. He reminded me of a kid sometimes. All full of energy and laughter waiting to come out, as if his love peeked around corners ready for the opportunity to show itself.

"I'll pick you up at eight," said Ben. "Hey, Cain. Maybe you need to call the professor. Make sure it's okay we can take our significant others with us. He actually might have allergies or not want an animal around."

"Sure thing." Cain was already on the phone, letting the professor know we were going in the guise of a weekend vacation.

They just wanted a vacation away. I knew that. I couldn't blame them. They'd been working insane amounts of hours on the cold cases, following every single lead, and retracing steps since we started together. They'd staked out the prison graveyard, yet never had Pew's body stolen. They started camping out at Mercy's lands on the back-dirt roads, saying they were working some deer hunting strategies but were really on the lookout for anything suspicious. Something.

And nothing ever came. One name entered a database but it would check out. One inner circle name crossed off the list. Alibis for the time of Katie's murder meant nothing to me. I knew this was bigger than just one killer. I knew Pew still had to be involved from the grave. Even his death couldn't hold back his influence.

I sighed. Who was I kidding? I needed a change of scenery, too.

Cain broke in my thoughts and said, "Just checked in with the professor. He's good with the dog, Maude, and all of us setting up the surveillance on his land. I told him he could keep a couple of the cameras for his security purposes as payment. I'll stop by the store and grab a couple more tonight and donate them to the cause. I also offered to pay him for allowing us to stay. He said it was his pleasure to help anyone that knew Jade. My girl did make an impact, didn't she?" His voice softened, making my heart catch in my throat.

"She did," whispered Mike, as he grabbed Cain by the shoulder. "I'm grabbing us some bait."

I protested. "Wait, didn't we say it was a working weekend?"

Mike said, "It is that. But we will need some Vitamin D at some point, Heather. The sun will do you good. I've got enough poles for you to join in. Don't worry. I've got you covered."

Ben said, "You've got enough fishing rods for the entire force to come along."

"And where are all of you off, too?" asked the Captain.

His presence startled me. In our joking, I hadn't even noticed he'd stepped into my closet of an office.

Cain stepped forward and said, "It's my treat, sir. I'm taking this group for a much-needed vacation. My friend has a lake house and we'll be staying there until Sunday. Back bright and early Monday morning with fresh eyes."

Captain McBride said, "I haven't said this enough to any of you. I appreciate all you've been doing for these cold cases. You're bringing them back into the light they deserve. But you can't go anywhere, Heather. I need you at a press conference. The mayor has it in his mind that a serial killer is now after him. Hired extra security and everything."

"Cover-up," I said.

"No proof he was involved in the bombing," said the captain, his voice warning me. He closed the door behind him. "The mayor is acting legitimately nervous."

"I bet he is," I said. "It's the fall of the year. The killer is going to strike between now and December. The mayor doesn't need to look at our case files to know the pattern. He knows the truth."

"Heather, I know you have your doubts about him and other leaders in this town. Don't think I haven't had calls from some top officials because I have. Snooping into their financial records. Whatever charities they like to write off, that's their business."

Mike said, "Not when it's a cult that has connections to Marcus Pew and Thomas Riley, both confessed killers. Then, it becomes our business."

The captain just shook his head and sighed. I knew it was all pressure from the top. I'd hate that job. "Just go meet the press, Heather."

"When, sir?"

"Now. They are outside."

"Some warning would've been nice," I said, and then I realized who I was talking to. My boss. "Sorry, sir. I'm just so swamped right now and . . ."

"And you're all going on a little retreat. I get it. Do this and then I'll keep your little weekend getaway under wraps."

"That means you'll cover for us," I said. "Nice of you to do that, sir."

"Just get to the bottom of this. Fast. Or I'll call the State bureau and they'll take it over."

Cain looked at me with a flash of anger. That meant he'd be out of the loop for Jade's killer. He needed in on this and the State would send their teams and possibly take our files after a review. Once they found out Cain was on the case, they'd remove him due to a conflict of interest. He was valuable to us because of that interest. Cain wanted to catch this madman more than any of us.

"Trust us," I said. "Let us handle this. It's Crystal Falls, we're talking about. Our home. We can do this better than anyone on the outside. Now, what's the script?"

The captain led me down the hall and briefed me on the mayor's frantic call. He wanted me to hold a press conference warning the public about a possible serial killer on the loose. He wanted families to be aware they needed to watch their girls. To watch themselves. In Crystal Falls, everything appeared to be so pristine on the outside, while darker things silently waited and hid beneath the surface of river rafting, hiking trails, and parks. A postcard, picturesque town with crime rings and serial killers. A bustling down-town with a mountain view, appearing as if we were right out of a Hallmark movie, but could be the next horror movie in the making.

I adjusted my eyes to the sunlight and scanned the steps of the station. Every major news source and the local paper, blogger, and couch cop hunters from Facebook were there. Questions started being thrown as soon as the captain made it up to the podium but he raised his hand to silence them. A few held up the pictures of the tattoo printed from the news website. I knew Dot's release was working. The attention was getting out even if the leads weren't coming in. Microphones out for the ready, arms extended, faces eager like seagulls secretly screaming, "Mine," as if the news that was about to be released to the public would be their greatest catch yet.

"I'd like to get started," said the captain. "Detective Moody is the lead detective of cold cases and has made some startling discoveries she'd like to address with the fine citizens of Crystal Falls. Detective."

I stepped forward to the podium, and he readjusted the mic, lowering it down for me. Just before speaking, I caught sight of Dot. She was to the left of the crowd, looking just as eager as the rest of them. She caught me staring at her and winked. "My team and I believe we may have a new serial killer in Crystal Falls."

The crowd of reporters exploded with a burst of questions that made me flinch from the blast of it. The captain stepped forward and told them to let me speak.

"Watch your girls. Watch your children. Watch your-selves. Be vigilant. We think he may strike by the end of December and we are working diligently to catch him before he does. If you know anything, call the hotline. If you see anything suspicious, call the hotline. Anything. Something. You never know how that could help us solve a case. It's going to take all of us to protect each other. We're asking for your help."

Captain McBride moved his hand to readjust the mic, covered it for a moment, and whispered in my ear, "Go on, now. You've got a killer to catch. I'll take it from here." He leaned over the mic and said, "The first question."

The noise escalated to full, frantic screams from the circle of reporters that also had families of their own to worry over now. As surely as I knew the Lord existed and worked behind the scenes, the devil was also doing his work to tear it all down. I could still hear the rise of their voices when I walked into the station. Let them feel the panic. That might save their lives. At least the killer would know we'd pieced enough together to connect his crimes. That might bring him to make a mistake, and we'd be ready when he did.

22

The knock on the door jolted me out from under my pile of comforters. The clock only showed 9:30 p.m., and I was surprised I'd fallen asleep so early. I usually fell asleep every night around one o'clock a.m., but I guess all the battles raging around me and in me had finally worn me down. *Pride and Prejudice* had fallen on the floor. My yearly read typically kept me alert. I pulled my sweatshirt over my pajamas and grabbed my gun.

One look through the peephole made my heart sink. Alex was pacing. What was he doing here?

"And you got my address how?" I patted my long hair down into some kind of place.

"Easy. I've got an inside lane on you, Heather. You just don't know it."

I opened my door. "Easy if you work at an office full of gossips and snoops. It's late. What's up? Why didn't you just try to call?"

"I did. Check your messages."

I looked down at my phone that I left on the kitchen counter and realized it had died. I've been doing that a lot lately. Running my computer and phone for multiple searches at the same time was draining the battery. I plugged it onto the charger and stared at Alex, trying to read him.

When he wasn't going to start the conversation, I said, "What's wrong?"

"Does there have to be something wrong for me to visit my old partner? I'm just checking on you."

"You saw the press conference? Live or recorded?"

"Live," he said. "I was out there listening and took in all the captain said, too. This case, Heather. I don't want you working on it."

"Wait. What?"

"You heard me. You need to get off this search for a new serial killer. You've brought the whole town to a level of fear we haven't seen since the Pew fiasco."

My face flushed with anger, and I started to try to pull my emotions back in check before speaking. "And what a mess that was. We needed to alert the public, Alex. It was the right thing to do."

"The right thing to do is to go away with me. Tonight. Let's just leave, Heather. Let's go anywhere. You name it. I have some cash saved up. We can just go."

"I'm not going anywhere," I said.

"With me. Go ahead and say it. You're not going anywhere with me."

"Can you please tell me why you're really here? I'm tired. I need some sleep. I'm sorry I canceled on you for our football duty, but I just needed a break."

"And I want to be the one to give that to you. A break. I want you and us to . . . for you to consider . . ."

Alex's voice trailed. I stared up at him, searching him out. His face was torn with emotion, clearly letting me see right away that he was hiding something. It couldn't have been romantic feelings for me. We'd worked together for so long. We were solid partners, and our friendship was always easy. Not this. Not now.

"Alex, I'm sorry. I can't get involved in anything right now. It's too hot and . . ."

"You mean Ben is too hot and his long hair and deep stare take your breath away."

Had I been that obvious around others how I was beginning to develop feelings for Ben? I'd sworn I'd been so cold about the whole thing, keeping him at arm's length as best as I could.

"Don't start creating scenarios that aren't there. Good cops don't follow false leads. You know me by now, don't you, Alex? I won't get involved."

"I see. So, you are not getting involved. If what you say is true, then how about trying with me? I think we'd be good together."

"We were good partners," I said. "Period."

"I heard were in there. We can be good partners again. Transfer back to us. The guys miss you, too, but not as much as me. I should have told you a long time ago how I felt, but I knew you wouldn't cross the line."

"And I won't now," I said. "We work together."

"Not technically. Different floors in case you forgot. Different units."

"Same boss. Same captain. Let us stay this way," I said. "I like it this way."

"Friends? No chance ever?"

"Don't complicate us, Alex. I like you as a friend. You're funny, smart, kind,

and . . ."

"Don't flatter me. I'm all those things but not enough."

"It's not that. I just can't get involved," I said. "That's all. I've got this case and . . ."

"And that's why I'm here. Stop the case. Now. Tonight. I couldn't bear to think you'd be hurt by this."

"And what makes you think I'm going to get hurt? What do you know, Alex?" I asked, watching his face with intensity.

"I know you almost died nailing Marcus Pew, and you wouldn't let anyone help you. You went all in there blazing glory and nearly got yourself killed. There is something called backup. And the protocol for waiting for it."

"'Almost' and 'nearly' are words you should hold on to. I'm fine, Alex. I can take care of myself." I started to walk to the door. My classic get-out-of-my-apartment move. It worked with Ben, and he never came back. Let's get Alex right out of the door the same way.

"Don't say I didn't try to warn you," he said, as he stormed toward the door with me. "Just come away with me."

"I can't abandon my team, and I'm not folding on the case. For Jade . . ."

"And she's dead! That's what I'm trying to say to you."

He grabbed my arm, but I pushed him back. I was trying to keep my patience with Alex because he was my friend, and I knew he had my back when it came down to it, but he had to understand this was my responsibility. I couldn't walk away now.

"Goodnight, Alex. Thanks for stopping by," I said as I lightly pushed him out into the hallway.

"You're impossible. Do you know that, Heather?"

"I've been told this before," I said, smiling at him, trying my best to ease over any anger he may be feeling or my own.

"And you're not going to change?"

"Not tonight," I said. "Too tired."

"Call me, Heather. Ask for help this time. And if you change your mind about us, I'll come running." He waved his cell phone at me. "And keep your phone on charge. Seriously."

"All right. All right. Got it. Goodnight, Alex."

I closed the door and heard him holler through the door, "Goodnight, hard-headed woman."

All of these feelings I'd been pushing aside, bulldozing aside really, for Ben, and now Alex saw them? And if he found out I was getting away with the team on our little 'retreat' as the captain called it, I was sure Alex would read way too much into it. This was a working trip and nothing more. That's what I kept telling myself. We needed a quiet location away from the monitors, possible bugs, and electronic taps. I figured we'd be driving to the university where the professor worked, not his private home. But out of those two options, I felt the lake house was the safer bet because that would make for fewer curious eyes watching us and wondering what a team of investigators and a flashy reporter were doing with a college professor who was an expert in anything religious cults. Until I thought about what that also meant. I'd be with Ben. I realized that was safer for the case, but I didn't know where that led me. Maybe not so safe for me.

23

I figured after last night's visit from Alex, he'd notice if my car was parked and abandoned over the weekend at the station. I didn't want to hurt anyone, especially Alex, because he'd been so welcoming to me when I first moved into town and took the position. He was the one that offered to be my partner and from that day forward, we were together. Until the captain moved me away from the team.

I tossed and turned the rest of the night, questioning if I had ever led Alex into thinking there might be more between us. Trying to read my book was of no use. My mind hopscotched all over the words. I desperately tried to create a list on my phone of all the reasons why it might be a good thing if I gave the two of us a true try but it seemed so hard to do. I came up with two reasons after hard contemplation: trust and the cute factor. Only one of them mattered, and it wasn't Alex's strong jawline or dark eyes.

I'd not had a serious boyfriend in such a long time. Maybe something casual could get me to feel again. Maybe something. Anything. But maybe not.

The doorbell rang and this time it was another guy. Two days in a row. What was the world coming to?

"So, you brought Heidi to rescue me," I said, as she found her way to my knees, sniffing and already showing signs she was the best snuggle dog in the world.

"She is Lassie's cousin," Ben said. "Ever watched those old reruns as a kid?"

"Yes," I admitted. "Here. Let me get my things."

"Let me," Ben said, and he grabbed my bag. "What else?"

I pointed to what he was carrying.

"And don't we travel light."

"And I'm thinking it was just for a weekend, right? Don't tell me you have matching luggage in the car?"

"Just kidding. I should've expected this. Let me guess. You've got all of your clothes folded and rolled."

He would never know. I was a stuffer, so I just smiled and shrugged. "Wouldn't you like to find out what's in that bag?"

"You know I'm going to be with you this weekend. I'll see the contents sooner or later."

I stopped him by the stairs. "Can I ask you a very serious question before we go any further?"

"You can ask me anything," said Ben. "Do I get a question in return?"

"Maybe," I said.

He smirked, those eyes of his almost glowing. "Go on, then, as long as I get my question. I'll take my chances."

It was hard to put it into words, but I knew Ben would be honest. "Do you think I ever send mixed signals at work? Like I like someone?"

"You like Mike," he said. "I know you like Cain. You better like me or this will be one awkward car ride."

"I mean like like someone," I said, biting my lip. "Like if

you've seen me around Alex, do I put off any vibes like I might like him?"

"Oh, that," he said, and went ahead down the stairs.

"Because I don't like him. I mean I do like him, but I don't."

Ben threw my bag into his trunk beside his tackle box, backpack with his work files and computer, and one small luggage bag. "So, do you or don't you like him?"

"No," I said. "Never mind."

"Okay, since we've cleared that up," he said with an exaggerated flair. "I get my question."

As soon as I got settled into the front seat, Heidi sniffed my hair and settled in on my shoulder. Sweet thing. "No, you don't. You didn't technically answer me. You said, 'Oh, that,' so that doesn't count."

"We're not stopping by the station. I figured we'd pick up some breakfast for the road, the old classic cops-and-doughnuts run. A tall coffee. What do you say?"

I knew I needed to tell him. Was it for my own purposes to see what response I'd get from him? To see if he cared? Or was it so there would be no secrets between us? Even though this wasn't technically his business.

"What do you say, you answer me. I want to know. I'm asking because Alex came here last night and asked me to try."

He pursed his lips together. "Try to like him?"

It was so hard to look at him. I wanted to see his eyes. What would they tell me? "Yes. Something like that."

His eyes were as warm as ever when he spoke but his tone was tense. "There's too many likes in this conversation. And let me guess, you told him you would for the sake of him being an old partner and loyalties and all that."

Second guess of the morning and was so wrong on both

accounts. "Tall caramel latte and a chocolate icing dough-nut," I leaned over and spoke into the speaker, ordering for myself, then realized I was so close to him I could smell his cologne. This time he didn't smell like Bill's hot dogs. Not a good idea.

"I don't think I can be in a relationship with anyone," I said as I breathed heavily, taking in his scent, and then turning away to hide my ridiculous behavior.

"Then, don't be. No one is forcing you to like Alex," he said. "You barely even see the guy with all the work we've been doing. I can clock your every move, pretty much, and you've handcuffed yourself to this case."

"The families deserve justice, and the rest of the town needs our protection. We are working to give the dead peace and the town hope as well."

He handed me the coffee, and I let out an audible sigh. I was too lazy this morning to make a cup. It was like he could read my mind on that but nothing else. Fine by me.

He said, "Where's your peace?'

"My glock?" I patted my side.

"No, your peace. Peace. Like peace out."

"I'm not important," I said. "Let's not get all philosoph-ical here. We knew what it was like when we took this job."

"Well, I don't know about that. Speak for yourself. I watched too many crime shows."

I laughed. "Please don't tell me you thought it was like SBI City with all its high-tech mystery gadgets to solve cases. That show is more like a sci-fi novel than real life, and we have the low budget of Crystal Falls."

He grinned. "I thought it would be exactly like it. Forty minutes later, the case was solved. The end. I'd guess the who-done-it before the last commercial run."

I said, "Just like you guessed all the Wheel of Fortune puzzles?"

"All right now. I can't be perfect at everything. That's your game. Now to my question."

I put my hand up in protest. "You don't get another question."

He had a look of mocked hurt. "Yes, I do. I haven't even asked it yet."

"You've technically asked me two. One was about breakfast and the other about peace. So, since we're keeping count, that means I gave you an extra one just for free."

"That doesn't count."

"I think it does. You said question. Period. So, let's just listen to some music for a while."

He turned on the radio and adjusted it to his playlist. *Korn* started blaring out of the speakers. Surfer. Rocker. Either way, Ben was more than just the cute factor. I wondered if I tried to make the same list that I made for Alex, but switched out the guy, would it be easy or hard to do? Was the thought of a relationship with Alex scaring me or was it because I didn't want one with Alex but with someone else? Someone who was trying his best to scream along to the music.

How Heidi or anyone could nap in the car with Ben was beyond me. He didn't drive as carefully as Mike and that was speaking nicely about Mike's driving ability. I switched off the music after a while and decided I needed to just get all of it out.

"What do you know about me?" I asked.

"Is this a trick question, because if you're trying to bait me into something, I'd rather just talk about the crickets Mike picked up on his way out of town to take with us."

"The last time I was in the car with Jade, she asked me about my parents."

"If you don't want to talk about your past, you don't have to, Heather."

"Because everyone already knows it?"

"Maybe not everybody."

"But you do," I said. "I'd like to hear what you know."

"I know you aren't originally from Crystal Falls. I would like to know why you chose North Carolina?"

"You mean to stay?"

"Yeah. Didn't you move away after all that happened?"

"Yes, I moved in with my grandparents, but after I finished getting my forensics degree, I applied to a few police departments and the Crystal Falls unit hired me. That's why I came back to North Carolina."

"I figured you came here to keep close tabs on your brother."

"That might've had something to do with it. When they reassigned him to the prison, I did consider that when I was applying. But it wasn't my only reason. I loved the falls the minute I saw them."

"Yet, you admitted you don't hike anymore."

I sighed and looked out the window. "I don't."

He turned the radio back on low but changed the channel to a soft jazz station. "Do you want to start back?"

"I would love to," I said, wistfully. Would I ever get that time? Just driving a couple of hours away to Lake Gaskins was a luxury for me.

"Why do you want to talk about your past? I respect your space."

"I know you do. I just wanted you to know about them. To know they were amazing parents. The best," I said. My voice caught as I stared out the window again. If I focused on the flashing trees long enough it was almost as if I could imagine myself running freely through them trying to outrace the Cherokee. Like I was back in Millbrook. Like I was about to run home to them, and they'd still be on the front porch, probably shelling peas and cracking peanuts to slide into their glass Pepsi bottles.

"I'm sorry for everything that happened to you. I can't imagine. My mom is still trying to live the high life. She's a little flashy and loud. Don't say I didn't warn you when you meet her."

That shocked me. "Are you planning on introducing me?"

"Eventually," he said. "Hopefully." And his tone was hopeful. Filled with promise. And then, he asked a tough one, "Why were you so reckless with Pew?"

"You mean, why did I run in there without backup? Funny you should bring this up. Alex reminded me of the same thing." I shrugged, still not looking at him. "I was young. First big case. I knew I had him and had to stop him. I was undercover and had no time to waste. He would've gotten away with another murder if I hadn't. Plain and simple. I did call my partner, but he was slow to the chase."

"How did you get into Pew's circle like that?"

"My brother. As you know, he's a big fan."

"Do you think your brother had something to do with Pew's hanging? Like he's the next Pew? That's why he changed his name?"

"You mean the resurrected spirit or reincarnated spirit of Pew to my brother? I can't say that's so absurd no one would believe that because I think all of this is the most far-fetched foolishness in the world."

"I've heard of some crazy tales out there," he said.

"Sometimes the truth can be stranger than the fiction we read."

"What's your favorite book?" I'd remembered he liked to read. I didn't want to talk about my brother anymore, or Pew, or my parents. I didn't know what prompted me to start.

"*Strange Case of Dr. Jekyll and Mr. Hyde.* The duality of man. Always been fascinated with that."

"And if you could only pick one?"

"Seriously? You already know the answer to that," he laughed.

"Yes, Dr. Jekyll."

He asked, "And your favorite book?"

Finally, we were on neutral ground. These questions were safe. I could breathe again.

"*Pride and Prejudice.* I read it every year."

He laughed. "Wait? The same book? Every year?"

"Why not? Tell me one that's better."

"Dr. Jekyll and Mr. Hyde. *Frankenstein. Dracula.*"

I should've known. "Oh, you're the horror, gothic literature type. Like Poe?"

"All in with that," he said. "Helps me to imagine outside of the lines of reality because with this job I realize not everyone we catch has a firm grasp of it. There is evil lurking in the world, too. Keeps me grounded. Reminded."

"I don't have to watch a horror movie or read a book to remember that," I said. "I just close my eyes."

He reached out and squeezed my hand, and I'd realized I'd said it out loud without meaning to. "Sorry. I don't know what's wrong with me."

Then, I started making the list in my mind of all the things I was sure of. I didn't have enough sleep and hadn't in months. I was overworked and exhausted from the cold cases just like I predicted I would be and couldn't quiet my mind. I was angry at myself for not finding the connections we needed to bring out an ID. I was sad it wasn't me in that bomb because Jade should've been the one to make it. I was worried I'd hurt Alex. I was staring at a man that made me feel all kinds of emotions just being beside him while listening to his sweet dog snoring loudly in the backseat.

"She's a keeper," he said. "A real keeper."

The way he looked at me made me question whether or not he was speaking about Heidi or me. He didn't let go of my hand and I didn't push him away. Just felt the way his hand fit perfectly in mine. For miles and miles. If this was what peace felt like, then I wanted more of it.

24

M ike, Maude, Cain, and the professor were already out by the lake when we drove up. Ben put Heidi on her leash and took her to the edge of the drive for a much-needed break. We'd stopped a couple of times for her, and I wondered how much time he spent at the office, how did Heidi deal with his absence. He told me he had an elder neighbor named Mrs. Potter who helped keep Heidi during the day as a joy. He paid her rent for it. I thought that was a pretty nice exchange. He said he didn't mind. He didn't have a grandmother, and his mom refused to take money from him. He said that was a way he could give back.

For someone who claimed he wasn't the most religious guy on the block, he walked with this clear integrity that was hard to describe. He didn't have to speak it loudly.

Maude gave me a quick hug. "How are you doing dear? No offense, but you look awful."

Mike screamed up at Ben. "What did you do to her? I knew his driving was bad. Messed your nerves up, didn't it? I should've warned you."

"I just didn't sleep well," I said.

Cain offered to make me some tea. That sounded lovely. He headed back up to the house, and I stayed a few minutes in light conversation with the professor, thanking him for his hospitality. He told me a little more about the property as I admired the beauty of the land and the house.

"I feel like Dragnet," he said. "Or Perry Mason. It's always been a dream to work with the police on cases. Maybe that's why Jade called me up in the first place. She was honoring an old man's wishes. I probably said it a time or two in the middle of lectures how I loved those good old days when I'd get called in."

"We do appreciate all you've offered," said Ben. "Not only this beautiful retreat for us because I must admit, we all need a little rest, not just Heather, but we thank you for your time."

"I live alone. I have no other relatives to share this with. Occasionally, I'll rent it out to colleagues and their families, but it'll be nice to enjoy this time with all of you, to be honest. And I must."

"Then, we will forever be in your gratitude," said Maude. "And I like to show my appreciation by cooking meals. So, get ready for some country cooking. Hope you like it. I've brought a cooler full of supplies."

"That would be a change to my box deliveries," he said. "I usually go for the light fare but will be delighted to get back to some of my roots food. It'll remind me of home."

Cain motioned for me from the large deck and held up my mug of tea. I excused myself and went up to meet him.

"Here you go, young lady."

"Thank you," I said, sipping it and loving how he'd added just the right amount of honey. "And thanks for already setting up the cameras. I saw them as we rode in."

"You didn't see all of them," he said. "Some are for obvious reasons as a warning to an intruder, you have a chance to turn around now, kind of signal. But others are hiding in case they decide to take those out. Better to have extra than not enough."

"I like that," I said. "But I think we're safe here. This is remote enough."

"Yeah. There is no internet or cables. The professor called it a blessing. I think it's a living shame to be in a place this grand without the finer things in life to go along with it."

"You mean we have no phones?"

"We have no nothing," he said, laughing. "This place is pretty much off the grid."

"I didn't know places like that existed anymore."

"Oh, yes. You'd be surprised. I just figured by the looks of the place it'd be wired with the highest of technology."

"So, how will the cameras work?" I asked, now worry crept in when my body was just relaxing with the warmth of the tea.

"They will," he said. "Trust me. I can still get Wi-Fi to my computer from the camera signals."

"Wait, I'm confused," I said, laughing at my complete lack of knowledge of technology.

Cain said, smiling, "Don't worry. I do my thing. You do yours. We all have our gifts."

Not only did Cain train Jade, but she also picked up his little quirks and his sayings. She'd told us that a time or two when we questioned how she was getting the data she was. She'd give us this 'stay out of it' look or warn us it was better to be out of the loop than in.

I thought about what Cain said, each one of us contributing in our way, and with all of us together, including Dot with her fancy investigative journalism flair, who'd now shown up to join all of us, we might have a chance of figuring out who the killer was before he chose his next victim. My greatest fear was that he'd already picked his prey and was stalking her now.

We gathered on the sectional. Ben made sure he sat by the arm of the couch and asked me to join him. Dot seemed a little disappointed that she didn't get the high dollar spot beside him in the auction, and it wasn't as if I'd even put in a bid. She honed in on the professor next. He'd taken her on the tour and let her know he was a little lonely and glad for the company. Single in the house. Let Dot find out. She might have her own romance brewing before the weekend was out.

Dr. Gates cleared the centerpiece from his large farm table. "I think we should start with a timeline of events," he offered his thoughts. "Could you start with that first case you were telling me about before?"

We'd worked the timeline and knew it by heart. Dot hadn't seen the files and did not know how we were pulling this together. Everything screamed within me to hold it all close to my chest and protect it. Never share it outside of the team, but I knew we'd built a wall as high as we could go, and maybe we needed to tear it down to see the truths behind it.

I handed the first file to Mike. Each one of us took one as I thought if one could become an expert on a cold case file and present it, comb over it relentlessly, our group meetings could high beam each case. Then as listeners, we might pick up on something that fits into the gap we found in our case file.

Mike said, "Maude, you might not want to see the pictures, sweetheart. You've heard the story enough."

"That's my cue. My ever-protective cowboy is trying to shield his girl, or he's giving me the signal by that stomach growling that he doesn't mind if I start cooking up that large pot of chili I promised him, with a side of cornbread, too."

"I can help while he talks about the case," I said. "I've heard it enough, too."

Maude swatted. "No, no. It's my pleasure. Already did a lot of prep before leaving. I've got my Tupperware." She pulled out all of her containers and it took me back to the day in the office when we had to navigate the smells of food, a nauseous stomach, and a missing member of our team.

Funny how it could be a word from Cain that sounded like Jade or the sight of Tupperware containers that would bring back the memory. I moved in closer to Heidi. She must've sensed my switch in thoughts and leaned her chin up against my leg. When I patted, she didn't hesitate to jump and curl up beside my lap, covering half of me and Ben. Her tail wagged, knocking on Ben.

"You'll spoil her," he said.

"She deserves it. She's a doll."

Mike went on to tell Dr. Gates and Dot all he could from the Emma Rose crime scene, and what we could piece together from sparse testimonies.

Dot stopped his presentation. "Didn't the uncle confess? Thomas Riley?"

"He did," I answered. "But we don't think he acted alone. If he did, then he shared his modus operandi and passed the torch to the next killer. I shudder to think it's that organized and multiple citizens in our town would be willing to go that far."

Professor Gates kept shuffling through the images. "See here," he pointed. "The neck swipe. They are holding her down with the straps before or after death?"

"Not sure," I said. "Didn't work these cases, so honestly, the details are few. The coroner wasn't as specific back then, either."

"Any victims bled out?"

"Yes," Ben said. "How did you know?"

"It's an oral tradition from the Jewish faith, not in the Hebrew Bible, which the Jews call the written Torah. This is in the Oral Torah. It's very similar to the way they slaughter their animals. You'll be looking for a distortion of the laws of shechita, clearly, someone has a disturbing ritual that is trying to mimic a sacred, holy tradition, but just with a human form. It's sick and a stretch, but just an observation you might want to note. Any murder weapon found?"

Mike said, "Sorry, but no."

"I'm guessing you'll find a chalaf. A long, very sharp blade. With someone with this kind of psychopathic obsession, I'm sure it is a weapon purchased multiple times because there can be no imperfections in the blade." He pulled one of the books from his shelf and flipped to the index, flipping wildly until he showed us all a picture of the possible murder weapon.

I said to Cain, "We can see where these are sold for butchering. Do we even have a butcher shop around town or near Crystal Falls? If so, check employees who might've been trained and run it against any hits from the cult. Run any inventory we can get our hands on. It's worth a shot."

Ben read over parts of the book about a bloodletter who also would drain the blood of diseased people. "We knew bloodletting was part of what happened to Katie. We figured they might be using the blood somehow with the other victims, but there was no evidence to back that theory up. We do have evidence that shows Katie's blood was smeared on a line of trees by a river. She was our last victim."

Dot said, "They are all so young. Poor girls."

I asked, "Were any of the girls sick? Health records seemed pretty normal. All went to the same physician and the blood type . . . Dr. Gates, what do you think the significance is that all of them shared the same blood type?"

"And did they have RH negative, rhesus blood or O negative?"

"Um . . ." I flipped through. "All we've got is O."

"So, the universal blood held some kind of potency to the ritual. Blood for all. The killer didn't just randomly pick girls out who happen to be type O. I'm thinking the killer had access to their medical records. A person of power or someone who could easily manipulate to access their information."

Mike said, "We felt the same way, but ruled it out after careful scrutiny. We couldn't see anything out of the ordinary at the pediatrician clinic they went to. Everyone seems to check out clean there."

"Seems," said Ben. "'Seems' doesn't mean is. We know we have someone that's probably within our community committing these heinous acts. It's so hard for me to grasp it, but we know it to be true. We have to reconsider all possibilities."

Cain said, "If I wanted to, I could get your medical records. So, maybe they have their own techie."

We opened up every file and spread them out in the timeline as Dr. Gates suggested. He went through each one quickly, pointing out the obvious connections to animal slaughtering that we'd missed. We had considered a satanic or occult ritualistic sacrifice. We also held the thought it was just a madman strangely posing bodies, knowing that alone could point to a serial murderer.

Dr. Gates moved back and forth between the files.

"Whoever is doing this has great power and social status within the community they've created."

Dot said, "And that's where I come in. I've got the files from The True Covenant of the Lambs."

"After supper," called Maude. "It's time to eat."

I broke through the file fog I'd settled into and realized the smells wafting from the kitchen. I'd forgotten everything else. Mike's stomach hadn't. His was growling.

"Let's clear this away," I said, picking up the files from the table.

Ben said, "How about we eat outside on the patio? I think some fresh evening air is what we need."

"Good idea," said Dr. Gates. "I'll help set everything up."

"I'll go with you," said Dot.

Sure thing. Just as I'd suspected. She'd moved her sights off of Ben and onto Dr. Gates. He was a handsome man, with slightly graying hair and a soft smile. The whole salt and pepper look going on was striking against the youthfulness of his face.

Ben pointed at them as they stepped through the patio doors. "She sees a story in there somewhere."

"I think she just likes him," I said. "I get the vibe."

"Well, since we are using the word 'like' again, can I finally ask you that question from this morning?"

Mike interrupted us and said, "Maude is a fine woman, ain't she? And that cooking! Love how she wants to always show her love for others by having a full table."

Ben laughed. "Is that a new love language we need to present to a panel? Food love."

"I think so," said Mike.

"I'm not disagreeing," I said. "Maude, you outdid yourself again."

"It is my way," she said. "Got it from my mother and her mother before her."

"That's it," I said, a little too loudly. Something clicked. It hit me like a ton of bricks and even though I had nothing to stand on other than a spirit feeling, I knew it had to be so.

Ben said, "What are we talking about now?"

"We are looking for the wrong gender. We've been focused on men. Thinking it took the muscle to carry out the plans, the body positioning, the acts of extreme violence. We've been driving on a one-way street. Time we get off that exit and hit a new interstate of possibilities."

Cain asked, "And you're saying what exactly?"

"It's a family. It's a matriarchal-type leader."

"Do you think a woman is behind this?"

"Very much so," I whispered. "A woman."

I stared out through the glass and saw Dot laughing away at something the professor said. "Let's keep this between us right now. Don't want to let the press in on this in case this is the next step for us."

Mike asked, "Why didn't we think of this before?"

"It took Maude's cooking to wake up my brain," I said, laughing at the absurdity of it all.

"Glad to know I'm good for something," said Maude.

Mike leaned over and kissed his sweet wife on the cheek. "Sweetheart, you're good for my soul."

"And you for mine," she said.

"Now, let's see if Dr. Gates comes to the same conclusion or see if The True Covenant of the Lambs information Dot collected might back up this claim," I said. "I can be totally off on this."

Even as I said it, my spirit felt so strong that it may be a woman. It's what we'd missed all along that was keeping us from discovering the real leader. We focused too much on the mayor and his assistant or Pew. We focused too much on the inner donation circle and ruling out suspects from that list. All male. But men and their mommas. A powerful thing. A queen bee to a working hive. It wasn't one of them, but a mother figure. A family tradition.

Ben filled up Heidi's bowl and started to walk towards the patio to lead her out with him. "You're not going to enjoy dinner, are you, Heather? Your mind will start backtracking on the timeline."

"Yes," I said.

"Put that for another time," said Mike. "You've got to learn to let some things rest a little before you jump into them. Enjoy the night. Enjoy our company and Maude's food. Let's just spend some time together."

"Be present," said Cain. "I think that's the wisdom he's trying to impart to you."

Present. That word only led me to think about the girls who weren't present at their dinner tables with their families or friends tonight. For Jade, who wasn't present with us. So many lives were taken. So much was at stake. I stared at each of them and saw how they all meant well. Being present meant I had to show up. Show up and feel something. That was hard. But maybe I should try it. I'd been granted a second chance at life. I walked away from that blast. Jade didn't. I owed it to her to sit here and look my team in the eye, listen, and care. She would've. I would be present. For her sake, I could at least try. What could one dinner do?

25

T he dinner left me exposed. No personal questions were directed my way, but I felt like I'd opened myself up anyway. I laughed. I felt the ease of conversation and the family vibe was strong between us, even with Dot and Dr. Gates with us, they seemed to blend right into our colorful hodgepodge conversations and teasing.

I hadn't remembered a time when I felt so relaxed. Whatever Cain had encouraged me to do, he might as well have put a spell on me. I felt it was working. There was nothing tense about me in those moments. And when it was over, I didn't know what to do with all of it. The rare look into normalcy was too brief. Could I put it in a box and hide it all away? Or leave it to work itself in me?

We cleared all the dishes away while Maude relaxed on the sectional with The Secret Ingredient, a novel by Nancy Naigle. She'd glance up now and then and say, "Really, Heather? You haven't seen the Hallmark movie yet?"

"I told you the boss lady doesn't have a TV," said Mike.

"Do you remember that time when you . . ."

Mike said, "Maybe I shouldn't challenge her on that. We could be here all night. It's a good movie. You should watch it sometime."

Ben started to comment on Mike watching Hallmark but then he was cut off again. This time it was by Dot. "I'm ready to show the professor what my investigative team of our own has recovered from the cult interviews."

"What I've been waiting for all evening," said Dr. Gates. "And, Dot, please, call me David."

Her eyes sparkled like diamonds. "My pleasure, David."

Cain watched Dot with wide eyes as she lugged the heavy suitcase toward the table. "What do you have in there? A member? Stuff him in your bag for an eyewitness insider interview?"

"I have my equipment," she said. "I know what you can do, Eric Cain. I've looked into you. Hands off my good stuff. Confidentiality and all of that."

Ben said, "Yeah, she's right. Cain will have all your files copied before you can wink."

She set up her computer and pulled out a couple of recorders of her own. Dot also had taken copious notes and had hundreds of snapshots organized in binders. Her organizational skills were impressive.

"Thank you for going to all of this trouble," I said. "We would've never had that judge's order to get this close."

"When I told Jason—my boss—that I had a local cult to uncover for the first time, he flipped. Literally, flipped."

I asked, "That means he flipped? Like turning a cartwheel?"

"Right in his office. Did this handspring thing. He's kind of a show-off."

"Sounds like it," said Ben. "Hey, Mike. Do one of those handstand thingies and try to keep your cowboy hat on."

"In your dreams, brother. I'd throw my back out before I could bend these knobby elbows and knees."

"Don't challenge him," warned Maude, as she looked up from her book. "I've told you guys about that before. He's a child. He'll take it."

"I said I wouldn't," said Mike. "I know my limitations."

"Yeah, just like that time when you . . ."

Mike coughed with an exaggerated humph at the end. "Dot, continue, please. You were saying."

I hid my laughter again. My heart was light and heavy at the same time. These people were lovely. They were my people. Somehow it happened over tragedy. Over a shared mission. But without a doubt, they had become a part of my life.

Dot said, "What I can surmise is that the organization is loaded with high-dollar backers, big rollers. The grounds are beyond immaculate and very well cared for by commune workers. Look at these pictures. The gardens alone look like you're at a smaller version of the Biltmore Estate."

She shared with us the video clips of the immaculate gardens. Meditation circles were marked with white stones and trellis structures were wrapped with vined flowers. There were groups of three at each one of the circles, holding hands, swaying, saying some incomprehensible nonsense.

"It's not surprising to see the groups of three here. Marks of Scripture are also noticeable from the symbolism throughout the garden. The fires by the shrubbery represent the burning bush as one remembering they can speak directly to God or that the leader itself may be claiming to be some kind of direct link to God, having heard the voice. Who knows? Maybe they claim Messiah status. It won't be the first time. That's not as uncommon as you'd think. And the water in the gardens could serve as reminders of baptism. Fire and water are strong symbols with this group."

Ben said, "That connects to our case files."

I asked, "When you got this footage, what did they say they were doing, exactly?"

"That's the thing. They were very open about their faith and their practices after about the fourth time I visited the compound. When I questioned why they weren't registered as a religious organization, they said they'd transcended the terminology and were without a label."

Mike said, "Tell that to the IRS."

"They have created their own language," she whispered as if that alone bothered her. "Code. It's the craziest sounding thing. Chilling. You know, like the vampires from *30 Days of Night*."

Ben said, "Let me guess. Alien beings? Alien language? They'll be taken to Zargon on their spaceship with track-suits." He clicked his tongue like he was right out of some sci-fi film.

Dr. Gates asked, "How do you know it was new? There are around 6,500 spoken languages documented. You can't say you . . ."

"Listen," she said. "It's a strange sound. So messed up, y'all. I can't even begin to tell you how it gave me the creeps when they'd exchange pleasantries or prayed or had announcements."

Dr. Gates leaned in to listen to the sounds. "Can you send me a recording of this? Can I take a sample over to my friend in the linguistics department?"

"As long as I can come for the analysis. We'd like to include it in the film we're making."

"Sure," said Dr. Gates, his face blushing. "I'm sure Wallace won't mind. He lives for the rarities."

"You are a gem," said Dot. "Now, they claimed they were out there calling for the three-to-be-one nonsense like they were chanting it enough times that whoever the three were had to be annoyed by it."

I walked over to the files and pulled out the Tracy Harrington file. The cave. I stared at her and wondered what was the last thing she saw. What did she hear? I whispered, "Three to be one. They went to the cave because they were being instructed there. Isaiah 2 makes so much sense to me now."

Dr. Gates read aloud from the Bible, "And there are three that bear witness in earth, the spirit, and the water, and the blood: and these three agree in one."

"That's what we found in the lamb," said Ben. When Dr. Gates turned to question him, he said, "Never mind." He didn't want to implicate the mayor out loud, and I'm glad he held back. For now.

I said, "And this cave wasn't Job or some symbolism to David's plight hiding from enemies. It was a teaching site, but also might be the bridge from the old to the new. The resurrection. The tomb. That's why she was lying down, positioned like that, and strapped instead of sitting like the others. Makes sense now."

"This serial killer thinks he's telling the greatest story ever told," said Dr. Gates.

I thought of trying to push my idea out there in the open without having to draw attention to my belief it was a woman. "He's got a sick way of storytelling. Imagine his mother reading him bedtime stories. Warped."

"Speaking of mother," said Dot. "See this woman right here? She's some kind of big mover in The True Covenant of the Lambs. They cross her when she moves by them, like an upside down version of it." She swiped her hands up and down to form the cross. "Just like that. Creepy. She just has the eyes of emptiness. Empty Eve when she smiles."

Dr. Gates said, "Women have led cults and organized crime. I wouldn't be surprised with the Mary figure being so highly honored in tradition."

"Then that might be the reason for this," Dot said, and she flipped through random shots to spread out a new collection. This time it was as if I could transport myself right into the frame space.

"Do you have this on tape? How did you get here?" Dr. Gates said, staring at each picture with wide eyes. "It's like she's blessing them."

"And they were young," said Dot. "We were able to get a few names. Many college students, all adults, and consenting ages, but still young and impressionable. Wearing these outfits with their hair all in buns. All of them. The same. Said it took away their pride. Made them as one."

I asked Dr. Gates, "Can you go back to that verse?"

"Sure." He reread it.

"We may look for three killers. The spirit. Marcus Pew. He's the spirit."

"You still think Pew is related to all of this even though he was locked away?"

"Yes," I said, with full conviction. "He had to be. He wasn't as organized as this group. Reckless. He was John the Baptist leading the way."

"Then, you were his willing convert, falling for him," said Dot, then added, "Or were you the one that asked for his head?"

"Don't you dare accuse me of anything other than doing

my job? That man was an evil murderer who took no care for human life and ..."

Ben said, "Dot, that was so unfair. I can't believe you just said that."

She lowered her eyes. "I can't believe I did either. I'm sorry, Heather. Please accept my apology."

I didn't lower my eyes but stared hard at her. How dare she accuse me of having feelings for that ... that ... thing. What had he told her before I got into that interview room? Disgusting. I knew that interview was a terrible idea. Pew was a monster.

Dr. Gates said, "If Pew was the spirit, who is the water or the blood? Do you think it's like that? You think it's that literal?"

"Yes," I said. "The water is on Mercy lands."

Mike said, "Not Mercy again. I thought we settled that. Maybe Thomas on the Mercy lands takes us to the boat killing."

I said, "He was just a disciple for the water figure."

"Now this sounds like some anime," said Ben. "Or maybe some villain in a comic."

I asked, "Who could represent the water? Thomas Riley? I'm doubting it was him."

"Funny one," said Dr. Gates.

Ben asked, "I didn't hear a joke. Did I miss something?"

"Doubting Thomas," said Dr. Gates. He saw his blank expression and said, "Never mind. A water figure could be someone from a family who has connections to the water somehow."

I asked, "Like you?"

His eyes widened. "Me? What do you mean?"

"No, I'm not pointing fingers at you, but just saying ...

look at this place. You inherited this or purchased it yourself?"

"My family left it to me."

"And their family left it to them and so on. Property deeds of Crystal Falls. Dot said big money. Lakehouse kinda money."

"I'm working off a professor's salary," said Dr. Gates, taking a defensive tone.

"I'm not trying to imply it's you, just gave me the thought we need to look into deeds. It's a family line. That's where I want to turn this investigation."

"Good idea," said Cain. "We can also sift through the rest of the images. I can do some facial recognition and might get some hits."

I forced myself to sound nice enough to ask the next question. "Dot, what else did you get?"

"So, they run this shop by Cooper's Landing. It's some kind of deli, an entertainment place that I think serves as a recruitment center of some kind. The crowd works and eats there. It has a small stage for poetry readings and open mic nights. We caught a couple of them singing. Sometimes it would be mixed in with their strange words and phrases and the next thing it would be a country hit from the radio."

I asked, "Open to the public?"

"Yep, right near the entrance to the compound," said Dot. "And the food isn't half bad."

"There's no way I'd eat from that place," said Maude. "They might be slipping something in their drinks. Getting them all loopy and stuff."

"I wouldn't put it past this group. Anything to be honest. The whole place appears so shiny and pristine but it's dark. It's wrong. Does that make sense that I can call a building wrong? A place they all claim is for prayer and relationship. A place for what they call reunion."

"To the one," I said. "We also need the earth leader. That's the killer behind the victim in the barn and Katie at the farmer's market."

Mike said, "I don't know how you connect the dots but when you were a kid, I bet you loved those pages in coloring books."

"I did," I said, and walked through the timeline. "Water. Earth three times. We may be back to water in the fall."

"Or the blood," said Dr. Gates. "Maybe there is someone that is the blood."

"Or that's the victims," said Ben. "The victims supply the blood and are represented in their O. Like universal purity."

"So, possibly just two killers then?"

"Two killers. Pew is dead. His work was somehow connected to this even without the obvious signs. He was the spirit. Freedom. The third is the leader."

Cain said, "Wait, what if they just are out there killing and are both the leaders. There have been serial killer couples in the past."

I said, "They could be a couple but they answer to one. Outside of the killing. Ordering it. And they obey like little lambs. And the way to join or have their reunion is to do the work of the leader, to somehow bring them all power or just the one to save them."

Dr. Gates read, "Revelation 12:11 says, 'And they overcame him by the blood of the Lamb, and by the word of their testimony, and they loved not their lives unto the death.'" He closed his Bible. "Don't you see? It will be finished. Revelation. The last book in the Bible. You can expect one more killing. A final battle with Satan."

"They are already answering to him," I said, turning to

my calendar. Counting down the days. "Funny if they think they're defeating him when they are the destroyer."

"You know what that means," said Dot. "We've got to go through the film. See who could be the Earth figure and who could be water. We know our community. We know our people. How can they be this twisted? How could they have been so vulnerable to this cult ideology?"

"We've been asking that for so long," said Dr. Gates. "Some things will always remain a mystery."

"Like when they will strike. It's like they are two steps ahead of us," said Ben.

I knew the killers were plotting just as we were planning to catch them. Evil minds were used to navigating in dark places. Hidden from the light. They couldn't stay silent much longer. They felt they were to be reunited soon, even if it meant dying for it. Just like Pew died for it.

"Why are you looking at the calendar," asked Dot.

"Because Jade left us something. She knew," said Mike.

I asked, "Knew what?"

Mike pointed at the upcoming dates. "This gives us only until Sunday. Sunday of this weekend. Or next Sunday ... or the one after."

"Are you saying all of these murders have taken place on a Sunday? You should've told me that a long time ago," said Dot as she pulled out a fresh sheet of paper.

"What are you drawing?"

"I'm about to send this to my editor," she said. "They'll run it at ten o'clock."

"The Sunday Killer Leaves Homicide Task Force Seeking Salvation," Ben read aloud what she'd scribbled on a piece of paper.

"You are not going to run that," I asked, already knowing her response.

"Oh, yes, honey. I am. That'll draw some attention."

"You get to name your first killer," I said. "That might put you down in the history of tabloid media."

"I am from a reputable agency," she said. "And I promise the American people the truth."

"And the truth is you are out for yourself, Dot. As you've provided us with key information, we'll continue with this review. But don't think that after this we'll . . ."

"What? Need my help? Because you've needed no one, Heather?"

"Meow," purred Cain. "We might just get us a showdown."

"At the HM Corral. She's winning this fight. My bet is on the boss lady."

"No bets. Stop being childish, Mike," said Maude. "Ladies, apparently we need a break from this work. How about some fresh air?"

Ben grabbed Heidi's leash. "Want to take a walk with me, Heather?"

I didn't answer him but didn't refuse him either when he lightly took my arm and guided me out.

I stopped. "Wait. Dot. What is happening here? Why are we being so against each other? I don't like it."

"Neither do I," she said. "I'm sorry I said that earlier. I guess I deserved that joke about the tabloid. That was a low remark I made. Classic headline from some trash paper."

"Then, I do accept your apology. No excuse really for my behavior. I know the case is heavy. We appreciate your help, we really do."

"And I've got more," she said. "I'm just getting started."

Ben said, "Then, we better get Heidi out and be right back."

I walked out into a cacophony of serenading sounds of

the night. How could things be so quiet here when everything else around me was so loud? I sighed heavily.

"I'm here," said Ben.

I frowned. "I didn't think you'd gone anywhere. I can still make you out. It's not that dark out here."

"No. I mean, I'm here for you, Heather. I'm like, here." He then laughed. "There's that word again. Okay, I'm just going to ask you. I've got to. I've waited all day. It's been a long time now."

"Back to questioning me? I thought the interrogations were over."

"Will you be my girlfriend?"

"People do that nowadays?"

He asked, "What? Do what?"

"Ask someone to be their girlfriend. It's been so long it just seems so . . ."

"Childish? Is that what you're going to say? Now you're starting to talk like Maude."

"It's not you, Ben. Really. It's . . ."

"It's me. I get it. It's not you, it's me. I know they still say that. I just had to ask," he said, nudging my side. "No weirdness between us, right?"

Heidi came bounding back between us and snuggling against me. "How can we be weird with this dog? This sweetheart? I might just say yes just to see her again."

"You don't have to pretend to like me to get to see Heidi. You can see her anytime you like."

"I might just do . . ."

My voice trailed. Heidi froze. Her ears picked up and laid back. Her eyes darted to the trees. I heard it. It was faint at first, so I passed it off as just an animal in its habitat. But this time it was a clear crack.

A break in a limb. A crunch of boots over pine straw and leaves.

"We aren't alone," I said.

Ben was still smiling, playing with Heidi. "I know. I told you I'm here for you."

"No, someone is on the property." I drew my gun.

Cain called, "Heather? Ben? You need to come back. You need to see this."

"Come on," I said, and I took off towards the house. We were only a few feet away when I heard a recognizable noise from my deer hunting days with my grandfather. It was the cocking of the slide of a shotgun. The boom rang out. The echo of it reverberating around me. My heart felt it. The tugging of everything reminded me of the day my brother chased me. It was the same feeling coursing through my body. I knew he was here. Somewhere.

"My brother is here. He's come back. He's earth," I said. "He's come to claim his own."

26

B en and Mike secured the lake house up tight with perimeter checks. Maude was visibly shaken, and Dot was thankfully trying to calm her with some outlandish story that I was sure she was making up about some animals caught on video having a conversation. Whatever it was, Maude cracked a smile. Cain leaned over the surveillance videos and rewound, caught nothing, then rewound them. The light flickered in the darkened room, and I prayed it didn't give our position away if there was someone out there still lurking around. There was only one shot, but it was enough.

Cain said, "The area hasn't been breached from the main road. We would have caught anyone coming in the drive." He continued to assure me it wasn't someone here to get us. There was no boogeyman on the loose.

I wasn't convinced. I knew otherwise. "They knew we had the cameras," I said. "Were any of you followed here? Did you tell anyone you were here?"

Everyone said not that they were aware of, and they'd told no one about the trip. There was no doubt in my mind it could've been my brother. I felt it. He'd escaped. That meant he needed outside help. I'm sure Pew had alerted his disciples, as he liked to call them, to another kindred spirit who could now lead them to the light since he'd planned his departure out of this world. That reincarnated spirit of Pew entering my brother in some sick, twisted psychological play now might be a thread to follow. I just wouldn't be the one to go and follow it.

"It's a hunter," said Ben. "That's all. He's night hunting when he shouldn't be. I just called the prison, Heather. It's not your brother."

"Are you sure?" I asked.

Ben said, "Heather, I just got off with the warden. Besides, if a prisoner escaped, we would've been alerted by now."

"Maybe you're right. I just don't know anymore."

Ben walked over to me and grabbed my hand. "Like you had to see the death certificate and video from the medical examiner to believe Pew was dead? You want me to call them back and put it on Facetime? Where you can see your brother locked behind bars? We can do that if it brings you some peace of mind."

"No," I said, a little too loud. "No."

Mike said, "What's this about your brother, Heather?"

I waved it away. If only it could be that easy like hand motions to the wind, nothing. It's nothing. "Ben checked it out. It's clear."

I sat down on the couch, my whole insides exploding like fireworks. I'd lost my cool. My control. I panicked and instead of calling out and checking, actually seeing if it was a hunter, my heart took the flight response and automatically went to my darkest nightmare. Not cool.

"I'm sending out the drone. We'll see for sure, Ben." Cain

flipped to a phone app and propped it up on the back stand. "Hold on. Watch this."

"You have a drone here?" asked Mike. "I feel like Army intelligence or something. Let me guess it has heat sensors on it and infrared."

"Everything but missiles attached. I could in the future, though, just to be safe," he chuckled.

Mike said, "And you can control that thing with a phone app? What is the world coming to? I still have my trusty ol' flip."

"Okay," I said. "Do it as quickly as you can. If you see anything out of the way, we'll need to call in backup. What's the neighboring town here? How close are we?"

"About twenty miles out from the sheriff's station," said Dr. Gates. "This is a huge hunting area. I'm sure that's it. We get hunters and fishermen passing through here all the time. Not right at night but it happens."

"See, he's walking away. It's one man. He has a beagle with him. It's a hunter. Ben was right."

I sighed heavily. Everyone was on edge, and it was because of me. "I'm sorry I got you worked up, Maude."

Maude patted my hand. "No worries, honey. You heard a shot. You wanted to protect us. I'd rather you be over the top than under the blanket."

"I wanted to run," I said. "For cover."

"As you should when shots ring out," said Cain.

Ben said, with a small laugh that made me smile, "She's used to running towards danger. She thinks it's part of the job description."

"It is," I said. "Technically. I'm sure Cain could find the manual. The job description. The protocols."

"Cautious while being alert. Clear-headed enough to

assess the situation," said Mike. "What was that about your brother again?"

"Another day," I said. "No more ghosts for me tonight. I've had enough."

"I'm bringing the drone back in. He's in his side-by-side and heading away from the property."

"Thanks, Cain. For all of this. You thought of everything. The ultimate peace of mind. State of the art."

"I told you to trust me, Heather. I've got an arsenal of tech and gadgets. It keeps me busy. I've been dabbling into some cool contract work and getting some of this as a part of the perks. Besides, staying still makes me remember my baby girl is gone."

"Then, let's stay still for a moment," said Maude. "Let's just have some silence for a minute. Let's remember her so you can remember the girls you're fighting for."

After a couple of minutes, Cain said, "Thanks for that, Maude."

"Now, this book is getting really good. I gotta see if the guy gets the girl and all that. And Mike, you're going to love this one. They mention some of your favorite country singers playing on the radio."

I hid my laughter. Whatever Maude could do to get Mike to watch Hallmark with her. She continued, "Y'all let me alone to do my reading. I think I might go settle in my pajamas and leave y'all to the dangerous police work. Falling in love is its own dangerous business. My spirit is still a little jumpy. I need to escape in The Secret Ingredient," she said. "Oh, and we can watch the movie after I'm done."

Mike winked at Ben when he sniffled and said, "No cable, honey. They don't have the channel out here. So sad we can't get to that tonight."

"It's on my Prime video account," she said. "No worries dear. I always find a way."

Just like my brother found ways to haunt me without ever having to lift a finger. Marcus Pew did the same, and he was dead. It was my brother who gave me the lead about Pew, when he thought what he was doing was trying to convert me to his maniacal ways. Like I was going to forgive him. "We are the same," he'd whisper to me with that scratchy voice. "The same, you and I." Then, he'd say, "Remember that time Daddy rigged up that old tire swing between those two big trees and we swung for hours." Like he didn't kill them. Like he didn't take everything from me. It was so hard for me not to hurt him, but I knew vengeance was the Lord's work.

I refilled my sweet tea and leaned against the counter, trying my best to gain my composure. If sweet tea and a moment of prayer couldn't do it, I didn't know what would. After my hands stopped shaking, I moved back over to our command station Cain rigged up. He did one more sweep of the perimeter to show me that it was all clear.

Dr. Gates was reading something out of one of his older Biblical texts, one among the hundreds from his collections of countless books. His deep mahogany bookshelves were filled with religious texts, classics, a full collection of Stephen King, and a whole section dedicated to cookbooks, mostly from Food Network stars. I knew if I stared long enough, I might be able to piece together Dr. Gates one-by-one by what he read, but I didn't have the time.

Dot, on the other hand, seemed to have all the time in the world for Dr. Gates. The way they would sneak glances at one another over the book reminded me of some high school flirtation. Did they still do that? I wouldn't know. I knew Ben was trying to get all fresh and clean with me, but that didn't mean I could handle it. I couldn't send signals back. It's not that I didn't want a relationship, it was that I couldn't have one. That meant I'd have to give more than I had. That meant expectation to do so.

I hated to break up their moment, but I said, "Dot, let's get back to all you had to show us."

She clapped. "Oh, yes. So, if you're thinking that there are two killers left, how about these as potential suspects."

She laid out a new set of images. All of the men were in white suits and wore a silver pin. It looked like the symbol that Mercy remembered from the tattoo. I passed them to Mike and Ben.

Mike said, "I recognize this guy. This is Jeremiah Anderson. He's a broker in town, been dealing with stocks and trades and community projects for development for years. He also works at the same financial office where Jade's boyfriend works. I met him when I went down to talk to Miles."

"What feeling did you get when you first met him?" asked Ben. "Heather always reminds me to go with my instincts. Anything creepy?"

Mike answered, "Fishy. Oily. Scaly."

Ben chuckled. "So, a catfish or a brim?"

"A sly cat," he said. "With whiskers, too."

I was going to say more about Jeremiah Anderson, but with Dot and the professor around, I knew I wasn't going to go any further with theories or discussions on our end. I needed us just to take what she had, all of it, and then put it all together on our own time. I acted absentminded and casually checked my phone, all the while sending Mike, Cain, and Ben a group text.

"Let's just get her info. No more brainstorming. Wait for it. Don't give anything away."

They all looked at me for a second after checking their phones and then tightened their lips. I saw how Ben's body shifted from being relaxed to tense. Maybe he thought I was overreacting, but the shot I heard reminded me we weren't out of danger. We couldn't reveal too much of the case to a reporter. We couldn't get comfortable. What were we doing letting our guard down to begin with? We were joking and cozy, settling in at a beautiful lake house, taking walks, and talking about having a movie night. We were here for business. Period.

I'd let her present everything she had to the professor. That's what we were here for. To gain his expertise on the cult angle. We'd thank them for their time, would leave first thing in the morning, and head back into the office. We could finish out our police work there, and all she had to give was a great benefit to us. I'd send her a card. Not here with a journalist out for her next line. No more detailed talk here. Not with Maude in the next room. I'd probably already given her enough to cause a nightmare or at least a restless night when Mike was looking for a getaway.

"Can we have all of this?" I asked, holding up her extensive filing. She was meticulous and her eye for detail gave us a lot to work with. There were maps and financial supports, a copy of the business plan that was on file as a public record, along with a list of names of all those she interviewed with personality sketches, notes on everything to who was friends with whom and who was dating whom.

Dot's eyes furrowed. "I knew you were going to ask for that. These are copies. Of course, I have all the originals. I'm going to put together a piece of my own."

When I started to protest, she cut in and said, "Don't worry, Heather. You can trust me. In time. I'm going with the Marcus Pew donation angle. Nothing else. I'll wait."

Cain said, "You mean after we catch them?"

Dot promised, "Yes. Once The Sunday Killer is in custody, I'm going to share all of this with the world. It might be the first book I write. I've always wanted to write a true-crime drama. I think with my inside track, it could make for an interesting story. I might even be on one of these shelves one day if David has room."

Dr. Gates pulled a couple of more texts from the shelf. One was on cult masterminds. He held up a chapter title, "Lambs to the Slaughter," and said, "Doesn't that seem close to The True Covenant of the Lambs."

Ben said, "I don't know anything about the history of cults, but isn't that also a short story by Dahl? That Mary giggling. That's a haunting sound."

"He was a double major. English and Criminology," said Mike. "Sometimes he likes to show off. I didn't get past the Archie comics."

"That's good literature right there," I said. "Always loved Jughead."

"Then, that explains it," said Mike, grinning.

I wanted to ask him what he meant, but Dot's voice grew louder as she leaned over the professor's shoulder and read the book he held. "It says from the late-1800s to the mid-1920s, there was a religious cult in the Pacific Northwest region. Based on accounts, the commune was very similar to Cooper's Landing set up. They based their traditional practices on the Bible. Animal sacrifice was reported. They had a storefront for recruitment, just like that place I was telling you about, but did horseback riding tours and cabin rentals as well for extra income and to get the strangers riding or camping out as recruitment to stay. An escape from the world's problems to a commune promise of community and togetherness. All you have to do is sell your soul. Lose your friends and family. Cut off ties to be one with them."

I looked at Mike. He gave me that disapproving look. He knew what I was thinking. Mercy rented small triangle shaped cabins all along the river. Mercy with his guilt. Mercy with his story of hiding in the truck bed with lambs' wool. The thought of it all just sent shivers down my spine.

Dr. Gates said, "And their leader was a woman in her late fifties, who'd stepped into the role of leadership after her father passed away suddenly from food poisoning. Sara Erlene Rogers."

Dot smirked. "She probably poisoned her father for power or had one of her henchmen do it for her."

Dr. Gates threw in another possibility. "Or, he knew he was to leave the world to bring his daughter to the next level and went willingly. We do have the Jones cult as a reminder people can take the juice for what they believe."

"Many were forced or were killed escaping," I said. "I do know a little about Jonestown. I want to know how they got Sara Rogers into custody. How did the story end? Does it say?"

"They were arrested for fraud, embezzlement, and multiple counts of child abuse. It just disbanded. Dissolved."

Mike said, "And the people of the cult? Just walked right back into society as if they had no prior attachment?"

"It's usually not that easy, but something like that," said Dr. Gates. "You could have a spin-off group here. They've settled themselves in the eastern region now, still along the mountain ranges. Still giving themselves a Mount Sinai. A sermon on the mount. From what I've seen, it's a new covenant. The old is gone and the new has now risen."

Cain wrote down the name of the cult. "We'll look into that."

The earth, river, spirit, and blood Bible verse kept bouncing around my head like the shuffling of cards. Images of suspects categorized themselves. I lined them up with a queen and king. Suites. Played solitaire in my mind. It was falling into place.

I would never ask my brother for help again. Getting the information from him about Pew's whereabouts was the only gift he'd ever give me. He thought I wanted to join him. He thought I'd finally seen the light. Now that he found out I betrayed him, he would never help me again. Since Pew was dead, he couldn't help me either, like I thought he'd relish in doing. I'd held strong to his chance to claim notoriety, and that book deal he so secretly desired. He thought he would be the next Ted Bundy. One less monster to breathe air.

That might've been why he was murdered in prison. The cult knew his weakness for fame and couldn't trust him to keep their secrets. They could've used the whole spirit theology to play their cards right. We had to play ours carefully. We had to stop showing our hands. Keep a poker face. That was the only way to play moving forward. If ever we were to have a chance in bringing this cult leader down with their murdering pack of psychopaths, that was the only way.

27

There was a special kind of quiet to be surrounded by so many books and holding a favorite in my hand. One day I'd want a room just like this one. The winter would hold even more contentment with the stone fireplace roaring. The house had its kinds of settling noises and anytime I tried to sleep somewhere for the first night, it always gave me trouble trying to settle my mind. I knew tonight would be no different, so I came prepared. I switched on the professor's desk lamp by his bookshelves and piled some pillows and chenille blankets from the couch to make myself a little spot between the bookcases.

I was about ten pages in and realized I'd read the same page twice. It wasn't a noise that was keeping me awake. It was knowing Ben was in a room down the hall. My mind wandered to where he was. Did he snore? Did he take the right or left side? Why did I even care? What was happening to me?

I could hear Elizabeth's voice talking to me from the pages of *Pride and Prejudice*. It felt as if she spoke my true heart and sadness crept in from words in ink to seep into my blood, always trying to turn the faucet to cold but it was warm as ever. I don't think I could kid anyone anymore, including myself. Who was I trying to fool anyway? Always at arm's length made me the fool.

I whispered the line from the chapter, "'There are few people whom I really love, and still fewer of whom I think well.'"

"Let me know how you think of me, why don't you? Not even one positive thought my way?" Ben snuck in and I hadn't even heard him shuffle across the hardwood floors. I was losing my edge. Soft and conflicted brought consequences.

"Hey," I whispered.

"Hey, why are you whispering? This house is big enough to get lost in. The bedrooms are far away."

"Apparently not far enough," I muttered, with a small smile. There was something about him that brought out the jab.

"Ouch. I can take a hint," he said. I knew he could tell my kidding voice now. It took a while because he said I was so serious all the time, but I think he's slowly figuring me out. He put on the fake pout. "I'll get my water and leave."

"You can stay," I said, still looking down at my book. I didn't want to see the way the night worked across his face. I didn't want to feel what would come with that knowing. He had a pair of baggy plaid pajama pants on, and I knew they'd fit very nicely on me. 'Stop, Heather. You will not imagine taking his pajamas. That's the first step to commitment.'

"You've got to talk to me sooner or later because if you didn't know this about me, you might as well know it now. I don't give up easily, especially when I know it's worth fighting for," he said, as he sat down on my pallet. He held out a water bottle he'd grabbed for me.

"I do talk to you. All the time," I said.

"Talk, talk," he said, flapping his hands together. "I want us to really talk. The kind that lets me know about the things that matter to you."

My mind couldn't move from the job. If it did, I might never get my shield back. "Catching these serial murderers matters to me."

"I know that. I know how important your job is to you. We all get that. But you've got to have more."

"Who says?" Even though I questioned it, I knew he was right.

"They say," he chuckled, pointing down the hall. "Look at Maude and Mike for a long minute, and that's all it takes to convince me there's more."

"My Granny and Grandpa, too. They are jewels of the rarest kind."

"I know where you were cut from," he said, quietly. "Heather, I'm falling in love with you."

Oh, no. Here it is. Love. Not like. Not 'I want to get to know you.' The whole 'will you be my boyfriend' speech was real. He's getting bolder. I'm letting him. How can I stop the waves from crashing? Do I even want to?

"You can't be," I whispered. I held the book to my chest and wondered if I could just disappear in the pages. "What book up on the shelves do you wish you could run into and hide away for a while. Not forever because that would be totally irresponsible, but just for a day."

He tugged on the book a little. "Does the one in your hand count? That means I'd be close to your heart. I could be Darcy. I get the girl in the end. No doubt, you're Elizabeth. I can see the similarities."

"Funny," I said. "You can't have my book. You get your own." I was stuck between the two shelves. He was in front of me. Dangerously close. Black t-shirt. Red plaid pajama pants. Hair all a mess and falling over into his eyes. If fine had a name, it would be Benjamin.

He kept trying to catch my eyes and hold them and all I could do was keep looking away. "Tell me about that book. It looks so worn."

"You haven't answered my question first. We need to learn the art of answering one at a time. I asked you which book on these shelves would you dive into. Let's start with that."

"I see what you've done here. Hold on. Let me see." He stood up and started to move across the shelves, tiptoeing ridiculously, until he finally landed on one selection and slid it out. He held it so gingerly, clearly knowing its value. "First edition. Just like I thought," he said, reverently. Almost as if he were a preacher delicately holding a baby at a christening.

"*Dracula*," I laughed. "You would get dark. Quick."

He cut his eyes dramatically. "Don't judge me based on what I read. I can't help I'm into horror."

"We live it enough," I said. "Give me another escape."

"But you read romance, but don't believe in it. That's a hilarious concept right there. What happened to you to turn you against the whole relationship thing? I need to know your story. Your book. Tell me about that book. Why?"

"I guess you remembered I told you I read it every year. Here's why." I opened up the book to the first page. My mother wrote:

For my beautiful daughter,

May you find love and happiness at every turn. May

sunlight forever be shining on your face. And the love you find never do you wrong. Love, Momma

"That was my momma's last Christmas gift to me. Now you know."

He leaned closer to me and squeezed my hand. I didn't want to cry in front of him. I didn't want to do it. I knew the words were there, but I hadn't seen her handwriting for so long. I usually skipped right to the first line of the novel, and hands down would fight someone if they'd say they didn't think that first line was a genius one.

He whispered, "Thank you for sharing that with me."

"Don't get used to that," I said. "Me sharing . . ."

He said, "Are you saying you don't play well with others?"

"Maybe," I smiled. The tears couldn't fall. He was making my heart smile again. The rollercoaster ride of emotions was so exhausting.

He put Bram Stoker back on the shelf and said, "Now, do you want to know about my particular interest in Dracula? I thought when I was younger if I had moves like him, those mesmerizing eyes that would bring a woman into a trance, I could convince any girl I wanted to fall in love with me. Ask me what I like to dress up for on Halloween every year. I have contacts and professional-looking teeth. The cape. I try the accent, like this. The whole bit. Ever see any of those black and white Dracula movies on Saturday morning specials?"

The accent was horrible, and I laughed a little too loud for it being in the middle of the night. "Oh, yes," I said, leaning back against the pillows and pulling my knees toward me, protecting my book again. "And did your powers ever work?"

He lifted my chin to meet his eyes and then swirled his

head around, crinkling up his nose. "No. But I'm not done living yet. I've still got time."

'I wouldn't be too sure about that, I thought.' They were working on me.

"To be bitten on the neck by a vampire and live for eternity? I doubt it," I said, jokingly. There was one thing I could say about Ben. He always knew the right weird things to say that brought me away from my protective shield and made me feel at home.

"Must be something I can mesmerize you with. Can I look into your eyes, just to check something?"

"No," I said. "That's weird."

"To stare at someone is to believe."

"Is that some quote you pulled out of a book?"

"Not that I know of. I just made it up. On the spot," he said, inching in closer. "Maybe I can sing you a song with lyrics like that, I can't go wrong."

"Can you sing?"

"No. But I can write lyrics. Country songs, mainly. About trucks and dogs and closing time. I'm sure I can rhyme some love ones out just for you that might just impress you."

"I'm not really into country, mainly instrumentals." I didn't want to tell him that lyrics made me think too much, made me feel connected to something bigger, or gave me thoughts about what I might be missing, and that was the all-time thing I was trying to avoid.

"Why are you trying so hard to impress me again? Are you trying to believe in something? Let me understand what's happening here," I said, trying everything I could to avoid his brown eyes staring at me.

"You've got golden flecked eyes mixed with green. They are so unique. I never really noticed the green in there before," he said. "Lucky Charms."

"Are you saying my eyes look like cereal? Write a song about that. You are the poet. Award-winning, for sure."

"I try," he grinned. "Seriously, though, Heather. Just look at me. It won't hurt."

I bit my lip. So much I could say. So much I was feeling but trying to hold in. The goodness in him was so present. So there. Warmth. Ridiculously warm, dog on it. Heat radiated off of his body, and before I touched his hand on the blankets, I knew how it would feel.

I reached out to him. I was the one that took his hand. His eyes widened when I met his gaze, and for the first time, I truly looked at Benjamin Caraway. His love sat there. So recognizable. So pure between us. I could see it so clearly. Like faith. I could feel him, see him, touch him. I couldn't look away even if I tried. This was a man I might start to think was worth fighting for, too. If only I had a fight left in me to try.

28

M ike grumbled, "She's keeping me from the catch of my life."

I smiled, but shot back, "How about I promise you the real catch will be when we solve this case?"

"She's so wise," said Maude. "Glad she's your lead, Mike. Have I told you just how much we think the world of you, Heather?"

I could feel the heat rising in my cheeks. Any kind of praise just felt unnatural somehow. I pushed through the uncomfortable. "I feel the same way."

Cain was busy packing up all of his many trunks of electronic devices and gadgets. Mike was carrying out Maude's bag, including holding her pink sequined purse for her. She still hadn't let go of The Secret Ingredient, and I imagined her reading it aloud to Mike on the drive home. Ben was putting away all of the dishes from breakfast. Not only was he someone I found I could be myself around and even confide in, but he was an amazing cook. His french toast was signature, for sure.

I was packing away all of Dot's work that she graciously

copied for us to take back to the office and thanking her again for all the trouble. She hesitated and looked at Dr. Gates. I saw the look pass between them and just knew.

It didn't surprise me when she said, "I think I might go into the town and check things out. Maybe shop or spend the day exploring."

An entry point for the professor. "Well, if you need a tour guide, I'm available. I was raised around here. Every summer my parents would . . ."

His voice trailed as they moved out on the patio to discuss more of the plans they had for the day. We all looked at each other and laughed.

Cain said, "Well, who would've thought our team could play Cupid."

Maude clapped her hands. "Me! I've already been playing it, ready with a couple of more arrows for a tough cookie I know," she winked at Mike. I figured she was talking about me when she gave me the next stare and wink. Me and Ben. Ben and I. Whatever we were, we were anything but friends. Something. Maybe more. One day.

More. I focused just on that word as we loaded up our cars. Ben and Mike were discussing getting a cabin rental or a fancy Airbnb soon so we could do this again without case files and surveillance cameras and such. Making future plans was new to me. I was feeling things and couldn't deny them anymore. I was used to wearing a bulletproof vest but realized I was also carrying around an invisible shield and wearing an internal armor plate around my heart. I was in control of it. No one else. Not Maude's Cupid arrows. Not Ben. Me.

Heidi took one last walk around the yard and jumped in the backseat happily. She gave me another sniff and snuggle, then settled back in for the long ride. Ben pulled out and waved to everyone, and we took the convoy back to the station.

Ben said, "And you just had to cut the fun short, didn't you?"

"We had time to relax." I felt the heat rise again in my cheeks. What was this with all the rushing embarrassment? Oh, comes with the feeling. Feel one emotion and another is bound to surface. Catalog and note them. Stick the ones in boxes, wrap them with a bow, the ones that need to go there, and let the others live free.

He said, "We stayed up until three a.m. talking. I haven't done that in years."

I admitted, "I've never done that."

"What? Talked until three? Let's do four the next time then. Let's keep pushing it for an all-nighter. Let's get every first that we can."

I looked at him and saw how the sunlight played against his features. He had small rings under his eyes, and it was my fault. I'd helped contribute to his tiredness. But through all of it, his eyes were bright. He had that sweet smile going on. It was as if it permanently lived there. Like he was always thinking of his next line or his next joke. Like he was always feeling that way.

"I would like that," I said.

"What? Wait? What would you like?"

"You were thinking about something just now. What was it?"

It was his turn to blush. "I was just thinking of firsts with you. I've been wanting to kiss you for the longest time. What would that first kiss feel like? But what did you mean by you would like that? You were thinking of kissing me, too? You know you can admit it. There's no weakness in that."

"I would like firsts with you," I said. "I was responding to what you said until you went to some fantasy land in your mind."

"Wait, but if you want the firsts with me then it's not fantasy. It's real life. But it's also magic, so magical realism?" He paused, then continued going through a list of genres. "Don't care what you call it, just as long as I get to call you mine. Does that mean you got no sleep last night, and you thought about what I asked you?"

"No," I said. "Wait. I mean, no I didn't stay up last night after you went to bed. I crashed. I slept so soundly. Like I can't remember the last time I slept that good."

"So, no or yes," he said. "Let's make sure I ask one question at a time. I don't want us to get caught up and lose this chance."

"Yes."

"Yes, you will?" He reached out and took my hand.

"Yes. I will," I said.

"Then, no more speeches necessary? That's a relief. I thought I'd have to write you that love song about Lucky Charms."

"You still might," I said. "You know that's a part of dating. Romancing the girl."

He laughed. "Oh, I forgot. You read romance novels. I better brush up on my skills. Gotta impress you and all that. Might need to grab me a couple of Nicholas Sparks books."

"You impress me by you being you. That's enough for me," I said.

"Fair." He brought my hand up to his lips and lightly grazed my knuckles. Just the touch brought shivers down my arm.

"But let's not tell anyone just yet," I said. "Wouldn't want rumors to spread through the office."

Ben laughed. "Um . . . sorry, but I'm sure everyone will take one look at me and tell I've fallen for you."

"What's so funny?"

"Turn around," he said.

I leaned back and looked out the back window. I'd forgotten we had the caravan behind us. Mike and Maude's hands were raised in the air, shaking. She was waving frantically, and it looked as if she was saying, "You go girl," if my lip-reading skills were on point.

I sunk in the front seat and covered my face. "Oh well. There goes that plan."

"They know anyway."

"Know what?"

"That I love you. I told them."

"You told them at three in the morning?"

"No, I told them when I first knew I loved you. We were out taking a walk down their dirt road. After dinner, Mike and Maude always go for an evening walk down their road and back. So, we headed out to do the driveway and back again and it just came out. I hope you don't mind."

"Well, it's done," I said. "It's not like they didn't just figure out we're together. How long ago was this anyway?"

He smiled. "Wouldn't you like to know?"

"I would."

He squeezed my hand. "Well, some things are just not meant to be known. You'll laugh at me."

"I will not," I said.

"The first week you became lead. The first time I saw you my chest was constricted."

I did laugh. "It was probably heartburn from Bill's spicy chili."

"Maybe," he said. "But maybe it was my heart telling me something I was waiting for had arrived."

"Sweet," I said. "But I still say it was heartburn or chest pains. You might need to go get that checked out."

"I'm checking you out. That's all the medicine I need," he said.

"Man, you're going to lay it on thick now, aren't you."

He shrugged. "Just want you to know how beautiful you are."

I sat on those words for the next few miles until I had the courage to turn to him. "I haven't had a boyfriend since high school. Josh Bennett. Junior prom. Don't ask to see the picture. My hair was ridiculous."

He acted shocked. "College?"

"That was . . ." I paused. "How do I put it? A rough time for me?"

"Oh. Dealing with your parents?"

"Yeah." I sighed, leaning back to pet Heidi. "I moved in with my grandparents when I was young. Transferred schools. Rough, you know. My grandparents are wonderful, don't get me wrong. But just rough. I saw my parents once a year when they could get away from caring for my brother. They were prisoners until they died, pretty much. I got lost in the books. Studied up to block the pain. Anything to take it away. Either books on criminology for tests or true crime for pleasure, forensic psychology, and then romance just to break me from all of the dark and at least know happy endings existed for some people out there. They had to. My grandparents. Mike and Maude. The writers of those things sure know how to pull my heartstrings and nothing else in the outside world ever came close."

I leaned over and put my head on his shoulder. "Until now."

He kissed my hair and then turned from me. "I'm not going to do you wrong, Heather."

"What if I ask you to pull over on the side of the road right now?"

"Are you feeling sick? You okay?"

"Yeah, can you just do it?"

"It'll scare Maude and Mike."

"They can pull over, too. Just now."

"Okay," said Ben. He turned on his signal and found the next safest place to pull over.

As soon as he put the car in park, I reached up and took his face in my hands. "Kiss me. Please."

He didn't hesitate or question, just leaned in and took his time, pulling me closer to him. The horns started honking, and I pulled back in a daze. My heart beat wildly in my chest, and everything was him.

He had the softest smile waiting for me when I opened my eyes. "I knew it," he whispered as he leaned in and kissed me softly again. "I knew it would be like that."

"Thank you," I said. "We can go now."

His laughter filled the car. "Well. Aren't you a surprise today, Miss Thing. Let's get on the road. I'll do whatever you say," he said with his voice hinting at playfulness but still thick with emotion.

He rolled the window down and stuck out a thumbs-up sign. Honks answered in return. Funny they didn't just call us on the cell phone or send a text. I turned and waved, sending them a heart-shaped sign. Heidi propped up on the back of the seat to get a good look, too.

"I think I might like you, Ben Caraway."

He turned the radio on. "Then, I think we've got something to look forward to, after all this. I'm still going to ask you for dates and steal kisses. Glad your office doesn't have any windows. Just saying . . ."

I laughed. "You can do all those things and I might just say yes to every single one of them. I trust you, Ben."

That was like saying I love you, yet it came out easier than I would've thought. Maybe because it was true. I did trust him. He was for me. And for a bit, a little drive longer, I could imagine we might make it in this ugly world. With Heidi enjoying the wind, sticking her head out the back window now and then to catch a ray of sun. In this car, with the radio up and blasting a 70s rock ballad, "It Had to be You," blaring on the speakers. I knew all was right with the world, if only for a moment. Even if I knew reality would hit and might change things. I'd risk it for this feeling. And that would be enough.

———

29

Ben had taken a long way home, and we all grabbed a bite to eat together in a small café right outside the county line. They kept snickering and chiding Ben. Thankfully, all of the attention was going to him and not me. They knew me enough to give me my space.

Holding Ben's hand in front of them was a new thing. We kept stealing glances at one another. I felt so shy. So aware, yet wanting to escape into the bubble, the pages of safety, but I knew that would take me out of the present. Cain's words kept coming back to me. Be present. I was trying. And it felt right.

After we ate, Ben took me to pick up my car at my apartment. Cain was headed over to the office straightaway, and Mike planned to drop off Maude and get a quick nap before heading back. I got a call from Cain before I could make it to the station.

"Be ready," he said. "Just know it's a madhouse in here."

"What's going on?"

"Just don't say I didn't warn you. Gotta go. Another call."

He didn't wait for me to say goodbye. I sighed. If the

captain was trying to reach me, he would've had a difficult time. The signal was patchy out at the lake house, yet the closer we moved towards town I still didn't get any voicemail alerts.

As soon as I turned onto Jefferson, I saw the zoo. Reporters from local, state, and even national outlets were parked at every available space. Was this all from the press conference? Tents were set up with barricade gates. People from the community were all standing around with signs and voicing their concerns loudly that we weren't doing enough to protect the citizens of Crystal Falls. Someone was selling blood-splattered t-shirts that read The Sunday Killer. A madhouse, indeed.

One officer waved me through, and I rolled down my window. "Is it like this inside? Cain called to warn me, but I would've never thought it would be like this."

"It's about the same," he said. "Town council just held an emergency meeting. Booted the mayor out."

I couldn't hide my surprise. "Wait? What?"

"Can you keep going in, Heather? You'll hear soon enough. You've got Ben behind you, and the reporters recognize him. They're starting to swarm the car."

"It's that surfer boy look," I said, trying to lighten the mood. "He even looks like a poster boy."

I rolled up my window and moved my way through to the back lot. Thank goodness, we'd had gates installed a few years back after the Delgado gang had come in and trashed a few of our vehicles and stolen a couple of vans.

Maddy was holding down the desk as best as she could. She yelled over the chaos. "Hey, Heather. Captain's waiting for you."

I waved. "I'm on it."

My first thought was to brace myself for the raging

storm. He was probably in the stay-away-from-me mood but you-better-listen-here mood all at once. That meant he wouldn't be nice to be around.

I wasn't wrong.

"Heather," he said, rocking his desk chair. "That press conference was . . . was . . . I don't know what it was. It's caused a hoopla, is all I can say."

I peeked through the blinds. They were constantly turning protesters out of the building, reporters were throwing passes, and the run-of-the-mill criminals were having a field day, cheering and throwing slurs as loud as they could at the officers trying to maintain some calm.

He yelled, "Can you believe it? Cain is shuffling through the hotline calls now. We've had over a thousand tips."

I sighed. Here we go. More false alarms to cipher through. More revenge calls or nosy false witnesses or those out there who wanted their touch of fame to become a part of the big story just for kicks. "Are you serious? Well, that's kind of a good thing, right? It means we might get a new lead."

He growled. "We don't have enough manpower to deal with that many tips. Or this," he swung open his door wide and yelled. "If the stragglers don't get out of here in ten seconds, I'm going to put you all in jail. We've got work to do. You're crowding our space. Give us space!"

He slammed his door back, and the force of it caused all the blinds to rattle and shake.

He then rubbed his face, almost as if it would come clean off, and took a long swig of coffee. Clear signs he didn't go home last night and hadn't had any sleep since the press conference hit. "And the mayor was asked to turn in his resignation."

"Yeah, I heard about that. What's that all about?"

"The car bomb in front of his office caused quite a stir. The news leaked out about Jade's lipstick message on your wall, so rumors are flying that the mayor is some conspirator and evil mastermind. It's a joke. Now I've got to worry about that mole. Leaking to the press. What else will he say? What else did he get his hands on?"

I told him what I knew all along. "I've always had a sneaking suspicion we had a snitch. I'll let the guys know to double down on trying to smoke him out."

"Don't waste your time," he said. "It's Alex. We got him. Caught him right by the entrance to Bill's taking a bribe for information to one of my old informants. Like we don't have our fair share of snakes in this place. We practically keep Bills' operational with so many of us stopping in to eat or pickup to go. Shows how dumb he was. The Bold and the Stupid. He could star in that show."

I sat down for that one. "Alex? Really?" It was as if I felt a blow to my stomach. "But he seemed so . . . so . . .

"Snake-like. Traitor." The captain held up a paper and the headlines already had it printed: "*Task Force Team Member Tells All.*"

Captain McBride threw the paper in my lap. "He got his thirty pieces of silver. He betrayed what we stand for. He threw out evidence to the sharks, Heather. The evidence we were holding. For what? Money? Look at his face. Pure evil. It's beyond me."

He was right. The look captured on Alex's face spoke volumes. Dark eyes. Menacing smile. Almost like, 'I got you.' Almost like he was manipulating it all . . . like Pew.

Pew.

"Sir," I said. "He came to see me. He was hoping to discover anything we might've put together. That makes sense now. I think Alex was working with Pew."

"What?" he whispered. "Keep your voice down. Saying he's a rat, and he is a rat, is one thing, but saying he was an accomplice to a serial offender is another."

It hit me so strongly. "Do you remember that night when I captured Pew?"

"We all remember it, Heather. You almost got killed."

"Yeah, and where was my backup? Where was my partner? He always threw that up in my face, but he knew where I was going. That's how Pew had one of his people waiting for me. That's how Pew knew. Alex told him and then decided to slowly make it to the scene. Knowing he'd come upon me dead and Pew nowhere to be found. The camera on my car catching it all. Him crying over me . . . looking like the innocent one calling it in. Don't you see that?"

The captain sat down. "Oh, Lord."

"You know it. You know it as well as I do. Alex has something to do with this cult, just like Pew was one member even though we didn't know it. I sure can't question him now."

The captain's nod told me he believed it, too. Sometimes you don't need to see the facts, just listen to the possibilities. They just made ridiculous sense. Sometimes the puzzle pieces just fit. "Alex did what he did because he was told to. Alex wouldn't jeopardize his career like this for money. He has a higher calling. That cult."

"That explains why he asked to be the escort for the mayor before we caught him like a red-handed thief."

"Glad the mayor did step down," I said.

"Oh, he was going to go either way. Peacefully or carried out. The town saw to that. Everyone's hot right now if you hadn't noticed on your way in."

"You should run for mayor," I said. "You could take over and clean this . . ."

Cain entered. "Don't give my job away. I'm thinking about staying in Crystal Falls and doing that myself."

I smiled. "Mayor Cain. No Cain. No Gain. Your new slogan."

"That's catchy," he said. "I might just use it. We've got something, Heather. I think you need to hear this."

With the door open, that allowed Ben to step inside, too. They'd given me my time with the captain, and now I was needed with my team. My guys. My guy.

"Sir, let me go and . . ."

He cut me off, as usual. "Get to work, you slackers. No more vacations. No more eating. No more drinking. No more anything until this is solved."

"But sir," whined Ben. "I've got to keep her hydrated. It's good for the brain."

"Get out, you three, and don't come . . ."

I said, "Back until we have The Sunday Killer. Yes, sir. We hear you. Loud and clear."

With his last dramatic show in front of his audience, he ripped the paper into shreds and threw it in the trashcan before clicking his blinds closed.

Ben whispered, "What was that all about?"

I stopped and pulled them close. "A lot has gone down since we left. Alex is possibly working for the cult. Tried to sell Jade's evidence. Asked to escort the mayor for protection. We've got to be careful. Even more careful now. All eyes are watching."

"Alex," sneered Ben. "I knew I never liked him."

"And I just thought it was because you were jealous. And I trusted him. He was my partner. He left me to die. That's why I didn't have backup with Pew. He withheld just long enough thinking his buddy could finish me off."

"Conspiracy. Accessory. Thief. Let's keep adding

charges," said Ben. "He'll never work in this town again. I've always wanted to say that."

"Are you serious about the mayor seat," I said, as we followed Cain down the hall.

"I've always had an inkling to join the political arena. With all of my experience and connections here from before I left town, I might have a chance."

"You've got my vote," I said. "It's an order. What I say goes."

Ben snickered. "You better listen to her. When you do, you win."

He winked at me, and I knew he was talking about when I asked him to pull off the road and he obliged for our first kiss. I couldn't dwell on how I felt so betrayed by Alex right now. I'd deal with him later. I also couldn't focus on the sweet way Ben kept looking down at my lips as if he wanted to kiss me again right there in the station. I felt the same but turned away just in time to see that Cain was leading us to one of the holding rooms.

"What's up, Cain?"

"One of the tips might've been just what we needed. He's in there." He pointed behind door number seven.

"That is my lucky number. You think we're actually about to catch a break?"

"It is Saturday," said Ben. "I'd rather it be today than tomorrow and we will be a little late if that is the date. With all this pressure, the cult might snap under it."

"Before schedule. Especially if Alex and the mayor are now exposed. They may be in a panic as we speak," said Cain, hopeful.

I said, "And panic leads to mistakes. Slip-ups. And we'll be there to catch them when they fall."

Ben turned the knob. "Let's go in, shall we. I'm curious. What's behind door number seven?"

As soon as the door opened, a deep male voice behind it said, "Thank God, you're here. I know you'll listen to me. I know who the killer is."

"Well, isn't it my lucky day," said Ben, turning to me with a smile. We all pulled up our chairs and sat down at the table with the disheveled man.

I leaned forward, seeing the urgency and fear spreading across his face. "It's okay. You don't have to worry. Tell us all about it. Tell us what you know."

30

Kaliq Ray owned Inked, a tattoo studio on the corner of Main and Elm. I knew about the place. A small yellow house was converted into a thriving business, and I'd often wanted to go in just to see what kind of design he could help me draw up in honor of my parents, but I never had the time to stop.

"I saw the drawing on the news, the one of the tattoo. I did that thing."

Cain said, "Kaliq, no. That was from way before you were born. You couldn't have."

Kaliq turned to me and said, "I've told this dude already over the phone that I did it just last week. He's not listening to me. Told me to come down here just to humor me. Wasting my time. I've got appointments until ten tonight. Just lost a five hundred dollar shoulder for this crap."

"Wait," I said. "Last week? Who was it?"

He unlocked his phone and started scrolling. "I've got a picture of the dude and his tat for my portfolio and the image of the receipt right here. We also have a cash app so I've got his email."

"Nice," I said. "We appreciate you coming down."

Cain said, "Sorry, I was a little grumpy with you earlier. I walked into the station to field false leads before you rang in. No excuse, but I'm sorry."

"It's all good," he said. "I know you guys have a lot of pressure right now. A serial killer and all. Man, in my shop. That creeps me out. I can't tell you how much that just blows my mind. And he's got my tat. If I would've known. He acted all normal and junk. Just a regular guy. Talking about hunting and fishing. Talking about going out this weekend to the cabins. He was going to catch his greatest one yet. He bragged about that."

"Did he say which cabins? Did he give a specific location? Here? Local? Out of town?" I asked, trying to hold the eagerness in my voice at bay.

"Nah," he said. "Sorry. Didn't say much else that I could recall that stood out. Here. Here it is." He held the phone to Cain, and he showed us the photograph.

The picture matched the description that Mercy shared with them. Not speculation. A real lead. After months of searching and digging and trying to piece all of this together. I held my hands tight to keep them from shaking.

"And his name?" I asked, trying to keep casual. "We'd like that receipt now."

"Sure thing," he said. "Can't believe I'm helping the cops. You think this might be the killer?"

Ben said, "We can't divulge any specifics about . . ."

He laughed. "The case. Yeah, yeah. I know. I watch crime shows. SBI City is my favorite show. Just crazy that I'm sitting here, you know. Metal desk. Metal chair. Interrogation room with the glass. Anybody behind that thing?"

"The name," I said a little too loud. He gave me a quick smile and pulled up the receipt. "Thanks."

"His name is Mason Wade."

We took down the information, and I handed him one of my cards. "Don't delete any of that," I said. "Can you send the snapshots to my email?"

"I can do it right now," he said.

"Thanks. We'll get in touch if we need you for anything else. You've been great."

"You look great." He stood to leave. "Think you might like to go get a drink with me sometime."

Ben started to snort and then turned to hide his smile.

"Sorry," I said. "I'm with someone."

"Sure you are," he mumbled as he left out. "All the best ones are."

"And the best one is mine," whispered Ben. "Now, let's go do some real detective work around here."

Cain laughed. "What do you think we've been doing for the past few months? Selling cookies?"

"We're wasting time right now," I said. "And if you talk about food, then that'll get Ben thinking about milkshakes that go with food, and we'll never hear the end of it. Call the judge, Cain. Let's see how many connections you still have left. We need the warrant to search Mason Ward's property. Let's get this done fast. Like yesterday."

"Got it," he said.

Ben said, "And while we wait, do you want a milkshake? I could run up and get us a to-go order."

I threw my hands up. "See, there. I knew it."

He laughed. "You were the one that brought it up."

"Maybe so. Let's go run a background check on this guy. See if he's in the system. I can't say it's nice to be back in the office after we just left that gorgeous lake house, but I can say it's good to come back to a fresh lead."

We zig-zagged our way around the press and people all

crowded in the building to get back to my office. Ben said, "That reminds me. We should alert, Dot. At least about the media coverage. For all she did, she at least needs to know about the mayor. The story alone would be worth her drive back in a hurry."

"I'll text her," I said. The reply came back, and I laughed. "Never mind. She's preoccupied. Got herself a sweet professor on her arm. Look at this cute picture. They look good together."

"I want a picture of us," he said when he closed the door behind him.

"Not like this. Not here."

"In your office. Just one. I know you've got one of those selfie sticks around here somewhere. We can hold it up and get this drab cinder block wall as a backdrop."

"Cut it out. Run his name, Ben. We've got time for all of that later. Gives you something to look forward to."

"Okay, I take that as a promise. Milkshakes and pictures."

He switched on his computer and settled in. I pulled out the new information from Dot and started looking at the member names. There it was, in her alphabetized list she so nicely arranged for us. Mason Ward. The last name on the roster. The first one we needed to find.

31

C ain led a convoy team to the location. Ben and I had another unit with us. We went over what we'd found one more time. It took Cain less than an hour and the search warrant was a go. Mike planned to meet us at the entrance to the Getaways Cabin Retreat. The cabin units had an access road and we wouldn't take it first until we were sure it was safe. I told him to let SWAT do a perimeter search first and not drive closer until we were cleared or had Ward secured.

There was no radio communication in case Mason Ward had a scanner. We didn't want any rabbits running through the woods he'd lived in his whole life. I was just about to tell Ben how I knew Mercy would feel the horrific pain of this. Bringing us the memory of the tattoo, giving us something to show the media during the press conference, and getting that tip led right to Mercy's grandson.

Mercy's only daughter, Jackie, married Sparrow Ward, a businessman in the next town over as soon as she graduated from high school. She helped her father run the properties along with Sparrow. He'd let them buy up piece-by-piece because they wanted to help Mercy, not just take an inheritance. Or that's how the story went. Ward wanted that land all right. Just like his father before him. His father was Jefferson Ward, executed for killing a family while they slept back in the early 1960s in South Carolina. He had a truck registered in his name that had been given by his father, Truvie Ward. It was an old Ford. The same one Mercy remembered rambling up on him and his father. The man who asked them to plant the trees. What could be learned from the internet today was amazing, and Cain was a genius. Jade would've loved to have worked side by side with her father. If only she could've had the chance.

And we may have time to stop the one that took that chance away from her. Without giving too much away, Mike called Mercy to ask about Mason bringing in that request for more surveillance tapes, even though we didn't need any more of them after Cain got permission from Mercy to set his equipment up. Mercy told Mike that Mason was out for the weekend on a hunting trip with one of his buddies.

Someone from the cult, no doubt. Once we got an ID on Mason Ward, we could easily pick him out of the photographs Dot had passed to us at the cabin. He was always close to one woman there. She had a shaved head in one photo and then different wigs in some others. But where she was, Mason was somewhere within arm's length of her. And where Mason was, there was always a shadow. Another person, but we could never get a good look at him or her.

I didn't want to go into the Bible verse with the guys in the van. They were already talking about the Braves and the Red Sox game, so I felt I'd let them take over the conversation while I thought more on the verse.

'And there are three that bear witness in earth, the spirit, and the water, and the blood: and these three agree in one.'

The spirit was probably Pew. Maybe not. Maybe I was wrong on that and gave Pew too much credit. Extending his reach to include the cult could've been just a farfetched idea. Me reaching for straws and already knowing how sick his mind worked. It was easier for me to put him in the box with all of this. But there are three. So, if it wasn't Pew, it could've been Mason Ward, the shadow, and the woman.

Mason was raised along the river. He knew this terrain like I knew my grandparents' property in Virginia. That didn't settle well with me because that meant he could easily evade us. If he heard us approaching, he would scatter like the wind.

"Ben, we can't pull in," I said. "Stop as close to the road as you can and find a place where we can conceal the vans. We need to walk it. I'm calling Cain."

Cain agreed. We'd spook him. The first dirt road Cain found close enough to the area we'd be searching for became our little hideaway spot. There were some old barns and a soybean field. Ben let Mike know our location, and we'd wait for him before we started.

Ben said, "And we're doing this because?"

"Because he is this earth. He is this land. Do you remember that night at the farmer's market? We came so close, Ben. And we almost had him. He got away because he's this earth. It can swallow him up for days if he wants it to. He probably hid out in one of these barns."

"She's right," said one officer. "I've known that boy since we were kids. He's crafty. Quick. Was a track star in high school, ran the 40 at a 4.2 and for as big as he was, that was a feat."

His house was just a half-mile in. He lived modestly. It

was neat. Small. He had a well-cared-for lawn. Nothing that would be out of the way. It was an old farmhouse style home, with a new tin roof and a patch of a garden in the back. The first team took the house. Just like I feared. It was empty.

One officer called, "Heather!"

I went in. The smell was so overpowering that my gag reflexes took over. I was going to lose it any second.

I covered my nose and mouth. "What is that?"

"He's got rotten meat out on the counter. Pig parts everywhere."

"I can't stay in here," I said. The blood on the wall was dried and streaked. 'Here Little Piggies' was written in the blood. He was calling for us. He knew we were coming.

"Search outside. Go," I said. "It's getting late. Already after four p.m. We have little daylight left and you know what he might do after midnight. It'll be Sunday. Understand?"

Ben said, "There's something over here." He opened up one of the equipment bags and pulled out cutters and snapped the chain and lock looped through a door leading to somewhere below.

"Give me a light," I yelled. "Hello," I called into the darkness. "Anybody in there?"

My ears focused on the drip, drip, drip of water. "It's Crystal Falls PD. Anyone there? I'm going down," I said, already putting my foot on the top rungs of the ladder.

Ben said, "I'm behind you."

The boards creaked under my feet and one board was bound to break at Ben's weight if I didn't warn him. I flashed the light around and saw a sheetrock bucket with a toilet seat attached to it. There was an old mattress on the floor in the corner, and a broken couch with the springs popping through in front of it. No one was there. Thank God. Yet, if she were, then we'd saved her. She was here. Gone again.

"Look at these," said Ben, pointing at the large metal hooks and bolts attached to the wall. The shackles were bloody and laying on the mattress, where I was sure someone was kept prisoner recently. The smell of urine was strong. Someone was just down here. In this dark hole. Oh, God, let us not be too late.

I called up, "Get forensics out here fast. We've got some blood."

Ben shuddered. "Let's hope it's from his mess upstairs."

"There's not enough to make me think he killed someone here," I said. "But he did have her here. Come on. She's gone with him. Let's hope she's still alive."

Ben asked, "Any missing persons on the database, Cain?"

"No," he said. "Not a word of a new one. We need to do a fifty-mile radius check, then state. He could've found a new victim outside of Crystal Falls. Knew we were hot on him, so he moved out of town."

"One of those young girls that Dot said looked like they were recruiting. They could've snatched her from there. If we get a confirmed hit this is blood, then we're going to Cooper's Landing. We've got a cause."

"You're stretching," Ben said when we made it back out into the sunlight.

My head was pounding. "We've got the footage with his face plastered all over it. I didn't say I would raid the place, but it's time we paid The True Covenant of the Lambs a visit and thoroughly search the place."

"And let me guess, you want to go right now?"

"We've got minutes until daylight turns to dusk. We wouldn't track him in the woods. We've got a map of the

Mercy lands. Let's all split up and check the cabins. Every single one of them."

"I like that idea better than moving from this place down to the commune. They wouldn't carry a body to Cooper's Landing. If they kill, it needs to fit the pattern. Out and away from the cult but of the cult. A boat on the river. A barn. A cave. A greenhouse. The farmer's market. To what . . ."

Ben and I looked at each other knowing. "To burn the fields."

I looked at Cain and grabbed his arm. "We need to call every farmer in the city limits. I'm calling the fire chief. I'm so glad I spoke with him before. I told him to be ready. When the car bombing happened, I thought that was it. I thought that was the fire reference. No. They're going to burn someone alive tonight and the three will become one, forged in fire. Purified by the flames."

"Lord, help us," said Cain. "Lord help us, now."

After I spoke with the chief, he assured me he'd be out with his men and everyone he could gather around the fields, scouting, looking, and with anything suspicious they'd call it in. A helicopter could be fueled and ready within the hour.

"I need the closest field to here, other than the one we parked in. Something higher to hide in. Not a soybean. One that wasn't cleared out for dove season. He's going hunting, so he'll be near corn plots. He's using his land as the cover, yet he needs to remain open to appear as if everything is fine."

Mike came up in a hurry. "Mercy told me about a place Mason and he used to hunt. It's got an old lodge on it that isn't mapped. It's been in an unlivable state for years, and guess what, it's near the farmland that borders up to Cooper's Landing property."

I said, "And when they catch the body on fire, they'll be able to witness it from Cooper's Landing, without it desecrating their holy ground."

"That's a cornfield, too," said one of the officers. "I know just where that is."

"Let's go," I said. "Now. Everybody." I raised my voice, and we ran down the dirt road to the vans. "He knows we're on to him. His little display there tells me that. Might as well get the chopper to meet us at that field. We may need it for an airlift to the trauma center. We might find the captive girl alive."

Ben tried to reassure me. "We've got time before midnight."

"We're so close, Ben. We can't let him get away. We can't."

Forensics and another unit were pulling into the long drive as we hit the road. I let them know to tell me what they found, even though I knew it was human blood. Someone had been shackled and chained. But who was she? And why wasn't she reported missing?

"There's no way I'm going in quiet this time," I said, checking out the map of the property Cain had sent over to my phone.

"I wouldn't have expected you to," said Ben.

"Then, I'm glad we're on the same page."

He leaned over. "And you aren't alone on this one, Heather. I'm going to be right by your side."

"I wouldn't have it any other way."

32

The farmland spread for miles and miles. Crystal Falls had it all. A beautiful museum of the falls, showcasing Native American art and local legend reenactments. A river community that opened its arms to vacationers and thrived under the thrill of rafting or sport. It was also a tight-knit community where everyone felt turned upside down with darkness lurking in the night. How could we have a cult here for so long with no flags being raised? And why now? Why all the killings? Was this new or something that had been happening for years and gone undetected?

Ben said, "What if we miss the field?"

"We won't," I said. "We're almost there. I'm so glad Tonya is meeting us with the K-9s. It is a lot of ground to cover out here, but this time I don't think it'll be done in secret. More out in the open."

Mike called and said, "Mercy's had a heart attack. Just got the call from Maude. He's in the hospital. Looks like he's in bad shape."

"Oh, no," I said. "I'm so sorry, Mike. I know he's your friend. I know you might want to go see him but I need you."

"No. He's unresponsive. Maude is with his wife, Carol, now. I just can't believe it's one of his kin."

Poor Mercy. I thought about his daughter. She might've married a man, thinking he'd love and cherish her forever, and all he wanted was the Mercy lands to wreak havoc and despair. She trusted him. For what? To only be hurt in the end.

I asked, "Do you think Mason Wade's father is the shadow? The one that is in the pictures."

"Probably," Ben said. "It makes sense, doesn't it? Raise your child in the way it should go."

I sighed. Knowing how much parents could mess up their kids. It wouldn't be the first time I'd seen it, but this was one of those outlier extremes. Raising a killer. Training a killer. "Even in the ways of evil. That verse was taken out of context."

Ben said, "Haven't they all been."

When we turned the corner, I motioned up ahead. "This is it. Right here."

Oh, my God. It had already started. I could see the flames lapping and dancing in the center of a field.

Ben accelerated, and the van jolted and dipped with the potholes of the dirt road. I put a call into the fire chief and reported what was happening. Thank God Mercy gave us this location. We'd be searching for a needle in a cornfield for hours. We might just. . .

An explosion lit up the sky, and black smoke billowed. What in the world was he out there doing? I texted the captain so he'd be aware we were moving in hot. There was no other way.

But this time I wasn't alone. I had teams with me. I had

Cain and Mike. I had Ben. He squeezed my hand. He whispered, "We're going to get him."

We hit the ground running, guns raised, commands blasting, and voices carrying across the wind. My heart beat wildly, thumping in my ears, blood rushing so fast I could feel it in my arms.

I heard it. A shrill cry. It was that of a woman, then it was followed by fits of laughter. A deep, bellowing kind. One that could only be categorized as having great joy. Joy at watching someone burn. The kind that let me know that whatever was happening in the cornfield might've already driven the girl mad.

We were close. I held up my hand. Voices were on the right and left. Chanting. That language that Dot had recorded at the compound hit me hard. We were not alone in the field. I remembered something from the New Testament and it almost made me stop to think about it. But I had to keep going. Jesus walking in the cornfield and plucking the wheat on the Sabbath.

This was another symbolic location. The ritual taking place wasn't going to be fulfilled until Sunday for the ultimate show. We had time.

A voice rose over the stalks. One that made my spirit revolt. It was the kind that held darkness and preyed upon vulnerabilities. It was the sound of delusion.

It was a woman. A clear strong voice of one who was on the fringes of ecstasy and madness. "We are here tonight to witness the final communion of the one. At exactly midnight, we will see the spirit, the water, and the blood unite in me, and I will resurrect, breaking the bonds that have chained this world for so long, and set all of you free. It is time for me to be nailed to the cross. I do this for you, my lambs. I do it all for you to live in union with me."

Cries rang out, like mourners being paid to all wail at once at some play. Ben caught my eye, and I could tell he was torn. What to do? I read it on his face. Rush in or wait. I held up my hand and signaled for the team to wait.

"Hush now, little children. It is my time to feel pain. But do not fear, and do not be afraid of what is happening to me now." I could hear them striking the hammer against the nail, and a long, shrill cry followed each pounding. I didn't have to see to know what they were doing. There were groans and loud protests. Through ragged breaths, she yelled, "What I do is for you and for the forgiveness of the sins you bear for the world. I will rise again at midnight. Let it be as it was written. I submit my life to thee."

I crouched low and whispered, "She's crucified. She's hanging in the middle of two others, serving as the criminals. I think we've got two more bodies. Call down the dogs for now. We've got to improvise."

Ben asked, "What about the burning? Will they burn the bodies?"

"I don't know. They might. But I think we need to silently take out these members, one by one. If we don't, they could ambush us. They may be armed. They may even know we're here and are expecting us."

Ben agreed and set off to relay the message. The voices were rising, and I knew that meant they were witnessing her being chastised and mocked. In the chaos, we could eliminate all the threats. Leave us with the ones in the center. Give us a chance to stop this madness before an innocent life or lives are taken.

The wind picked up my hair and waved the surrounding stalks. My hands rested in the dirt, and I sifted through the earth. Planting myself to something real in all of this insane show.

My thoughts went to me and Rory building our first scarecrow with Grandpa out in the cornfield outback. Rory gave away his plaid, patchwork Christmas sweater Granny had knitted for him. He was so happy to contribute to the cause, but I was sure it was because he'd never be caught dead in that thing, anyway. Rory said, "Sis, you do the honors. Tie the neck together. Wring it. Like this." I watched as Rory's eyes glinted with a hint of mischief and awe, as if he were imagining his first killing then. At such a young age. In the middle of the cornfield, torturing hay and paper. Probably imagining it was me.

I wiped my hands on my pants and rose. Even the innocent memories held a faint hint of disease. I got a tap on my shoulder from one of the team members. He nodded and pointed ahead. There was only one way to move. One way to go. We had to do this now.

We moved all at once. SWAT had positioned themselves in a circle, mixed in with my team. We walked quickly and with stealth. Our sounds intermingled with the rushing of wind and the sounds the stalks make when they dance.

I could see them through the last two rows. They'd created the circular clearing. Three bodies hung. The center stage belonged to the bald woman. She was upright, whereas the other two were inverted, hanging upside down, clearly dead. Eyes wide. Faces contorted. Jaws wide open. They were not nailed as she was. They were tied with large ropes, still securing them into their place on the planks. Their heads were both turned to face the middle cross with one nail between their eyes burrowing their skull in place.

I didn't recognize the men beside her, but I saw Alex busy at work anchoring down a young girl on a platform brought in to conduct the ritual. She was dressed all in white. A tube was hooked into her arm and blood was dripping into a gold bowl on the ground. Mason was lifting a sponge that was dripping with her blood and rubbing it on the woman's mouth and face. She licked it and shook her head like a wild animal, acting as if she were refusing it but then taking the blood from the sponge with delight.

SWAT rushed in with flash bangs. The stun grenades echoed throughout the field and smoke billowed around the semicircle. They swarmed them armed with shotguns with 12 gauge bean bags, shooting any member moving towards them to attack, dropping them to the ground. My team was at the ready for anyone else who might have signs of a weapon.

I yelled, "Stop! Police! Put your hands up. On the ground now."

Mason dropped the sponge and spun around, dazed. His pupils were dilated. He was on something. As if trained for this moment, his reaction was lethal. He went for his gun, but before he could get a shot off, one rang out instead. Mine. Right in his shoulder, making his arm go limp. One more shot fired.

I turned and saw Alex on the ground. He'd done the same. His gun lay at his side. But he would not survive this one. He didn't have a shoulder hit. He had part of his face missing.

SWAT rushed in and collected the weapons, and I headed straight for the girl, falling to my knees, and calling for the EMS to hurry. They'd all set up at the perimeter. We had the whole support crew backing us up. Fire. Ambulance service. The helicopter sounds mixed in with the cries of the members, wailing in defeat.

She didn't lift her head. It was limp, hanging at a side angle. Her matted and sweaty hair hung over her face like a veil. I could feel the crucified woman's eyes on me the whole time. She was speaking in that bone-chilling language, calling out, desperate for someone to return her call. I didn't need an interpreter to break down what she wanted. She wanted someone to come in and save her. To stop us.

There was no one left. SWAT took care of that.

It was over.

The girl barely had a pulse, but she was alive. EMS rushed her away. I moved from the clearing and stood three rows into the cornfield again. The cult leader screeched and wailed, gasping for breath. With her violent movement and jerking, she may quicken her experience. Her lungs may collapse before we could get her down. She must've skipped the part that Roman-style crucifixion caused intense pressure on internal organs and was a slow death for hours. Some say that could be categorized as the worst torture imaginable. She cried out for anyone. Someone to help her. It's not like we had a manual on how to remove a body from nailed boards without causing more damage. SWAT didn't have that in their formal training. We let her hang a little longer. I'd let the captain decide how to proceed with her.

"I can't stay here," I said. "I can't watch." Each time she cried out, my stomach lurched. "This is insane, Ben. Insane."

Mike came up. "We've got another body to add to the count. Maude called. Mercy just died. What in the world?" he said, shaking his head.

Pictures were being snapped. The crime scene was already being roped off. I watched as an EMS worker zipped Alex's body into a bag and parts of his face were being collected to carry out with him. Mason was laughing hysterically as they carried him through the cornfield. His voice mingled with the crows. Eerie. Haunting. The clicking sound and gargled language rose like the black smoke.

"I don't know if I can move," I whispered to Ben, and he leaned in close.

"You have to. We have to. It's getting dark. I don't want to get lost out here in this cornfield with you. Don't get me wrong. You are the best kind of company, but the thought of it is already giving me anxiety. I got stuck in a maze once. One of those roadside Halloween mazes set up with zombies. It was an experience I don't want to relive."

How could I move? I closed my eyes and began to pray.

When I felt I was able to gather some strength again, I said, "Will you lead me out of here?"

He took my hand and said, "I told you, you wouldn't be alone, Heather. You're not alone."

"I never was," I whispered. "I just didn't know it until now."

We walked together, single file, through the cornfield. I did not let go of his hand. Even when we made it out on the other side and met the frenzy of the media, the captain running with a team of medical professionals, it all felt like a blur.

Dot was one of the first ones that screamed when she saw us emerge. "Detective Moody, give us a statement. What was it like in there? What did you see?"

I shook my head. "You don't want to know," I said. "Trust me."

"Ben, tell us something. Anything."

"Tell Bill I'm coming. Get my place ready for a table for two tonight. After today, I think I need a meal on the house."

A couple of the reporters laughed and took it down. Cameras were snapping. Reporters were screaming questions I couldn't answer. Time would tell. Who was responsible? Who was the killer? Was the girl alive? Would she survive? Who was she? We would soon find out all of the answers we needed to know, right now I needed to get as far away from the cornfield and get the warrants for Cooper's Landing.

We slid into the backseat of Mike's Bronco. "I heard the plans. This table for two? Tell me more about this? We can call the judge on the way."

"Well, I say we get ol' Mike here to drop us off. We shower. Change. Give me time to take Heidi out for a quick walk. And then, I'll pick you up. We'll hit the town. We'll do it big. We'll ..."

"Get milkshakes and hot dogs?"

"Exactly," said Ben, leaning over to give me a quick kiss on the cheek. "A perfect first date."

"This guy," I said to Mike as he turned onto the highway. "What am I going to do with him?"

"Just love me," said Ben. "That's all I'm asking for—my lucky charm."

I laced my fingers through Ben's and leaned my head against his shoulder. "That, I think I can do."

DEAR DETECTIVE MOODY

Dear Detective Moody,

I have been at such a loss for words for so long holding a pen to force myself into this place of forming them is strange. I've stared at this plain piece of stationary for so long, praying that God would just let the words come. But here I am again. Just a paper collecting words that will never match up to emotion. But I must try anyway so I apologize for my rambling. I'm trying to gather my words that could express what my wife and I feel. Relief. Grief. Torture. Gratitude.

All of those things. I'm trying to say thank you, but that doesn't seem like enough. How can it be? You brought my daughter's killer to justice. I know you're shaking your head and saying it wasn't you alone, and if you want to share this with your team, please tell them all the words that still fall short. But you. You looked at me when the others couldn't. You listened when others failed to do so. That alone made you different somehow. Like you saw through the file and into the very heart of our precious daughter,

Beth. Our family. For that, I'm forever grateful because maybe that's what brought that monster down.

If my family and I can ever do anything for you, do not hesitate. We owe you a great debt. Free vacation. A plane ticket for you and your team. Whatever you want, it's yours. It will not pain us if you walk through the travel agency ready to go. It'll bring us joy because we can at least repay you in ways we know how.

Sincerely,

Jones and Ruth Black

ABOUT THE AUTHOR

Dr. Jennifer Lowry is from Maxton, North Carolina. She is a fan of all things horror, UFC, and binge-watches episodes of The Mentalist. When she isn't literacy coaching, author coaching, or homeschooling her son, she can be found sharing her author journey online or hiding behind the pages of a new book. She's a traditional and self-published author/poet over twenty nine books. Grab a peppermint coffee, a Reese's cup, and check her out @jenlowrywrites.